WAGER LATE

WAGER LATE

TOM FARRELL

Printed in the United States of America
Railbird Publishing LLC

Editing by Steve Parolini
Copy Editing by Susan Brooks
Cover Design by David Ter-Avanesyan
Interior Design by Susan Brooks

www.tomfarrellbooks.com

1

I was taking a break from my usual duties at O'Connell's Tavern when Nicole walked up to the bar, her jaw set, an empty coffee cup in her hand. "Eddie, Jessie texted me. She's coming over. She never texts me—she always calls."

I shrugged and grabbed the coffeepot from behind the bar. "Maybe she's busy."

"Couldn't you tell? The other night when we were over there for dinner? The way Dad and Jessie looked at each other. I felt as if we'd walked in during a fight."

"A fight with Sal would be business as usual." Sal Nicoletti, Nicole's father, was a longtime trainer at Thornton Racetrack, and his job required a certain degree of toughness. Jessie Rivera, his partner at home and his assistant trainer, would naturally fall into the crosshairs.

It had been an uncomfortable Sunday night dinner, and I was

glad we'd found an excuse to leave early. Jessie served her specialty, carnitas, and usually I loved it. But this time it was dry and overcooked. Still, I ate my usual quota. The conversation had been strained, focusing upon the weather and Sal's software problems with the payroll, although we could tell there were other problems simmering beneath the surface.

Nicole swiped a stray hair away from her face. "I know what Dad's like, believe me. He can be a handful, but this is much worse."

Nicole had worked in Sal's barn until she decided to pack up and try her luck at the poker tables in Vegas. The move didn't meet with Sal's approval. Jessie, who had become like a big sister to Nicole, had supported the move.

"Any idea what they're fighting about now?" I filled her coffee cup and added some cream. The lunchtime crowd was light. Usually, Jessie stopped by after lunch.

"If she leaves Dad, you know what that will mean—he'll try to draw me back in. That's my biggest fear. Just when things are going well."

"C'mon, that won't happen."

"I knew I shouldn't have come back to Chicago. I'm too close."

"Now, wait a minute." Nicole had come back to live with me.

"You don't know what it's like. Taking care of those horses. You can't help yourself. You want what's best for them. It's a twenty-four-hour-a-day job. Maybe Dad and Jessie are having money issues."

Nicole strutted back to the alcove where she worked mornings. She had taken the town by storm. The story of her heads-up poker game against a billionaire in Vegas had been played up across the media by WagerEasy, the British sports betting conglomerate and sponsor of her sports betting show. When Nicole ran the table on her top picks the first week of the regular season, the show's viewership took off. When Nicole's "best plays of the week" hit at an alarming rate several weeks in a row, she became an instant celebrity. They even featured Nicole on a billboard for the show.

I shouldn't complain, but a guy has his pride. Sometimes I'd hoped she'd at least misfire on a few picks, instead of defying the law of percentages week in and week out like a magical diva sent by the gambling gods from Vegas.

I flipped through the employee schedules on my laptop, then checked the stats on last night's game. Uncle Mike would be happy. Nicole's pick had won, and she'd been right about the "over."

O'Connell's Tavern, my uncle's bar, had grown its customer base over the past few years. We had a good crowd every night, especially on weekends, and the servers and the kitchen were kept busy. The food and liquor receipts hit a new monthly high, and everything was running smoothly, but people weren't asking me about receipts or talking about how well the bar was doing. They talked only about Nicole.

In their eyes, I was my uncle's bar manager and a part-time PI, who just happened to luck out with Nicole. The crowd at O'Connell's didn't know about the jobs Uncle Mike and I had done for Burrascano, the mob's gambling boss. You don't tell tales about solving murders for the mob if you want to enjoy a long and happy life.

I heard a few snickers and comments like, "What does she see in that guy? He doesn't make any money." It's not good to start fights when you run a bar and are the bar's bouncer, so I ignored all their bullshit. Nicole knew about the jobs Uncle Mike and I did, and that was enough.

A woman in jeans and a black windbreaker entered through the front door. She wore a worn White Sox hat pulled down over her face. She looked up, and I saw it was Jessie. Nicole gave her a short wave from the alcove.

"Hey, Jessie," I called out. "How you doing?"

She closed her eyes, clenched her fists and yelled toward the ceiling. "Fuck."

Nicole ran over. The two of them hugged, a long consolation hug. The few lunch customers in the bar turned to look.

"Just another day at O'Connell's," I explained and then turned to Nicole. "Let's discuss this in private."

Nicole guided Jesse to a seat at her table. In a soft voice, Nicole asked, "What is it? You can tell us. We're family."

I grabbed a glass of water and brought it over. Jessie wasn't usually one to let things get to her. She was the rock in Sal's operation.

Jessie Rivera had been working with horses since she was a teenager. She caught the bug in New Mexico with quarter horses, then graduated to thoroughbreds. She'd even done a stint as a jockey. After more than twenty years in the business, she'd put on some weight and height, but plenty of muscle. Her long black hair complemented her brown skin and quick smile. She and Sal had grown into a power couple in Chicago horse racing. Jessie was Sal's eyes and ears. She'd work the horses in the morning and tell him if a horse was ready to run its race.

"It's Sal, not me," she cried out, throwing her hat on the table.

"Slow down, slow down." Nicole stood over her, a hand caressing her shoulder.

"We've been fighting. He's impossible." Her hands were balled into fists, her head down, her entire body clenched. "I want to stay with him, but he won't listen."

Nicole gave me one of her looks and sat down. We'd let Jessie talk it out.

Jessie slammed a fist on the table. "Your father has ordered me to leave. Tells me it's time I went out on my own."

Jessie spat out these words one by one, as if each one was poisonous. Her shoulders began to shake. It wasn't uncommon for a longtime assistant trainer to eventually go out on their own. But Sal and Jessie were different. They had been a team for years.

Except for the license and a ceremony, they were an old married couple. I didn't get it.

"He never smiles anymore. Never takes me in his arms." She looked at each of us, tears in her eyes. "You don't know. We haven't been in bed together for a long time."

"I'm so sorry," Nicole whispered.

Jessie looked at her as if she was a stranger. Then she looked at me the same way. "I forgot. You two don't know, do you?"

"Know what, Jess? What?" Nicole said.

"Sal is facing suspension. Clients are talking about leaving us."

Nicole stood. "For what?"

"Juicing."

"That's nuts. Dad would never drug his horses. It must be some mistake." Nicole bent at the waist as if she'd suffered a body-blow. A few sheets of her handicapping notes floated to the floor as she sat down. "And why am I hearing about this for the first time?"

"It was Sal's idea to keep it quiet. It had to be a mistake, he said. We got another test, but that didn't help. We went to the hearing pleading contamination, and lost. Sal wants me to save my good name."

I was dumbfounded. I'd heard of other trainers being suspended for juicing, and all I had to say was "good riddance." Horses had suffered, and some had died during a race. Now I saw it from a different angle.

Jessie took a sip of water. "He wants to protect me. Protect me from what?" She pulled out a tissue and dabbed at her eyes. "Shit. Maybe he did finally give in. Maybe he did it after all. Everyone just wants to win. He'd never tell me if he did."

I knew Sal made his share of bets on questionable races, but he always drew the line when it came to drugging horses.

Nicole went over to the woman she considered her older sister and threw an arm around Jessie. "Damn him. We'll get you something to eat, then you go home and rest. We're going to the track later. Let us talk to Dad. We'll get to the bottom of this."

I hoped we could find out more, but the suspension of a trainer was a serious matter these days.

2

I DROVE MY THREE-YEAR-OLD DODGE CHARGER through what was now a steady deluge of rain. Fall could turn ugly in a hurry in Chicago.

I swung around a city bus stopped at a forty-five-degree angle, blocking my lane. A long line of drenched passengers tried to squeeze into the packed vehicle.

Traffic was bumper to bumper. Getting from the near north side to the west side of Chicago was like traversing a minefield because of construction and potholes, and the weather only made it worse. My route to Thornton Racetrack had evolved over the years into a complex network of back roads, shortcuts, and detours. I took one.

The track was once my second home. I was introduced to the races when Uncle Mike bought a piece of a racehorse. I'd be out there for the early morning workouts with my stopwatch. Even after Uncle Mike got out of the ownership business, I stuck around to play the horses.

Nicole had been unusually quiet during the drive. I thought we'd made progress with the old trainer. Now I wondered what else Sal had kept from us.

I glanced over. Her arms were folded over her chest, and her mouth was tight. "Maybe it isn't a good time to visit Sal," I said. "He just had it out with Jessie, and then you show up."

She looked out the passenger window. "We talked about that already."

"I know you're upset. All I'm saying is now might not be the time."

"It's the perfect time." Nicole had a lot of Sal's blood in her. She had his temper, too, and it was now directed at me.

"Okay, okay. But you've been trying to reconnect with him—"

"And Dad's been an asshole. He's kept up this act long enough, Eddie. This bullshit that I betrayed him. Like, I went rogue when I moved to Vegas. As if I was some stripper, instead of a top poker pro. He can't deal with my success. And don't even get me started about the house."

"The house isn't your fault."

"You're damn right it isn't. It was a smart move to invest in a house. Can I help it if the developer went under? My house is surrounded by half-finished homes. No one will even rent the place—it's a haunted neighborhood. The realtor sent me a picture—kids have been busy spray-painting graffiti. He wants me to drop the price again. That ought to make Dad happy."

"Take it easy. It's not Sal's fault either."

It was the house she'd bought in Vegas, her pride and joy. She hated chaos in her life. Games had rules and odds and results. Maybe that's why she worked so hard to predict the outcomes in sports. It brought a certain order to a Sunday of uncertainty.

If she'd let off some steam on the ride over, maybe she wouldn't say something to Sal that she'd regret later. I had to think about my role in this—right now I was providing a public service by keeping my mouth shut.

"He's pissed because I didn't stick around to work at his barn—as if he'd built it up over the years just for me," she said.

Sal inherited the training operation from his father, Nick Nicoletti. Sal's older brother, Nick Jr., had run things until his untimely death. Family tradition was hanging over all this.

Nicole elbowed me as if she couldn't sit still. "He's the one who complains about the business all the time. He's the one who feels trapped. And what does he want from me? To take over and bow down before him like he's God almighty, when all he's done is hand off this crappy job to me? Well, he's the one stuck, not me."

I knew she dealt with guilt. "It's a family thing for Sal."

"Remember, *he's* the one who sent questionable bets to *me*— to place at Vegas sportsbooks. All so he could avoid affecting the track odds. He got me banned at a lot of those casinos. The sportsbook employees—my friends—almost lost their jobs. Then they looked down their noses at me like I was robbing them. If he juiced his horses, I'll kill him."

"You wanted to reach out to him when you came back."

She turned her firestorm on me. "Thank you for throwing that in my face. This is what families do—they have it out. I know you had it rough, growing up without parents and living in your aunt and uncle's house, but you and Uncle Mike are always good old boys."

It was a cheap shot, though accurate. My mom had been raped and murdered when I was a baby. It was something I lived with—the devil under the bed.

Her anger was constructive and logical, while my anger could turn dark and uncontrollable. I'd listen to her vent.

—

We parked in the employees' parking lot along the backstretch.

Nicole stopped at security outside the gate and flashed her badge. Then she marched in the rain toward the Nicoletti stalls and office, and I tried to keep up. Sal would be on his own in the upcoming scrum. I was there to ensure a fair fight—no punches below the belt or eye gouging.

We walked past the shedrows. A steady stream of people shuffled past the stalls—owners and their guests, trainers and staff, vets and assistants, probably in attendance due to the upcoming Thornton Derby this weekend.

Nicole didn't even stop to say hello to the horses as she always did. Alejandro, one of the barn's grooms, stood beside an empty stall wearing a yellow raincoat and heavy boots. He waved but didn't smile.

Nicole stopped to say hello.

"Miss Nicole, go back," he said.

"We need to talk. And Sal is going to listen to me for once," she said.

"Eddie, tell Nicole now isn't a good time. He's been fighting all day with Jessie, and he's not himself. Jessie just told me —"

"Jessie is here?" Nicole said. "I told her to go home and settle down."

Alejandro shrank back toward the stall. "Yes, she's still here. I've never seen her so mad. She's got demon eyes. She asked if I'd quit Sal and come work for her, but I don't know." He cowered, probably from Nicole's demon eyes.

"Just don't do anything yet," Nicole ordered him, then turned to me. "C'mon."

What a cluster fuck this was turning into. I slipped in the mud and horseshit. If Sal and Jessie were going their separate ways, it would be a landmark moment in Chicago horse racing—what was left of Chicago horse racing—and I was in the middle of it.

Nicole hesitated outside Sal's office. I wasn't sure if she was waiting for me to catch up or if she was rehearsing her opening salvo. She knocked and then threw the door open.

The office was nothing more than a ten by twelve-foot room at the end of the stable area. The one important luxury item was a window air conditioner that made the office a refuge of coolness during the summer. Today, the room was cold; water dripped from the ceiling into a bucket to the right of the gray steel desk.

Sal sat behind the desk, his glasses low on his nose, a piece of paper in one hand. His weathered, deeply lined face showed his age. His bloodshot eyes glared up at Nicole. "Look what the wind blew in."

Nicole stood her ground, hands on her hips. "You know how to welcome a person."

"Get off it. I know why you're here. If you're looking for Jessie, she's not here."

His speech was slightly slurred. I spied a glass near a stack of papers. It was half-full of a brown liquid, most likely Sal's favorite bourbon.

The office floor was concrete. Sal's slick raincoat hung from a hook, and his heavy boots, caked in mud, had been tossed in a corner. Horseplayers had no idea of the time a trainer put in or the extent of the operation. Horses were like two-year-olds and craved constant attention from Sal and his staff.

"How could you?" Nicole demanded.

"How could I what?"

"How could you treat Jessie this way after all these years?"

Sal shrugged. "I know you two talk—behind my back."

"So what? You're being suspended? You don't think that's something you should've told me? C'mon, Dad."

He reached for his glass. "Hey, Eddie. Want a drink— bourbon? It's all I got to offer—no inside information today."

"No thanks," I said, wanting to fade into the background.

"I'm waiting," Nicole said.

"You want some explanation, some story? When they're after you, they're after you. It's my turn."

"You always swore—"

"Wait just a minute, little lady. I didn't admit nothing. You think I'd do this to *my* horses? After all these years?"

"What about those bets I made in Vegas? You're telling me those were all on the up and up?"

"Other guy's horses. People tell me things. You want me to go begging during the winter months? I've still got bills to pay. Of course, I don't have a money-pit mansion in Vegas, either."

"I knew it. I knew you'd make it about me and Vegas."

Sal spread his arms. "You could've had all this."

Nicole laughed. "All of what?"

"Something my father built and my brother handled before me. It's a lot."

Nicole took a deep breath. "Of course it is, and as I said before, I appreciate it. But it's not what I signed up for, okay?"

"You could've made it even better. Taken it to the next level."

"Chicago racing has another level?"

"It is what it is. It could've been a jumping-off point."

"To the Kentucky Derby and all that glory? The chance to suck up to billionaires who only want to check things off their bucket list? It's a dying game."

"Maybe." Sal gulped his drink.

Nicole said nothing.

They'd been down this road before, about the business of horse racing and succession, and this was the first time Sal had given an inch. He'd always stirred the embers and fired back before.

"What is it, Dad? Why would you do this to your horses?"

He stared at her for a long minute. I'd become invisible. "They'd have to shoot me and bury me out there in the infield before I'd let any one of those fuckers with a needle get anywhere near—"

"Nice talk, Dad. Nice. What am I supposed to believe?"

There was no need for me to mention that all trainers

injected their horses with therapeutic drugs prescribed by a vet; the bad actors were those who injected prohibited substances—the dopers.

He picked up the glass, noticed it was empty, and set it back down. His face became contorted in pain and rage. "I've been framed."

Nicole stepped forward and leaned on one of the chairs that fronted the desk, her shoulders slumped. "Framed? Who would frame you?"

"They do it when you're not looking. You think I've got my people standing guard twenty-four hours a day? I got more than sixty horses here. Anybody can slip something to them. Now I've got a black mark against me. Your grandfather is rolling over in his grave."

Who was he talking about? Who were "they"? Did Sal's enemy pick a horse at random to wreck his operation? I knew better than to ask questions at this moment.

Nicole and I had looked up Sal's suspension. The horse involved in the suspension was a cheap claiming horse. Sal's attorney had obtained a brief "stay" on the start of the suspension for ten days to allow for the filing of a motion to reconsider with the court.

"You must have some idea. Did somebody come to you? Attempt to get you to go in with them on some scheme? C'mon."

"Yeah, I got an idea. But it won't do any good."

"You owe money?"

"To the wrong people?" He shook his head. "I'm not that desperate. I know how to play this game."

"Then who? Why won't it do any good?"

"I think it's Jesse's brother."

Nicole tugged on the back of the chair. "Ramon? He's in prison."

Ramon, a drug dealer, had flipped on the cartel for a

reduced sentence.

"Ramon's friends are out there. You know what he thinks of me. I'm living with Jessie. He's hated me for it."

Nicole shook her head. "Why now, Dad? Why would Ramon set you up? He's been in prison for over a year. He could've done this when he was riding high, working for the cartel."

"I got a call. Somebody with a Latino accent. They said to 'Let Jessie go or else.' I ignored them, of course. Then, my place got ransacked. Then I get the positive result on one of my horses."

"Did you tell Jessie this? She's out there thinking you—"

"It's for the best, Nicole. It's the only way. And you're not going to tell her. Let her take my best clients. I don't care anymore."

"I thought you always said giving up wasn't in our DNA? Where's Jessie? You two need to sit down and work this out. I won't stand for it."

"No way. Stay out of it. Jessie deserves her chance. Our clients love her." He waved a hand of dismissal, stared down at the mind-numbing stack of paperwork, and then settled his gaze upon the rows and rows of framed photographs tacked up along the walls—winner circle photos of the barn's major victories. Winners brought to post by Sal's father and Sal's dead brother and then Sal.

"It can't end this way, it can't," Nicole said. "I'm going to find Jessie. I don't care what you say. Where is she?"

Sal leaned over, and one arm dropped behind the desk. His hand must've searched around inside a drawer, because a moment later he pulled up the bottle of bourbon and set it on the desk as if to make a statement. It was still half-full.

Nicole checked her cell. "She's not answering my texts."

"I'm not surprised. She's pissed. And she doesn't want you getting in the middle of our breakup."

"Well, I'm in the middle of it now —"

"Fine. Go. She's meeting Isabel at her dorm."

Nicole turned and stomped out. I followed. Isabel was one of the exercise riders for the stable. Jessie was clearly making her move to hire away staff—first Alejandro and now Isabel. On second thought, I rejected that idea. Jessie wouldn't give in so easily.

As we walked past the stables, Nicole stopped to see Winning Spirit, one of her favorites. She walked up to the stall, and the horse came over. "Hey, boy, how you doing? How you doing, boy? You ready to run your final race? Then you can retire in style. You deserve it. Good boy."

The horse bobbed its head and nuzzled up to Nicole. She stroked his muzzle. The thought that someone could dope a horse fired up my anger. What might be a slight impairment for a horse could become a real problem during the running of a race. The jockey could notice a horse was in pain and take the horse back. A doped horse was robbed of that safeguard because the drug masked the pain.

After she'd spent time with the veteran claiming horse, Nicole tore herself away, and we hustled outside into the heavy rain. We ran the twenty yards to one of the dorms, a squat, two-story, block-long building.

The track, now officially called "Thornton Racetrack and WagerEasy Sportsbook," had planned improvements to the grandstand and clubhouse to entice sports bettors, but no improvements were in the works for the dorms.

"Where is Isabel's room?" I asked.

"The next building over. We can get there by walking through this dorm."

The dorms were no place to raise children, but the workers had kids and whole families crammed into these concrete pillboxes. Most of the rooms were ten-by-twelve and half of them didn't have a bathroom. The majority of the six hundred track workers—grooms, hotwalkers and exercise riders—were migrants, many of them women, and they hoped to give their children a better life. But that American dream seemed far off, since the workers were barely paid minimum wage and often cheated out of overtime.

Inside the first dorm, music I'd hear in a Mexican restaurant echoed across the floor. A child rode her tricycle down the hall, supervised by a short-haired, brown mutt. The child stopped and waved. The dog gave me the once-over. I tried to look innocent.

A group of workers and kids had congregated at the end of the corridor. A woman screamed, and there were loud cries. Nicole started running; she knew Spanish from her years working on the backstretch. I didn't. I took up the chase. The agitation of the crowd caused my adrenaline to spike.

Nicole twisted through the crowd, past people who recognized her, and backed away in shock and fear of something outside.

They let me pass as well. Some stepped back into their rooms.

When we got to the door at the end of the hall, we slipped through a phalanx of silent workers. A lone security guard stood outside the door.

The guard recognized Nicole and shook his head. "Take a look." He pointed to an area near the corner of the building.

More security personnel were driving up in golf carts, talking on walkie-talkies and shouting orders. We stepped outside and walked around a couple of parked cars. Near a bike rack against the wall, several workers were on their knees, huddled around a figure on the ground. I swear they were praying.

Nicole shrieked my name, then fell into my arms.

I looked down at the body beside the bikes. It was Jessie, spread-eagled on her back, with a bullet hole in the side of her face. Her eyes stared up into the rain, her face frozen in a death mask.

3

I ESCORTED NICOLE BACK INSIDE AND DOWN THE hall. She was in shock and crying uncontrollably. My anger trumped any shock.

We could stand here in the dorm hallway amid a crowd of frightened, grieving people or keep moving. Maybe we should go back to Sal's office and tell him, but by now, he'd probably already heard. News traveled fast around the backstretch. Sal would be at the scene any minute.

I recalled what Sal had said about Ramon. Ramon had been a rat. When the cartel was out for revenge, they didn't draw the line at family. That would explain Jessie's murder and the frame-up of Sal.

Why was Jessie going to meet Isabel? Did Isabel know something? Maybe she'd talk now. If the cartel was responsible, they might get to her, and then she'd refuse to talk to anyone. None of the workers would be willing to talk once the cartel sent out word.

I assumed Jessie's murder had happened only minutes before we'd arrived, but maybe not. The heavy rain had kept people inside, and the body was in an obscure place—the parked cars would block the view of anyone running through the rain from one dorm to the next. I should've asked those gathered around the body. But I couldn't go back now.

I should just get Nicole home. Let the police handle it. Maybe somebody had seen the killing, and Jessie's murder would be an open and shut case. Still, it didn't seem right to leave the track. And Nicole would rightly kick my ass if I didn't investigate.

We turned around and walked back to the end of the hall. Nicole trudged along beside me—one arm tight around my waist for support.

She was no longer crying. "Eddie, who would do this to Jessie? Jessie, of all people."

"I don't know." Nicole wasn't really expecting an answer.

Once we got outside the dorm and past the security guard at the door, I had an arm around Nicole, and with the other, I pulled out my cell and called Uncle Mike. I explained to him what had happened.

"Oh, my God, Jessie?" I heard his old desk chair creak. He let loose a string of cuss words and then asked, "Why?"

I told him I didn't know and about my plan to see Isabel.

"We need boots on the ground. I'll come right over."

"What? The traffic—"

"I have friends on the force, remember?"

"Okay." I hung up.

The loyalty shown by other officers toward my uncle, a retired homicide detective, never ceased to amaze me. I imagined Uncle Mike in a squad car, siren blaring, racing across town.

Nicole and I kept walking through the rain to the adjacent dorm. I stopped once or twice to look back. The scene was now crawling with emergency personnel and police. The workers were walking back to their dorms, shooed away by the uniforms.

"Eddie, where are we going?" Nicole asked, as if she'd just awoken from a deep slumber.

"We're going to see Isabel."

"No, not now. We have to go to Jessie." She tried to pull away, but I held her tight.

I tried to talk sense to her. "Track security won't let us. The police are here."

Nicole stopped and looked around. "I can see that. I'm not stupid," she hissed.

"Of course." I wanted to echo her anger and confusion, but I needed to maintain control.

We reached Isabel's dorm. It was eerie. There was no music, no children playing in the hall. Men stood in groups, talking in low voices. They recognized Nicole. One reached out and touched her arm without saying anything.

The near-silence bore down on me. Why did I insist on meeting Isabel? Nicole was hunched over, taking a series of small, quick steps, then staggering along, willing herself to move forward. Me, the big honcho investigator who knew she must be hurting, seemed only intent upon magnifying her heartfelt pain.

We stopped outside one of the closed apartment doors. Nicole knocked twice. A part of me hoped we had the wrong apartment or that no one was home, and we could shuffle away and lick our wounds.

The door opened slightly, and a woman bent at the waist with sunken eyes looked out and whispered, "Yes?"

"Isabel," Nicole cried.

"Oh my God, Nicole, come in."

Isabel grabbed Nicole, and they clung to each other. I squeezed in behind them and shut the door on the hall of grief.

In the corner of the room, a young girl, maybe ten years-old, sat on a stool before a desk, her attention focused upon a small black and white portable TV playing a soap opera in Spanish. A box of Cheerios and stacks of groceries crammed the desktop and the space below. Above, a dying plant hung from a hook in the ceiling. The walls were covered with posters of male and female teenage idols, sports figures and horse racing photos, except for a foot-long shelf above the bed with a cross and a statue of the Virgin Mary. The floor was covered with colorful rugs. A small bathroom off to the side made this apartment one of the El Primo residences in the dorms.

After several minutes, the women composed themselves somewhat, and I asked, "We heard Jessie was on her way—"

"Eddie, not now," Nicole said.

"No, it's okay," Isabel said. She seemed eager to talk. Her hair was wet, and her track-issued windbreaker, hanging from a rack beside the door, dripped water. She wore a light blue hoodie, and she wore her black hair up. "Yes, Eddie. Jessie wanted to talk to me about her trouble. You know?"

Nicole took Isabel's hand and held it tight with both of hers.

Isabel glanced her way. "He can be trusted?"

"Yes, he's okay. Go ahead. Eddie can help. It's me. I'm not thinking," Nicole said. "It's just that…"

"I understand," Isabel said, reaching over with her free hand and gripping Nicole's shoulder with a quick hug. "It's terrible."

The young girl turned around and studied the pair. Then she glanced at me, took a deep breath and returned to the TV.

"You were outside?" If I could've dug a hole through the floor, I would've tunneled my way out of the place.

"Yes, I heard people scream and cry and went outside. Jessie and I …" She stopped, lost in thought. "We always talked. We came here to America about the same time." She picked her words carefully and enunciated each as if translating on the fly. "Jessie did everything for Mr. Sal. More than everything—she ran things. I was…we all were proud of her. She lifted us all up. We were part of all this because of her, you see? Jessie was the one we ran to when we needed—"

Isabel began crying again, and Nicole joined in. I hunted for that escape hatch.

After a moment, Nicole gathered herself and whispered, "Tell us about the trouble, Issie."

The longtime exercise rider for the Nicoletti barn composed herself and blew her nose. "It's too much. Jessie was getting pressure from Ramon. We thought things would settle down when he went into prison, but they got worse."

"Pressure? From Ramon or the cartel?" I asked.

"Yes," she nodded, "from both. Ramon's friends came around. They wanted her to leave the barn and leave Mr. Sal. Ramon believed she was being used. Ramon is a proud man. A proud man. And a proud man is the worst kind of man. All it's done is cause his family evil."

She stopped as if she'd lost her train of thought and then continued. "Jessie and I were very close. She came here every day, or we'd meet for coffee at Elena's or—"

The girl at the desk turned abruptly in her chair. "Are we going to eat now, *momi?*"

Elena's was the local kitchen, grocery, and cafe, run by the Karras family. It was open before dawn to serve the backstretch crowd and would usually be closing about now. I bet it would stay open tonight to serve the cops.

"No, *mija*, not now. Later." Isabel said.

The little girl looked at me again and then turned back to the television.

I needed to choose my words carefully. "What about Ramon's previous employer?"

Isabel hesitated, digesting my code. "Yes, the cartel. My daughter knows. She has to learn early. Jessie insisted. Hugo would come around. His people sell the meth. My daughter understands why. People work long hours and some rely on the drug. Not me. Never. My daughter knows this.

"But when Hugo came by," she stopped as if picturing Hugo's presence at the backstretch, "he'd sneak up behind you at the barn or around a dark corner after a long day and always laugh and say, 'Why so surprised? You don't like me?'" Isabel made a face. "He is no good. Evil. Could he be the one who shot Jessie? I ask myself. I don't know. When Mr. Sal wasn't around, he'd threaten Jessie. I think he wanted to hurt Jessie to get back at Ramon. But I don't think the bullet is enough for those people."

"You saw Jessie?" I gestured in the direction of the murder scene.

"I heard and went out to see for myself." She threw her head back and closed her eyes, her lips moving. Then she crossed herself with her free hand.

"How did you hear?"

"The Lopez child was getting his bike. He was going to Elena's. He found her."

"Do you know what time?"

"The Lopez boy?" She looked at the radio alarm clock on the nightstand by the bed. "It was about a half-hour ago or less? Juanita's show was just starting."

Juanita turned around in her chair. "My show starts at four o'clock every day."

"Thank you, Juanita," I said. The body was discovered between four and four-thirty, but from the look of Jessie's fatal wound, the shooting must've happened much earlier.

"Watch your show," Isabel told her. "You'll miss something."

I prompted her. "The Lopez boy told—"

"Yes, his family lives across the hall. The news spread. You don't think the police will talk to me? I have Juanita to take care of. No one will talk because Hugo will hear."

"It's okay," Nicole said. "We won't talk to the police about you."

"That's right," I said. "What about Jessie's trouble with Mr.

Sal?"

Her eyes grew wide. "You heard? The suspension has us worried. Jessie planned to take over while Mr. Sal appealed. She would never leave him or go out on her own. She loved him with all her heart. But that's what Sal wanted. He's not himself."

"How?"

"Mr. Sal has pressure, too. The suspension is only one thing. Jessie says the bills are piling up. Some owners don't pay or make trouble. Times are not good. Things are not like in the old days, they tell us. Why did this have to happen? The police will find no one. Nothing will change. It will only be worse. I'm stuck here with Juanita and no place to go."

The child turned in her chair. "Don't worry, *momi*. I'll do all my homework."

Nicole smiled at the child and raised an index finger to her lips. "It's okay, Juanita. I'm here. You and your mother can talk to me. Eddie will sort it all out for us."

Isabel and her daughter studied me as if looking for some invisible power they hadn't noticed before.

"We'll find out who did this," I said to reassure them.

"You?" Isabel pointed at me. "You can do something about all this? Something about my poor Jessie, the cartel, the owners who don't pay, Ramon?"

I nodded because that's what investigators do, even when they don't have a clue.

Isabel turned back to Nicole. "Please don't bring us into it. Please, my daughter. We have no family. People are scared. Immigration might come. Miss Arlene has always protected us and got us papers, but now…"

Arlene Adams, the track owner, somehow managed the ongoing carnival that was the backstretch. Harness in the winter then a thoroughbred season in the spring; harness again in the heat of summer, and thoroughbreds back again in the fall—with different owners and trainers and many of the workers changing location each time the meet switched from harness to thoroughbreds and back again. Kids changed schools, trainers moved to another track, and sometimes workers were left without jobs.

"Don't worry," Nicole said. "It will all work out."

"Thank you, Nicole. Thank you."

Nicole threw her arms around Isabel, and they hugged and cried, and I swore I wouldn't forget this moment.

—

Nicole and I trudged back through the muck. The police had begun to set up a makeshift tent and lights around the murder scene.

Uncle Mike waved to us. He was in a crowd gathered a short distance away from the tarps, the group huddled beneath the overhang of an equipment shed.

We walked over.

Uncle Mike stood with four uniformed officers whose job, it seemed, was to maintain the perimeter. "Eddie, Nicole, let me introduce you. Nicole was good friends with the deceased."

He named the officers in the group. Each officer smiled broadly, perhaps in appreciation of the recognition given to them by my uncle, a legend in homicide, or because of Nicole's celebrity status. I shook their hands while they offered condolences to Nicole. She was in no mood for small talk. As a result, the officers found excuses to slip away, and the three of us were left alone.

"You made it here in record time," I said to Uncle Mike.

"Yes, thanks for coming, Mike," Nicole said.

"I told them to take it easy on the way over, but they didn't listen. I hear Detective Saboski and his new partner have drawn the case. They just got here." He nodded toward the tent.

Saboski had been the junior partner to Liz Zelinski, Uncle Mike's old partner in homicide. Liz had retired from the force and moved to Wisconsin after her husband passed away.

"Did you talk to Saboski?"

"Just for a second. He's still all business."

Saboski thought Uncle Mike should take up golf instead of "playing detective." He liked me even less. The fact that Saboski had wormed his way up the ladder to lead homicide detective made me wonder how any murder case in the department ever got solved.

"Nicole, can you excuse us a minute?" Uncle Mike asked.

"Sure, Mike." She continued to stare off at the scene.

Uncle Mike nudged me along until we were a safe distance away and then, in a low voice, asked, "How's she doing?"

"Not good. She and Isabel had a good cry."

"We can talk later about Isabel. You better get Nicole out of here while you can."

"Why?"

"They're looking for Sal. They want to question him."

"Because he and Jessie were arguing? There's no history of any rough stuff, at least nothing I know about."

"I know. I know. Just take Nicole home. Look, I've been on plenty of these murder scenes, and it doesn't go well for anyone to be questioned at this moment. There's simply too much emotion, and it causes unnecessary issues. Get her out."

I knew all that. "Screw Saboski. Nicole and I won't stand for—"

"See?" Uncle Mike placed a hand on my shoulder, his eyes wide. "If you're like this, what will Nicole be like when Saboski starts in? That's not the everyday victim over there in the mud—it's Jessie. But for Saboski and others—"

"Right. It's Jessie." I was surprised by my flood of emotion. Shootings happened every day in Chicago; no big deal. This one was different, but Saboski wouldn't see it that way.

"Your job right now is to take care of Nicole. It won't be easy. I called Maureen. She'll bring some food over to the apartment. Sit on the couch. Watch TV—"

"Okay, okay." I took a step toward Nicole, then stopped and turned back. "Thanks, Uncle Mike, for coming out."

"Sure. Now get going. I'm going to find some coffee. I'll let you know what I hear."

4

THE NEXT MORNING, I RAPPED ON UNCLE MIKE'S office door at O'Connell's and heard his booming voice. "It's open."

I carried my coffee into a cloud of cigar fumes. My uncle sat back in his chair, his feet up on the desk. The office ceiling fans funneled the cigar smoke outside.

"You're here early," I said.

"Where have you been, sleeping in?"

"No, I was with Nicole."

"I know. Just kidding. She's here? Good. She's working on this weekend's picks?"

"Yeah. She didn't want to, but I convinced her that keeping busy is the best therapy."

"Good idea."

"Nicole says her father called. He wants to see her. Apparently, he almost apologized."

"No shit?" Uncle Mike leaned back in his rickety swivel chair.

"I guess when the cops show up at your door at eight in the morning to ask you about the murder of your lover and you're trying to sleep one off, it makes you eat humble pie."

I sipped my coffee. "That's not all. The owners want to meet with Sal. They're nervous."

"When do they want to meet?"

"They haven't set a time yet. Nicole and I are going to see Sal."

"Sal is going to need support. I'm glad to hear Nicole is going to work with him."

"Saving the Nicoletti Barn hit a soft spot after all. I hope the crisis will bring Sal and Nicole together."

"She's a good woman. Try not to fuck it up this time."

"Working on it." I needed Uncle Mike's trash talk. My mind had been spinning. I'd thought through all the possible angles—the cartel, Ramon, others present around the track—and I couldn't eliminate Sal. Sal and Jessie had a lover's quarrel and an employer-employee fight, a fiery combination that could lead to murder. All last night, I'd thought about our conversation with Sal. If Sal shot Jessie, it had happened only minutes before we met with him. I thought of the wet raincoat, his muddy boots, and the golf cart parked outside his office.

When was Sal told about the murder? Uncle Mike said Sal was a "no-show" at the scene. What could he do? I suspected that he went home or to a bar and tried to drown out his misery.

The more I considered Sal as a possible suspect, the more I worried about Nicole. If Sal was charged, how would she take it? She was already overwhelmed by Jessie's murder. Nicole had eaten a little of Aunt Maureen's casserole so she could tell my aunt how much she liked it, took a sleeping pill and sat in front of the TV, and passed out.

I asked, "What about Saboski? Did you learn anything last night?"

"I learned that I should've worn my long johns. I was

freezing my ass off."

I laughed. Uncle Mike had worked murder cases that could pull the heartstrings to the breaking point, yet he was still able to maintain his sense of humor. His skin was thicker than cowhide.

I hoped some of his means of coping would rub off on me. Last night, I imagined grabbing Hugo and beating the truth out of him—not exactly a smart move to make with the cartel's resident dealer.

Uncle Mike sipped his coffee and puffed again on the cigar. "The preliminary report said that the shooting occurred about an hour before the body was discovered. I guess a witness said he heard a shot, looked outside, but didn't search around behind the parked cars and the bikes. Maybe due to the rain."

"The body was discovered later by a boy named Lopez?"

"Right. Around four o'clock. That's what Isabel told you as well?"

"Yeah."

"What else?"

"She thinks it could have been the cartel, but she didn't think a bullet would be enough."

"Right. When the cartel takes revenge, they send a message to others who might think about spilling their guts to the police. Isabel is pretty smart. We need to keep in contact with her. What else?"

"She thought it might be Ramon. Ramon's friends have pressured Jessie to leave Sal. Ramon thinks Sal was using Jesse. Ramon is one of these proud guys."

"That's not good. Maybe one of Ramon's friends argued with Jessie and things got out of hand. If so, Ramon will probably have that friend killed."

I hadn't thought about that scenario. I'd been more focused on Sal.

"Isabel also mentioned that Sal and Jessie had problems with some of the owners. The owners aren't paying their bills."

"Interesting. You were right about those folks in the dorms—they didn't have much to say to Saboski. They're worried about their jobs and the cartel. What time are you and Nicole going to meet with Sal?"

"Around two."

"Maybe I'll tag along."

I appreciated Uncle Mike's interest in Jessie's murder. Once he got wind of a murder case, he wouldn't let go. "You think it's Sal, don't you?"

"I reserve judgment, but Saboski has Sal in the crosshairs. And what do you think is going through Ramon's mind while he lies on that skinny mattress staring up at those prison walls?"

"He'll get his friends to kill Sal for sure."

"We'll be busy. You've got Tim to handle O'Connell's today?"

"Yes, I changed the schedule around." I could always rely on Tim, my assistant manager, to keep things running smoothly.

"I assume Nicole is okay with us sticking our nose into this?"

"Last night, she asked if we'd investigate Jessie's murder. I told her yes."

"Good. We'll need to bring her up to speed when you think the time is right. Meanwhile, let's get a list of Sal's horse owners. One more thing—Burrascano wants to meet."

"That's a surprise."

"If you're the mob's gambling boss and a murder occurs at the last race track in town, you get a handle on it."

I should've thought of this angle. "I'm sure Arlene would insist." We suspected that Burrascano and Arlene were co-owners of Thornton and that Burrascano was the silent partner. "When?"

"I don't know yet." Uncle Mike puffed on his stogie. "There's talk of Saboski getting a search warrant for Sal's office and other offices."

"Arlene will hate that." Arlene Adams kept an orderly backstretch and didn't tolerate outsiders, especially the police.

5

UNCLE MIKE, NICOLE, AND I MET UP WITH SAL AT his office at the track. As we went over Sal's list of owners, he took a phone call.

We had hoped for another venue—maybe a room inside the track or a restaurant—some neutral place where Sal could focus on his problems without the distractions of the office, but Sal insisted. He'd told Nicole, "It's where I do business day in and day out. That's not about to change." He planned to spend every "damn spare minute" in the office until they dragged him away.

Unfortunately, it would change and soon—he had to start serving his suspension in less than ten days.

Nicole, Uncle Mike, and I sat in the chairs that fronted Sal's desk, a desk loaded with stacks of invoices, lawyer pleadings, race schedules, and payroll records. The local newspapers were looking for a comment from Sal about the murder.

"Jessie was with me for many years. My suspension? It's a travesty," Sal said into the phone.

"Don't talk to the reporters, Sal," Uncle Mike told him. "Just hang up."

Uncle Mike's patience was wearing thin. We didn't have time to waste. We'd agreed to focus on the barn's owners and the upcoming suspension, rather than grill Sal about Jessie's murder, and yet Sal was talking to reporters.

Sal was the number one suspect. He didn't have an alibi witness—Nicole and I had arrived too late the day of the murder. Surveillance cameras around the track took note of the time, although at Thornton, surveillance didn't include the dorms.

Uncle Mike would be watching Sal closely.

Helen St. Clair, the criminal attorney, had also given me a call about a job for my PI business. Since her law firm was a good source of investigative work, I couldn't afford not to meet with her.

When Sal finally cut the phone call short, Nicole began, "We wanted to go over the transition—"

"Don't I have enough problems?" Sal said. "The murder of my top assistant and the suspension—why bother? Let those owners find their own way."

It was a lot to process—Jesse's murder and the suspension. It wasn't easy for Nicole either. If she hadn't gone to Vegas, she would've been in a position at this moment to step in and handle the barn, but five years away was too much. It was another layer piled on top of what was for her already a heaping mountain of guilt.

Nicole straightened in her chair. "C'mon, Dad. That's a shit attitude to take. Eddie and Mike are here to help. You know as well as I do that a two-year suspension is nothing in the world of horse racing. Others have stepped back from the job and then returned. So can you."

"Fine." Sal took a deep breath. "You've got the list. Keep going."

Nicole read from a printout. She'd made copies for me and Uncle Mike. "How about the Willinghams?"

"Sorry about my attitude—this is a lot. Thanks for helping me out, Mike. Saboski and his questions—he's got me tied up in knots."

"I understand, Sal. I assume he came down on you kind of hard?"

"Yeah." Sal looked at each of us. "Left me wondering where I stand. I mean murder, for God sakes."

"I assume you have a gun," said Uncle Mike. "I'm worried about Ramon's friends. Maybe we can talk about getting you representation."

Sal almost stood up out of his chair. "I don't need a lawyer. If Saboski gives me a fair shake, there won't be any need for lawyers."

I saw the vulnerable side of the trainer for the first time. It was an eye-opener. As a small-time horse player, I always felt that in each race I was forced to match wits with the trainer. Meanwhile, it seemed to me the trainer's job was to shuffle their horses around in class or from turf to dirt, or back, and from sprints to routes—all with the specific intent of driving up the odds on their horse and causing me heartburn.

"I'm always available if you need me. Stop by O'Connell's later. We'll talk," Uncle Mike said.

Uncle Mike was treating Sal like a victim, giving him that sympathetic cop voice. Yet Uncle Mike wasn't taking a stand against Saboski, either. Uncle Mike was walking a fine line to get at the truth.

Sal scratched at his gray hair. "Good. I'll do that, Mike. Thanks. Now, where were we, Nicole?"

"The Willinghams."

"Damn Willinghams." Sal stood and paced behind the desk. "We only get the stock they're trying to move or maybe one of their projects. We never get their stakes horses or top two-year-olds anymore. I always thought they gave up too soon on their horses. Like Freedom Rider, for instance…" He stared off in the distance. "Freedom Rider has true potential. He showed it in that move he made in his last race." Sal's lips tightened. "It doesn't matter anymore. The Willinghams, you know how they are—rich clients who can't afford to have their reputation dragged through the mud—their new trainer in Kentucky emailed me today. They're pulling all their horses from us."

"I'm sorry, Dad," Nicole said.

"That's tough," Uncle Mike said.

"You did an awesome job with Freedom Rider," I offered.

The Willinghams had assigned the horse to the Nicoletti Barn from their top local trainer. They required Sal to drop the horse into a claiming race, but when it didn't get claimed, Sal moved him into optional claiming races and then up to the allowance level. The horse had found something and had put together a nice string of wins. A stakes race was not out of the question.

The backstretch was the same as any business arena—ruthless decisions were made on a daily basis. A trainer had to establish a relationship with each owner. It was a two-way street, and to be successful, each had to listen to the other. As a horseplayer, today I had that rare chance to hear about the owner—trainer dynamics, and I gobbled up every morsel.

"What about Ray Marshall?" Nicole asked, moving on to the next owner on the list.

"He and his brother Terry—shit, those guys are party animals. They used to be all-in on the claiming game. Cigars and scotch whenever their horse won. Paid on time. Now they're easing out of it. I can't tell you how many of the top owners have left over the last few years."

I recalled the Marshall brothers. I'd bet on a number of their horses in the past. The fact they'd decided to leave horse racing turned my stomach. "Why are so many owners leaving?"

Sal laughed. "Pick your reason. There's the *joy of ownership,* but that wears off fast. After a few trips to the winner's circle, the afterglow is gone. When they enter the winner's circle, they take the opportunity to bitch at me about their bills. Everything is going up—the feed, the help, the vet bills—"

"We'll need a list of your receivables, Sal," Uncle Mike said.

"Sure. While you're looking them over, give them a call and tell them to send a check. Then you can listen to them bellyache and find out for yourself. You know what doesn't go up? The purses. Lot of risk and no reward. I always figured I'd be like a lot of the trainers out here—I'll own most of the horses I run. *Owned and trained* by Sal Nicoletti. I already have a few."

"Ronnie Orman does that, doesn't he?" Nicole asked.

Orman was the trainer who had agreed to take over for Sal during the suspension. It was a risky move for Sal—owners might decide to stay with Orman, instead of returning to Sal once he'd served the suspension.

Sal sat back down and sipped his coffee. "Yeah. He's got a few owners, though. I feel sorry for them. Orman likes to claim horses and then hike them up too far in class. Then he drops them a couple of races later and expects them to win. But the horse has learned to lose during his jump up the class ladder against tougher horses. You have to be careful. Plus, he likes to run his horse at the wrong distance or tries them on turf as if he expects to find a jewel in the rough. Orman ends up screwing with the horse's head."

"Haven't you claimed some of Orman's horses?" I asked.

"Yeah. I give the horse a month or two off and train the horse back."

I nodded. "Like that horse last week? Alto Blue?"

"That's right, Eddie. Did you have that horse? He paid good."

"I did." Uncle Mike gave me a sideways glance. He didn't approve of my gambling, and with good reason—I'd gone into debt several times. But a guy has to keep his hand in. I tried to limit my bets, stay in control, and keep a close watch on my bankroll. Whenever I felt like I was slipping back into my old habits, I took time off. Alto Blue paid thirty dollars to win, and I had a C-Note on him—a good day.

Sal smiled, impressed. "Good. Well, keep that strategy between us. I expect that after a long dose of Orman, my owners will welcome me back with open arms."

"Let's hope so," Nicole said, making a note on the clipboard.

"Your secret is safe with me," I said. Orman had a lot to gain. The suspension and then the murder of Sal's right-hand assistant played into Orman's hands. Did Sal and Orman already have a working relationship? What kind of person was Orman? I kept these questions to myself for now.

Uncle Mike sighed as he made some notes on the owner list. I wondered if he was thinking the same thing I was.

"Next, Diamond V Farm," Nicole said.

Sal got up again. "Good outfit." He stepped up to one of the winner's circle photos. "This is the latest winner," he pointed. "I don't know them all that well, but I'll tell you one thing—they pay their bills like clockwork, and they win. Professional. Jessie worked with their representative. I'll look them up and give you a name and phone number."

I made a note on the list that the owner was "current."

"Fine," Nicole said. "What about Crescent Farm?"

Sal's expression switched in an instant. "A bunch of bums. You can send them a termination letter for all I care. I don't know how much they owe, but it's probably at the top of our list of receivables. Send them to Orman. Put them on your call list, Eddie. Call them in the middle of the night. Those ungrateful bastards."

"What about Ridgewood Racing Stable?" Nicole asked.

"Hell," Sal said between gritted teeth. "That's another one that Jessie kept close tabs on. No problems."

"Let's move on." Nicole said.

We continued down the list. There were the golden owners, the ungrateful bastards and those looking for the exit. I had a number of calls to make.

After that exercise, Nicole said, "That leaves Mr. Van der Walt."

Pieter Van der Walt, known as Vandy, was the owner I wanted to hear more about.

"Yeah." Sal rubbed his forehead and squinted. He stared at the wall to his right, lined with those winner's circle photos. "You can find Vandy's horses all over the wall. We wouldn't have a barn without him. We need him. Jessie is the one who held his hand. She knew this track backward and forward, kept in touch with other exercise riders, and knew every horse down to their shoes. She could tell us what horses to claim, where to spot our horses and even when and where to ship them. She could also tell Vandy how to make the most money betting his horses."

Sal had lost an indispensable employee and lover. He was cut in two. He must be dying inside. What would he do during the upcoming suspension without horses to train and a business to run?

"Maybe Eddie could help," Uncle Mike suggested.

I almost fell out of my seat. Uncle Mike recommended me?

"What?" The old trainer studied me as if I might be a spy for another barn. "Nicole, what is this?"

Nicole seemed flustered at first and then exchanged a quick look with Uncle Mike. "Eddie's been following the horses here at Thornton for a long time."

"He knew about that horse you claimed from Orman. Alto something," Uncle Mike said.

"Alto Blue," I said. What were Uncle Mike and Nicole up to? Vandy was the claiming wizard—the man making magic behind the scenes. Vandy used his horses like chess pieces, placing bets as he moved them around the board at record speed. He bought horses in California and elsewhere and shipped them to Thornton. He also shipped horses from Thornton to tracks all over the Midwest, found easy spots to win, and then shipped them back. He was the kingpin of Chicago racing and, no doubt, made the Nicoletti Barn the envy of every other trainer on the grounds, and they wanted *me* to advise *him*? I was a track bum who tried not to lose his shirt. I just happened to luck out with the Alto Blue pick.

Then I thought again. That lightning-quick handicapping brain of mine began spinning, and I glimpsed what Nicole and Uncle Mike were hatching. It was Vandy's horse that had tested positive. I liked it. In fact, it was genius.

"Sure," I said. I wanted in.

Sal shook his head. "Why would Vandy listen to Eddie? You're pulling my leg—"

"What if Eddie meets with Vandy first?" Nicole said.

"Yeah. Maybe do a test at the track," Uncle Mike said. "See if the two of them can work together?"

Nicole leaned in toward her father. "You can't afford to lose Vandy."

"Alright, alright," Sal said, raising his hand to signal stop. "I've got to do something, and God knows I can't be talking horses to anyone with all this shit going on. I'll ask him. If he and Eddie can work something out, then fine. But don't expect me to force his hand. The guy tends to do the unexpected."

It was what we needed—a chance to work with the Wizard of Thornton and learn more. Vandy and Jessie had been close. He probably wanted to find the killer as much as we did. It could be the perfect partnership.

6

NICOLE WASN'T ABOUT TO VISIT THE BACKSTRETCH without saying hello to Isabel. After our meeting with Sal, Nicole called her and set up a meeting at Elena's, the track diner. Uncle Mike and I were happy to go along. Isabel's insight into the workings of the backstretch would be invaluable.

We needed to walk more than a couple of city blocks, past the shedrows, and then past the dorms on our left and the equipment sheds to our right. Owners with golf carts zipped past to pick up drinks and snacks from Elena's. Backstretch workers hauled plastic grocery bags from the parking lot to the dorms.

Halfway to Elena's, a woman screamed. It came from our right—one of the equipment sheds. I ran over.

A man stood over a woman. He wore fancy jeans, a leather coat, and a white cowboy hat. Isabel was kneeling in the dirt, her coat hanging off one shoulder. The man uttered a stream of Spanish and then bent over and slapped her face.

I shoved the man off her, then reached down to help Isabel.

He lunged toward me. "Hey, gringo, you know who I am?"

I turned as he threw a punch at me. I blocked it with my left arm and stood up over him. He was only five-ten, and I was six-four. His anger-filled Spanish told me he wouldn't back down. He threw a wild punch at my gut.

I dodged the effort, swung around and caught him with a right hook, flush to the side of his head. The cowboy hat flew off.

He wobbled like a bobblehead and reached into his coat.

"Eddie," Nicole yelled.

I didn't need the warning. I bolted forward and slugged the guy hard enough to propel him backward off his feet into a tractor. He was out for the count. I reached into his coat and grabbed his gun.

Another man ran into the shed screaming and yelling something in Spanish. He wore the same fancy jeans and cowboy boots, but he was a head taller and heavier.

"You want what your friend got," I told him.

When he saw the gun in my hand, he raised his hands and backed away.

"Take your friend and get out before we call Security," Uncle Mike said. "I don't want to see you two here again."

Nicole and Uncle Mike helped Isabel out of the shed while I kept watch. I assumed the second man also had a gun, but he didn't try anything.

"Thank you," Isabel cried. "I don't know what he'll do. You should leave. That was Hugo."

I knocked out the cartel guy? Good.

7

UNCLE MIKE AND I WALKED INTO THE SEYMOUR Professional Building at the south end of the Loop for our appointment with criminal attorney Helen St. Clair. It was an ancient three-story office building located alongside a Green Line "L" stop.

I nudged Uncle Mike. "I like these attorney appointments a whole lot more when I don't have criminal charges hanging over my head." I'd fought charges of battery due to a fistfight a number of years ago when I was young and stupid. A last-minute plea deal got me off the hook, but the experience haunted me.

"Yeah, visits to a lawyer are even better when they're paying you. The way you clobbered that guy yesterday—"

"I did Hugo a favor. Look at all the trouble he would've gotten into if he'd shot me."

Uncle Mike laughed. "I was impressed with Isabel. She got up and brushed off the dirt."

"She'd told me Hugo stalked her. I'm worried about her." It

wasn't only Hugo and the cartel; Isabel had to find another job.

"Do you think the cartel will take revenge?"

"I hope not. It wasn't her fault. I told Isabel to call us." I pressed the button for the elevator.

"Your PI business is beginning to work out, Eddie."

I welcomed the note of pride in my uncle's voice. Although St. Clair was a repeat client for my PI business, she had asked for Uncle Mike to join us. Maybe I should've been insulted by her request or, at the very least, a bit miffed that she didn't trust me to handle things on my own, but when I analyzed it more closely, I realized Uncle Mike and I were now viewed as a team by certain parties around Chicago, and I should simply accept it.

Uncle Mike, a former homicide detective, had connections to Burrascano, Chicago's gambling boss, a relationship that we didn't boast about, yet seemed to have found traction. To a prospective client, it meant we could offer a pipeline to the criminal element.

Mob guys could be tight-lipped and unpredictable, but we didn't bother to enlighten anyone of this fact. We found the murky rumors about our connections useful.

We still hadn't received a follow-up call from Burrascano about Jessie's murder. Burrascano often had information that could jump-start our investigation. I hoped the gambling boss would come through for us again.

We might need Burrascano more than ever. When you deck a guy who works for the cartel, you need all the underworld help you can muster.

I'd started making calls to Sal's owners this morning. So far, I'd left a number of messages, describing myself as Sal's assistant working to coordinate the move of the horses in Sal's care to trainer Ronnie Orman. Those who owed money hadn't called back.

Today's meeting with Ms. St. Clair sounded interesting. The criminal attorney had told us that certain property had been stolen from her client and that the thief demanded a ransom for its safe return. We would be expected to handle the payoff and the successful return of the property. We'd asked St. Clair about the nature of the property, and she told us the information would be revealed to us at today's client meeting.

Of course, Uncle Mike and I couldn't help but speculate upon the nature of the property on our drive downtown. What property was so unique that a thief would take such risks? Why not simply fence the stolen goods? Perhaps the "property" was a stamp collection or a special painting; some family heirloom with great sentimental value. We were eager to find out. We didn't come cheap.

Uncle Mike glanced around the vacant lobby and then back at me. "Helen St. Clair could do a whole lot better than this shitty building."

"She's been here for years. She's a smoker."

"I should've thought of that. Hey, who is Nicole picking tonight?" It was the Thursday night game.

"I get it. You want to bet the game before her telecast. Whoever Nicole picks might move the line."

"Just a small wager. When you're hot, you're hot."

Inside the elevator, I hit the button for the top floor. "I'll call her right after the meeting."

"No reason not to jump on the bandwagon."

We walked into the Spartan lobby of the law office and were greeted by the smell of cigarette smoke. The rounded, art déco, elongated counter of the receptionist desk made me think about sitting down and ordering lunch. High-backed wooden chairs were lined up against the wall as if a crowd of defendants was expected. The office lobby was empty except for the receptionist. Our mystery client must be late or possibly seated in one of the other rooms.

The receptionist led us down the hall to a conference room with a long table and cushioned swivel chairs. She asked if we wanted coffee, and we accepted. The windows were covered with tightly closed blinds.

After we'd gotten our coffee and checked our email, the conference room door opened and Helen St. Clair walked in slowly, holding the arm of her younger law partner, Pam Ferguson. St. Clair was in her mid-sixties and I was surprised to see that she needed assistance.

Ferguson was at least a foot taller than St. Clair and, from what I'd heard, was an avid windsurfer. Ferguson's deep tan and physique showed she'd managed to find time on the water this past summer.

"Gentlemen, don't get up," St. Clair said before dropping into the chair at one end of the table, out of breath. "My back acts up from time to time, and today is one of those days. My doctor tells me not to work so hard, but here I am."

She slipped on her thick glasses with the pointed frames that hung from a chain around her neck, took a deep, wheezing breath, and opened a manila file folder. She nodded toward us and forced a smile, her sharp blue eyes evaluating us. "Mike, good to see you. Eddie. Thank you both for coming."

"I had nothing better to do this morning," Uncle Mike said.

"You heard about Jessie Rivera's murder at the track?" I asked.

St. Clair nodded. "Yes, of course. You and Mike are working on it, I assume? I wouldn't think you'd have the time for my case as well—"

"We can make time," I said.

"A piece of cake," Uncle Mike said.

St. Clair smiled briefly. "Good. Thank you, gentlemen." She turned to Ferguson. "You left Professor Kovalenko in your office?"

Ferguson checked her watch. "Yes. Don't forget, we have court this afternoon—the prelim on the Robertson case."

"I know, I know." St. Clair brushed back her silver hair, cut in a short bob. "I wanted to talk to you two about the professor before we bring her into the meeting. She's a powerhouse in the field of biochemistry. She's Ukrainian. I don't need to tell you how sensitive that can be. Her full name is Yana Kovalenko, but please address her as *Professor* during our meeting."

Ferguson wrote notes on a legal pad, although she had a laptop nearby. I assumed her contemporaneous notes of our meeting could be considered business records of the law firm. It impressed upon me the serious nature of the matter.

St. Clair referred to pages she'd pulled out of the folder. "I have to go through our usual confidentiality talk, so listen up. I'm sorry for all the intrigue surrounding the nature of the client's matter, but I couldn't take the chance of telling you over the phone. It would be best if the professor told you about the exact nature of the stolen property when she joins us." She pointed a finger at Ferguson. "Pam, you want to do the honors?"

Ferguson read from her laptop about the importance of maintaining attorney-client confidentiality and how this extended to me and Uncle Mike in our capacity as investigators for the firm. After a long-winded review of our responsibilities, Ferguson slid some paperwork to us concerning these terms and conditions, including our fees.

After we signed the documents, St. Clair leaned forward. "Enough of that. You know the drill. I met the professor a few years ago at an alumni function. She has received a number of grants that have funded a lot of research for my alma mater. Her work on blood disorders has attracted attention." As she talked, she pulled a Marlboro Light from a pack she retrieved from her coat. At the same time Ferguson reached back and flipped a switch. A series of fans, positioned at far corners of the room, came to life, forcing air to circulate and funneled the smoke into a duct behind St. Clair. I felt like I was sitting in a wind tunnel.

St. Clair talked and smoked, as if the noted attorney couldn't do one without the other. I wondered how she managed in the courtroom, where a smoking ban would be strictly enforced.

She tapped the cigarette at the edge of the ashtray. "The professor's research has brought considerable prestige and money to Lake Shore University. Her work is extremely valuable to various industries supporting her research, and she holds a number of patents. I don't have to tell you the professor provides lots of jobs for many people connected to the university."

The build-up only added to my eagerness and growing anxiety about our investigation.

St. Clair stared first at me and then Uncle Mike. "I want you to know who you're dealing with. The professor comes from a family with *real* money. As you know, it's clients like the professor who keep the lights turned on around here and the fans humming. It allows us to take *pro bono* cases for those who are in dire need of our help, keeping them out of that damn criminal law factory they run over there in the courts."

"What do you mean, 'the professor comes from a family with *real* money'?"

My question drew a wry smile from St. Clair. Ferguson shook her head.

"It's quite strange, Eddie," St. Clair said, shifting in her seat. "I guess it's because I've never met anyone quite like her. She's a puzzle. Other people I've met in positions of great family wealth are born and bred to *be above the fray* and taught to accept a more luxurious lifestyle. Their focus is usually on charitable foundations as opposed to more serious endeavors such as— *cripes!*—biochemistry. Just when I thought I'd seen it all, I can still be surprised."

"Thank God there are a few people out there who can surprise you," Uncle Mike said with a laugh.

St. Clair laughed along with us. "Life would be pretty dull, wouldn't it? Pam, would you fetch our client? I'd like to get to court on time for a change."

After Ferguson left the room, St. Clair leaned forward as if she had additional secrets to pass along. "I don't have to tell you about the legal mess the professor could fall into. Her failure to contact the police about the theft could end her career. School policy is quite clear about what is expected. Reporting is mandatory. The thief could pose a danger to others, making a failure to report into a full-blown scandal."

She took a deep drag. "You see what the professor is risking. I can advise a client, but the client makes their own decisions even when those decisions pose a threat. That threat could point to both of you as well, you understand that?"

"I've spent years on the force," Uncle Mike said. "You don't need to lecture me."

"I'm beginning to like the professor." I wasn't one of those who made it a habit to follow rules either.

I didn't like the fact that we were still in the dark about the stolen property, but if Uncle Mike could take it in stride, I could. A little suspense might be good for me.

St. Clair shrugged. "You'll see. I only set the wheels in motion. I'm the facilitator, the troublemaker. I envy you, gentlemen. I might be wrong; this case might be less than nothing. But if my old instincts are right, your journey might just be beginning."

8

FERGUSON HELD THE DOOR OPEN. A WOMAN stepped tentatively inside, clutching one of those handbags rich women haul around. She was in her forties, thin, with her auburn hair pulled back in a braided bun. Her tweed skirt and matching blazer, high cheekbones and upturned nose, made me think "model" instead of "scientist," but then I recalled that the ravishing old movie star Hedy Lamarr had been a scientist and world-class inventor.

We stood as St. Clair made the introductions. Her voice caught as she said, "Gentlemen, allow me to introduce you to Professor Yana Kovalenko." It seemed Chicago's finest criminal lawyer was slightly in awe of the Professor.

We all nodded back and forth. The professor's hands continued to tightly clasp the handbag as if she suspected she was in the company of purse snatchers, but her expression didn't betray a case of nerves. In fact, she appeared to be the calmest person in the room. A casual smile suggested that she was somewhat amused. She held her head aloft and paused to make eye contact with each of us across the table, her eyes a startling shade of chestnut.

I sat down, somewhat in awe myself.

"Well, let's get to it," St. Clair barked, bringing us all to attention.

St. Clair lit up, and then the professor reached into her fancy bag and produced a cigarette as well, complete with a shiny black cigarette holder. She caressed a thin gold lighter with her long fingers and manicured nails. The click produced a powerful butane flame that kissed the tip of the cigarette with practiced elegance. Beneath long lashes, she looked directly at me as if the entire procedure had been part of an experiment to gauge the reaction from her improbable "detectives."

Ferguson, caught between competing cigarette clouds, rubbed her eyes and slumped in her chair.

St. Clair continued, "I want you to know, Professor, that our firm employs a number of investigators, each with various areas of expertise, although I can say without equivocation that you have the A-Team."

I appreciated the fact that we were the A-Team, but who were these other investigators? What work did they get that I didn't? The type of work St. Clair doled out wasn't easy for an investigator to find.

The professor extended her swan-like neck and exhaled smoke. "I appreciate that, Helen." Her Ukrainian accent struck me as exotic and expensive.

"If you could explain to them the nature of what you've lost and how you've been contacted, Professor, we can proceed." St. Clair said. "I've kept them waiting."

"Of course. I suppose the theft of my item will seem strange and hardly worth all this trouble, although it is, gentlemen, a most valued possession, so please, bear with me."

We nodded.

She glanced down the end of the table toward one of the windows covered by the tightly closed blinds. "The property stolen from me was a lab book, or journal, in which I keep my most important notes." She hesitated and took a deep breath. "These are not lab results, per se, which are always entered into the LIMS system, but rather my impressions of certain experiments, including stray thoughts, new ideas, research I may need to consider, and extraneous notes."

A hush fell over the room as Uncle Mike and I digested this information. My sixth sense told me that Ferguson and St. Clair awaited our reaction.

Uncle Mike broke the silence. "Was it just one book?"

The lawyers sat back. Uncle Mike's question signaled to all of us that the theft was, in fact, a grave matter and that we could proceed.

All this trouble over a notebook of doodling and scribbling seemed like a waste of time to me, but what did I know about the scientific method or patents? I didn't flinch. I was determined to play along. This table could easily pass for a poker table where each of us played for unknown stakes—maybe within the pages of her lab book one could find a shimmering jewel outlining some new discovery.

"Just one book, Mr. O'Connell."

"Can you describe it?"

"It is black and leather-bound. They are custom made. Other books are at home in my safe."

"We're talking about one stolen book then?"

She glanced at the blinds again. "Yes."

"What happened? When did you notice it was gone?" Uncle Mike asked.

"I always place the book in a locked drawer in my office when I go out. Then, I lock my office door. Otherwise, the book is with me. Yesterday morning, I came into my office and someone had jimmied open my desk drawer. The book was gone."

"Was the door still locked?"

"It was."

My uncle scratched the back of his neck. "Have you been contacted?"

"Yes, I had a message on my cellphone. A person said that they had the book and that I would have to pay."

"We'll need to listen to the message."

She stared at the blinds again. Upon closer examination, I noticed that two individual slats of the blinds were turned in the opposite direction from the other slats. Maybe the Professor felt compelled to get up and flip the unruly slats back in place to restore order.

"I can play it for you." She reached into her purse.

"Go ahead."

The room grew silent.

She held her cell in the palm of her hand. "*Professor, you shouldn't be so reckless. I have your precious notebook. You'll need to be taught a lesson. I'll be in touch.*"

It was a woman's voice, low and taunting. Payment for the lab book could be inferred from the words, "*I'll be in touch.*"

"Do you recognize the voice?" Uncle Mike asked.

"You think it's an inside job?" The professor smiled, and we shared a slight laugh. "No, I didn't recognize her voice."

"Is your cell number out there for the employees —"

"Yes, of course."

"When was the phone call made?"

"Later. Last night. I'd already called Helen."

"You didn't call back?" Uncle Mike said.

"I wanted to call. But Helen reminded me about how people record calls, using it to trap or harass a victim."

I thought of what St. Clair had told us when we were alone; about how the professor's failure to report the incident could lead to a scandal. I wondered what that initial conversation between the professor and St. Clair had been like.

"It's probably a burner phone, but we'll need the cell number." Uncle Mike said, continuing his line of questions.

"Of course."

"Are there surveillance cameras?"

"In the lab, not in my office or the hallway."

"We'll still need to look at the surveillance tapes."

The professor squirmed slightly in her chair. "I'll pay whatever—I can afford it. I don't want to press charges. I just want my journal back as soon as possible. Tomorrow at the latest. Surely—"

I interjected. "We need to cover all the bases."

She turned toward me as if she'd forgotten about my presence. "Of course." She pulled out another cigarette and fixed it in the holder.

Uncle Mike nodded. "You contacted Helen when you discovered it missing?"

It was like Uncle Mike to repeat a question.

"I couldn't go to the police."

Uncle Mike nodded. The thief could destroy the lab book if the police got involved.

"We'll need a list of the employees," Uncle Mike said.

"Is that necessary? I don't want—"

"I'm afraid it is, Professor," St. Clair said. "I realize theft is difficult. Being forced to pay for the return of your property only adds to the sense of being violated. How are you doing? Are you okay?"

The professor shifted slightly in her chair and placed one elbow on the table. "Yes, okay, I guess."

"You have someone to drive you back?" St. Clair asked.

"Yes, my chauffeur is here."

"One of us will go with you," Uncle Mike said. "It might seem a little too much, but I think it's warranted."

I assumed that the thief would make it their business to

follow the professor and might be waiting outside this very moment.

We couldn't have Professor Kovalenko talking to the thief. She was emotionally attached to her work. The perpetrators would try to exploit that. If we negotiated directly with them, the situation could be reduced to a cold-hearted transaction and increase the chances of recovery.

"We're going to the Lake Shore University Labs, correct?" I asked.

"Yes." The professor gave me a long look, and a slight smile creased her lips.

"It's a plan then," St. Clair said. "I have to run to court. Mike, Eddie, let me know what else you might need from us. Good luck."

The matter sounded easy enough, yet had its complications. My future work for St. Clair would depend upon results.

I knew the reason behind the professor's smile and the reason we'd been assigned to investigate the case. St. Clair had mentioned the professor's work with blood disorders. The Lake Shore University Lab was well known to those who followed the horses. The lab ran blood tests on horses running at tracks across the country.

9

I FOLLOWED THE PROFESSOR'S CHAUFFEURED limo in Uncle Mike's truck and managed to get caught in traffic on the way across the Loop. By the time I found my way to the lab building, located in a commercial warehouse area on the north side, Uncle Mike, and the professor had settled into her office. It was a large room with a big oak desk and jam-packed bookshelves lining the walls. They were talking like old friends. The professor had taken off her blazer, and wisps of hair hung down, framing her high cheekbones and penetrating eyes.

I took a seat beside my uncle in one of the two chairs that fronted the professor's desk. "I hope I didn't miss anything."

"Not much," Uncle Mike said. "Just a tour of the lab and the professor's life story on the way over."

"Please, Mike." The professor laughed. "You make me sound like one of those women who won't shut up."

During my walk from the main entrance to the professor's office, with a security guard beside me, I took notice of dozens of small rooms, each crowded with personnel, glassware, and instrumentation. The guard told me there were more lab buildings around us; the cluster was located several miles from the main campus. People in lab coats had walked past us down the hall, each person giving me a long look. I probably didn't pass for the scientist type.

I didn't need a tour inside each lab. What did I expect? That I'd walk into a lab room and spot the guilty party hunched over in a sweat?

No, but at least our presence on the heels of the commission of the crime might get the thief worried about who we were and what we knew. The perp might wonder what missteps they may've made or if someone suspected them and had come forward.

We also wanted to get the professor out of St. Clair's law office and back into her own office, where she could relax and tell us more. In a lawyer's office, people were generally afraid to talk as if whatever they said could come back to haunt them in court.

"St. Clair is a character, isn't she?" Uncle Mike said.

The professor shook her head. "Yes. We bonded over our smoking habit. We were AWOL from an alumni function, where Ms. St. Clair was the scheduled speaker. We stood outside in the night during a rainstorm, huddled beneath an overhang, puffing away like teenage criminals."

She was comfortable, but embarrassed. Her office door was closed, and I could only guess what her staff might be thinking.

"I was ready to light up my cigar in that conference room," Uncle Mike said.

"That would've really upset Ms. Ferguson," she said. "Ms. St. Clair is so lucky to have her."

Perhaps the professor would be even more comfortable if we settled into a designated smoking area outside, where Uncle Mike could also light up. I preferred her office, in close proximity to the scene of the crime. We needed to get a look at the drawer that had been jimmied open.

"You must have a 'Ms. Ferguson' you rely on," I said.

"I have several."

Uncle Mike leaned forward. "Have you shared with them—"

"No." She shook her head. "Never. I don't dare. School policy."

"Was anything else taken from your desk drawer?" I asked.

"No, nothing."

Uncle Mike snapped his fingers. "Maybe we should take a look at that drawer while we're here." He made it sound like an offhand suggestion.

"Of course." The professor stood and stepped away. "It's the top drawer." She pointed.

I walked around to the heavy oak desk and examined the lock. "May I?" The professor nodded. I pulled out the drawer. It was empty. The heavy grooves and splintered wood around the lock weren't the signs of a professional.

"Where did you get this desk?"

The professor blushed. "It was one of the few items my father brought over. It's been in the family for years."

"I wouldn't keep anything valuable in that desk," I said, taking a look at the other drawers, outfitted with similar locks. "The locks aren't much good."

"I'd listen to him, Professor. Eddie has a way with locks," Uncle Mike said. "Who else has keys?"

The professor took her seat behind the desk, while I opened the office door and took a quick look at the outside doorknob. If the door had, in fact, been locked at the time of the theft, someone had done an excellent job of picking the lock. Upon further examination, I did find some marks. Compared to the jimmying of the desk drawer, it looked like the work of a pro. I returned to my seat.

"I suppose school security, administrators, and some of my

office personnel have keys. A lab doesn't operate on a nine-to-five schedule. Tests must be run at odd hours and need to be monitored. But I believe that I have the only keys to my office."

"Of course," Uncle Mike said.

"Why keep your notes in a lab book instead of on a computer?" I thought of the advantages of encryption.

She pursed her lips. "I'll tell you why." Her anger caught me by surprise. "We've had several incidents. Hacking. We had a ransomware demand. I've complained to the school's IT department time and again. I've been more than a pest; I've been highly critical. I've met with the school's administrators. The money needed to withstand the attacks hasn't been allocated."

It was a good lead. As a means of revenge, someone might try to strike back at the professor. The thief's message had accused her, "*You've been reckless.*"

I did wonder why the professor didn't simply pay for a better system in the labs. If the lab's computer system was integrated with the school's IT for purposes of management and control, then, I assumed, "buying her own" wasn't an option.

"Who in particular in the IT Department?" Uncle Mike asked.

"I don't usually play the snitch, but I'm at the end of my rope." She stood and leaned over the desk. "My lab book includes notes that could be taken out of context. Certain ideas that could prove valuable for those trying to reverse engineer what I do here. As I said, we've been hacked before. I've lived the nightmare of having my data held hostage. My lab book—my own handwriting—was my last resort."

She trembled, her face red. "I'll give you their names. We've fought and argued. It's no secret." She pulled out the empty drawer. "When I found that drawer empty, I cried. The lab book gone. My last hiding place ransacked. I need your help."

10

OUTSIDE THE LAKE SHORE UNIVERSITY LABS, WE got into Uncle Mike's truck. As usual, I was behind the wheel.

Uncle Mike pulled out a stogie. "I got enough second-hand smoke at the lawyer's office that I might as well smoke a cigar."

"Thanks." I cracked the window. The weather was still sunny, but a cool breeze from the north confirmed that the expected cold front would arrive as predicted.

"It won't be easy, but we have no choice but to sit around and wait for this scumbag to call. That's what good detectives do— they learn to wait."

I grew up in my aunt and uncle's house. Many nights I heard my uncle digging through boxes of old case files as if there might be something in a file that he'd forgotten—cold cases from his days in the homicide department. He knew how to wait.

"You got the professor's life story, right? Is she married? Kids?"

Uncle Mike clipped the end of the cigar. "Nope. She's fully

dedicated to science."

"Maybe she's not always doing experiments. I've got a hunch about this lab book," I said.

"What? You think there's something in the lab book about the professor's love life?"

"Like a little black book of phone numbers?"

Uncle Mike chuckled. "Right."

"No, no little black book. Other scientific stuff."

"This ought to be good. Didn't you flunk chemistry in high school?"

I'd never live down that "F" in high school and laughed. "Forget about my shitty high school transcript. I was thinking about why St. Clair would contact us on this case. I know she talked about us as the A-Team and all that jazz, but I think we were retained for a particular reason, and I think the professor requested us."

"Interesting." He lit the cigar and filled the cab with smoke. "Okay, let's hear it."

It was Uncle Mike's cop voice. He was headed down that dark hole where clues lurked. Meanwhile, I headed west on Dempster toward Milwaukee Avenue.

"I think the professor heard from St. Clair about our connection to the gambling world. I think that lab book has some high-octane stuff."

"I'm listening."

"When you're a horse racing fan like me—"

"A fan? You mean a junkie."

I wasn't going to let the crude comment sidetrack me. Plus, I probably deserved it. "When you follow the horses, you can't help but read about horses being drugged."

"Like Sal's horse?"

"Right. Now that the feds are running the tests, horses test positive and trainers are getting suspended more often."

"Good. What does that have to do with the professor and

her stolen lab book?"

"I looked it up just to be sure. The Lake Shore University Labs run blood tests on horses. Not just Thornton Racetrack, but all over the country."

"Shit. Labs, horse racing. What the hell?"

"I know she told us that lab book has her notes and ideas, but it might also have a lot of stuff a horse player would want to know."

"You gamblers are all alike—you see a conspiracy around every corner. But this time, Eddie, I think you're right. Thieves don't usually lock the door on their way out."

11

THE NEXT FEW DAYS WERE FRUSTRATING. WE'D called the professor each day to ask if she'd heard from the thief, and she told us she hadn't. We had told her the delay was part of the thief's game to gain leverage. The professor seemed to be having second thoughts about giving us the list of IT names at the school, saying that she didn't want to make a big deal about it. All we could do was wait.

Our other case, the murder of Jessie Rivera, was not on hold. Detective Saboski had been busy with his homicide investigation, conducting a search of Sal's office and his house. According to Uncle Mike's contacts, no incriminating evidence had been found.

We'd tried to meet with some of Ramon's friends in the backstretch, but Saboski was keeping a tight lid on things. We'd have to wait.

The presence of the authorities on the backstretch had one benefit—Isabel told us she hadn't seen Hugo or his buddies around.

We'd heard from one of Burrascano's men. Burrascano wanted to meet with us, and we'd set up a meeting later tonight.

Nicole, Uncle Mike and I went to Thornton Racetrack during the day for Winning Spirit's last race. Sal had arranged for his top owner, Vandy, to claim the horse for ten thousand dollars in its previous race upon Nicole's urging. It was agreed that after today's race, Winning Spirit would be retired to aftercare, where the old warrior could graze hilly pastures and ease back; a chance to smell the roses.

Nick Nicoletti, Junior, Nicole's uncle, had claimed Winning Spirit during the horse's four-year-old season and had won a couple of races before losing him to another barn. Nicole worked with the horse back then, before Nick Junior passed away, and Sal, Nicole's father, took over—before Nicole moved to Vegas. Back then, Nicole had become attached to Winning Spirit.

In a claiming race, a horse could be bought outright by anyone filing a claim prior to the race. If more than one person filed a claim, a shake of the dice would determine the new owner. Claiming races were the lifeblood of the track. The allowance races and stakes races, featuring the big stars of the sport who attracted publicity and TV coverage, took place at the end of the day's races. The claimers were the working-class heroes of horse racing.

Nicole, Uncle Mike, and I stood along the rail as Winning Spirit was loaded into the starting gate, hopefully for the last time. Officially he was a gray horse, but when the light hit his coat just right, like today, he was a silver color.

The jockeys prodded their mounts into the gate. I saw the look of anticipation in Nicole's eyes, a look that showed me her love for the horse, and maybe just a bit of fear and hope as well, praying the old war horse would make it around one more time without incident.

"What do you think, Eddie? He's at fifteen to one—no one thinks he can do it," Nicole said.

"The money is still flowing in. The odds could change." I tried my best to sound optimistic, though Winning Spirit's past performances told another story.

The nine-year-old had run sixty-seven times, and amassed total earnings of three hundred and twenty-four thousand, one hundred and eighty-four dollars, with twelve wins, fourteen seconds, and six third place finishes during his seven-year career. It averaged out to four thousand, eight hundred and thirty-nine dollars per start. Last year he ran fifteen times and won forty-seven thousand dollars. This year he'd run six times and hadn't finished better than fifth.

Other horses acted up in the gate as the last horses were being loaded. Winning Spirit stared straight ahead—all business.

The records showed every race he'd run since his two-year-old campaign, when he broke his maiden, and then ran in the allowance ranks, where he didn't quite cut it. At the end of his three-year-old season, he was dropped down into the claiming ranks, where he'd stayed for the remainder of his career.

Winning Spirit never made it to the top tracks on the West Coast or East Coast, though he'd been everywhere else. Claimed by one barn after another, he'd been shipped around from Chicago to Arkansas, Oklahoma, Ohio, Philadelphia, and New Orleans during his career.

"He always gives his best," Nicole whispered to me like a prayer.

The last horse was loaded, and the starter waited for a couple of other horses to settle down. Then the bell rang, and the gates crashed open, and the eight-horse field took flight.

"C'mon, Spirit," Nicole screamed, slapping the top of the rail. Uncle Mike and I echoed her cheers.

The jockeys' silks flashed a wide array of colors in the afternoon sun. Winning Spirit broke sharp and raced forward, the jockey guiding him over to the rail for the one-mile contest. Eight furlongs had been a winning distance for Winning Spirit throughout his career, and he liked to run close to the front, stalking the leaders. The odds had gone up to seventeen to one instead of down—never a good sign.

Sal had given Winning Spirit a couple of months off, and the freshening seemed to be paying off as the horse settled and bided its time down the backstretch—the straightaway alongside the stables and dorms. Other horses moved up behind Winning Spirit. The pace had been brisk, and I hoped that would work to Winning Spirit's advantage when he made his move down Thornton Racetrack's long stretch.

"C'mon," Nicole yelled. "C'mon, Spirit, you can do it."

"Hang in there, Spirit," I screamed.

Uncle Mike chanted, "Go, go, go, c'mon."

A few old, tired horseplayers along the rail looked over at us and then checked the tote board to confirm the long shot odds, and then turned and smiled at us, shaking their heads, probably concluding we were "rookies," instead of seasoned horse players. We had purchased token win tickets as a matter of faith only, because today wasn't about the money or the career earnings or exactas or trifectas or any of that; it was about saying goodbye.

Of course, that didn't sit well with Sal. "Saying goodbye" wouldn't make a trainer a dime, and he'd complained about Nicole's "harebrained scheme" since claiming the horse. It hadn't helped their already frayed relationship.

"C'mon, Spirit, c'mon," we yelled together.

I tried to convince myself that the pack of cheap claimers, the bottom rank of horses that Spirit now raced against, had lost interest in winning and would be satisfied to trudge along behind to the finish line. Maybe the field had gotten together and bought a gold watch for Winning Spirit, and none of us horse players had a clue. But the favorite began moving up fast on the outside, full of run.

"C'mon," we yelled.

At the top of the stretch, Winning Spirit made his move, getting the first jump on the leaders. The favorite followed right behind Winning Spirit. Along the rail, the old horseplayers shot us a sour look and yelled in tandem for the favorite. Nobody got a free ride down the stretch.

By mid-stretch, Winning Spirit dug in and passed the leaders, who were done for the day. The favorite gained momentum, a half-length behind Winning Spirit, who was in the lead. They'd be eye-to-eye soon, and the mind games would begin.

The valiant claimer needed us more than ever. "C'mon, Spirit. C'mon."

The horses came together in front of us, Winning Spirit maintaining a nose advantage.

We were all screaming. The pounding hooves filled my ears as the horses charged past toward the wire. Nicole jumped up and down beside me, grabbing hold of my shoulder for support, as if the higher she leaped, the better the chances were for victory.

They battled all the way to the end. The announcer's frantic race call said it all—"too close to call, a photo finish."

The old horseplayers shook their heads, and one of them said, "I hope you got it."

I grabbed Nicole in a bear hug, and she slung her arms around my neck. Did the stellar effort really matter? For Winning Spirit, it had, and for those around us it had, and maybe some people in the stands, and others betting through simulcasting, but everybody else, everybody else, had simply missed out.

There wouldn't be a replay on a sports channel. At seventeen to one, it was the perfect ending, and struck the highest note any horse player could ask for. We made our way down to the winner's circle.

"Damn, Eddie," Uncle Mike said. "Are you sure I should go down there? I'm not an owner."

"Neither am I," I said. "I wouldn't miss it."

Uncle Mike smiled at me like a guy getting away with petty larceny.

After the race, Winning Spirit came back first, his head held high, and pranced around before the tote board. The favorite trotted up later and circled before the tote board, waiting for the decision on the photo. It didn't take long. Winning Spirit's number was posted first.

My heart was pounding. The three of us joined Pieter Van der Walt—Vandy—with Sal and Alejandro before the camera. Isabel held a loose rein on Winning Spirit, the jockey, all smiles, still on board.

Vandy was unshaven and wore an old leather bomber jacket. A few inches taller than Sal, Vandy took the opportunity to shake everyone's hand. He looked up at me from beneath the brim of a Churchill Downs cap and said, "I hear you're the expert. We need to talk." Then he moved on.

I didn't have a chance to respond. Instead, I relished the scene. The horse was breathing heavy. How many times had Winning Spirit posed for this picture? It was his thirteenth win. I hoped that didn't mean bad luck. He knew how to win. As the horse bobbed its head and stomped its feet, it seemed he knew exactly what this game was all about.

After the photo, as they walked off, I heard Vandy tell Sal, "This horse is a winner. It would be a damn shame to retire him now. He's still got plenty left in the tank."

I didn't dare tell Nicole what I'd heard. She might've grabbed the jock's whip and chased Vandy out of the track.

12

THAT NIGHT, UNCLE MIKE AND I HEADED WEST ON the Eisenhower Expressway. Usually, we'd meet with Burrascano in his private suite at Thornton Racetrack, but due to Jessie's murder and the ongoing investigation, Burrascano had chosen another venue. The mob's gambling boss shunned publicity, and the old track was in the midst of being showered with its fifteen minutes of fame. The meeting would be held at the Old Shagbark Country Club on the west side to avoid all that.

The media loved the moniker "Backstretch Murder." Even the word "backstretch" brought to mind a shadowy, dangerous world, unknown to those who only played the horses once a year on Derby Day.

The story had all the angles—the lover's quarrel involving Sal Nicoletti, the trainer of the legendary Chicago Nicoletti Barn, and boss of the victim—the forgotten history, the sport, and the quirky characters. The media posted pictures of past champions trained by the barn, including grainy black and white photos of

Nick Nicoletti Senior standing in the winner's circle forty-five years ago before a massive, adoring crowd.

Attendance at Thornton had even increased slightly due to the publicity, despite its location in one of those "dangerous neighborhoods" near abandoned factories, where drug gangs allegedly prowled by day and by night. Suburbanites would now risk a trip to the track to see things for themselves and get a taste of Chicago's past. For some, it was their past as well—their grandfathers had taken them to Thornton Racetrack years ago.

I couldn't believe yesterday's article about track owner Arlene Adams. They used her publicity stills from long ago—the sex kitten who had her own show in Vegas when she wasn't doing movies—and mentioned that "Ms. Adams might be available on Thornton Derby day to sign autographs."

Ronnie Orman had been interviewed about how he planned to handle the horses from the Nicoletti Barn while Sal served his suspension. He talked a good game, but Uncle Mike and I planned to meet with Orman later to ensure that his temporary stewardship of the Nicoletti horses was just that—temporary.

The media hadn't taken an interest in the dorms or their residents, but it did a culinary piece on Elena's. The Karras family had brought out its special Italian Beef for the occasion, even though high-priced breakfast burritos were the everyday staple.

I suspected the WagerEasy area manager kept the publicity mill running. There was an article about the sportsbook and casino currently under construction beneath the grandstands, a joint project by the track and WagerEasy. Like all Chicago construction projects, it suffered from "unforeseen delays," but the article offered splashy graphics of "what would be." I'd worked briefly at WagerEasy several years ago, and I knew how much they hated to go over budget. I'd be shocked if the project was completed during my lifetime.

Sal had learned his lesson and dodged the reporters, leaving the media types to interview other trainers in a vain attempt to unravel the new federal laws cracking down on the horse racing industry and the use of prohibited drugs. Contamination could happen these trainers argued—a groom with a meth habit, a groom with diabetes, or a groom with a head cold, spraying antihistamine—anything could happen, and the poor trainer would be saddled with strict liability, which meant, by law, that unless there was proof of innocence, the judge or arbitrator must return a finding of guilt. The laws, a last-ditch effort by Congress to clean up the dying sport, were another work in progress.

I wondered if these articles would change the way people thought about horse racing, but I didn't hold out much hope. Any minute, the public's attention would leap to another viral target—a three-headed chimp or a UFO.

We had more important concerns than the welfare of horse racing. Uncle Mike and I were trying to convince Nicole and Sal that Sal needed a criminal attorney. What if Sal was charged with murder, we asked. We needed to be prepared. We recommended St. Clair, but Nicole and Sal were still in that "what do we have to hide?" stage.

It was close to ten o'clock by the time we arrived at Old Shagbark Country Club in the western suburbs to meet with Burrascano. The lights were off in the long, four-story brick building that reminded me of a castle. Any of the golfers who had braved the fifty-degree temperatures during the day would be long gone. We drove toward the back of the parking lot, where three limos were parked. A tall, heavyset man in a black overcoat waved us over to a parking spot. I spotted another man standing in a row of stately trees at the edge of the lot.

I parked and then rolled down the window of Uncle Mike's truck.

The man in the overcoat bent down and flashed the end of a penlight in our faces. "Your names?"

Uncle Mike leaned in closer. "How you been, Lou? Keeping your nose clean?"

The large man with a bent nose smiled and nodded. "Yes, sir, Mr. O'Connell."

"Good lad."

"I'll show you guys in," he said.

I hated to admit it, but the cloak and dagger stuff was kind of cool. Lou led us through a back door, into the men's locker room, past an elevator, and then up a narrow stairway, used by the help to deliver drink orders. We stepped into a dark room. As my eyes adjusted, I realized it was a large barroom. Rows of liquor bottles gleamed behind the long oak bar. Another man stood at the end of the bar, his back to us, staring out the windows. Lou led us past the bar and up another narrow flight of stairs into a meeting room, where the lights were on. There were a few circular tables with chairs.

"Make yourselves at home," Lou said. "I'm afraid the bar ain't open."

"That's okay," Uncle Mike said.

I sat down. "You were right, the room above the Hickory Pub."

"I knew it," Uncle Mike said, taking a seat. "I would've bet money on it. Joey L and I met here a few times back in the day."

We needed to find out as much as we could from Burrascano, because he never told us more than he thought we needed to know, which didn't amount to much. Assuming the gambling boss hired us to find the killer, we'd lose what little bargaining power we had to gain information.

Of course, we didn't want to share much with Burrascano either. Although we assumed the gambling boss made it his business to know the day-to-day activities on the backstretch, we didn't assume he knew everything.

There was a brief knock on the door, the kind of quick knock a doctor makes before they step in to see a patient. The door opened.

Vic DiNatale stepped inside. "Eddie, Mike, thanks for coming. Do you mind standing? Routine."

We stood.

DiNatale's massive frame made the room that much smaller, and his husky, garbled speech made it difficult to understand him. He'd been the mob's chief enforcer, sent to quell any threat to the mob's interests. If he showed up in Vegas, rest assured a rival gang had tried to make a move on the mob's territory. His mere presence would cause the gang to rethink their strategy. His success had not gone unnoticed, and I assumed he would succeed Burrascano when the time came.

"Hi Vic," I said, raising my arms. "Have you been busy?"

"We haven't seen you since Vegas," Uncle Mike said.

"You should drop by for a beer," I said.

DiNatale didn't smile or say a word in response. He gave us a frisk, and I got a whiff of his heavy cologne. He grabbed our phones, and his fingers hunted through our clothes for any hint of a wire.

"Thanks, gents. I'll leave the phones just outside. Mr. Burrascano will be in shortly."

We sat back down as DiNatale left and closed the door.

"Vic is all business tonight," I said.

"Fairly hospitable, I'd say," Uncle Mike said. "It's a nice gesture. Getting frisked by the second in command is their way of showing respect."

DiNatale had never appreciated our role in these jobs for Burrascano. He felt that using outsiders to do mob business showed weakness.

There was a knock on the door again, the door opened, and then DiNatale wheeled in Burrascano. The mob's gambling boss was bent over in a wheelchair, his lap covered by a heavy green wool blanket. His hair had thinned out, and his face was so white, it was almost translucent. I bit my bottom lip to squelch my reaction—I recalled how Burrascano once stood ramrod straight, his steel wool hair and bespoke suits suggesting a man in full, a Wall Street titan or captain of industry.

We knew he'd been in and out of hospitals, undergoing treatment for cancer, but that's all we'd heard. We weren't told what type of cancer he had or his prognosis. On our last job for Burrascano, a few years ago, we'd spoken to him over the phone while driving in a limo with DiNatale. What was so special about today?

"Eddie, Mike." Burrascano whispered.

We scooted our chairs closer to hear him.

"Hello, my friend," Uncle Mike said.

I knew my place and stayed silent. DiNatale remained standing, one hand on the handle of the wheelchair—his face solemn and unreadable.

Burrascano turned toward Uncle Mike, and a wisp of a smile stretched his features. "No cigars."

"No." Uncle Mike shook his head. "No cigars."

Burrascano took a deep breath. "This murder at the track. I'm staying out of it. Changes…" His eyes closed and his mouth dropped open. We waited, and then I began to worry if he had expired right then and there.

DiNatale didn't flinch.

Uncle Mike rubbed his chin and gave me a worried glance. "Rosario?"

When I was about to suggest we call an ambulance, Burrascano opened his eyes.

"I know you guys—you'll look into it on your own. Okay." One hand reached out, and he tapped his chest. "I can't. For now. Bullshit commitments. Ippo…"

I tried to memorize every word so I could string them together later to analyze their meaning.

Burrascano's fish eyes glanced at each of us. "Not my call. Fucked up. Vic will be able to handle…" He froze as if in a trance and then his eyes closed. His shoulders slumped over even more.

Vic will—what? What was it all about?

DiNatale tightened his grip on the wheelchair.

Uncle Mike tried to get answers. "Rosario, what—"

"That's all." DiNatale took a deep breath, shaking his head. "He's out. He wanted to be here. You'll need to leave. Thanks for coming."

"What did he mean by 'you'll be able to handle'?" Uncle Mike asked.

DiNatale shook his head. "Later."

Uncle Mike and I stood. Burrascano had fallen asleep, his head hanging, his breathing heavy and labored. He must've wanted to tell us more—but what? Why go to all this trouble?

Uncle Mike reached out and touched Burrascano's shoulder on our way out. "Goodbye, old friend."

—

On the drive back toward the near north side and O'Connell's, I waited for Uncle Mike to comment about the meeting. He hadn't bothered to light the cigar that was firmly clenched in his jaw. His window was cracked open as if he'd intended to light it, causing the traffic noise from the interstate to flood the cab.

Uncle Mike's connections, first Joey L and then Burrascano had been the source of our jobs for the mob. What was different about this murder? Or why set a meeting in the first place? I had a stream of questions, but I had to remain patient. I flipped on the radio.

Finally, Uncle Mike spoke. "Interesting. In the past, Burrascano has always given us some valuable insight or a contact."

He allowed the comment to hang. I waited. Uncle Mike shifted in his seat. He seemed to be going through a mental progression. What must it be like to see an old friend with one foot in the grave?

"My guess," Uncle Mike said, then hesitated. He took the cigar out of his mouth. "Burrascano isn't his old self. In the old days, he'd never have allowed us to see him like this. The track has faded in importance for the mob, but it has always been near and dear to his heart."

Burrascano kept a private suite at Thornton Racetrack. He had a long relationship with Arlene Adams. We speculated that Burrascano even held an ownership interest in the track. The dying crime boss loved the horses.

What "commitment," what "changes"? I bit my lip and waited. Sometimes a detective did his best work with his mouth shut.

"Let's think this through," Uncle Mike said. "We have a murder of an important assistant trainer for one of the track's top barns. We know the trainer, Sal, through Nicole. Burrascano knows all this—knows of your relationship to Nicole. He knows we're all-in on finding the killer. Hell, Jessie was family for Nicole, and Nicole is like family for us."

"Right." I hadn't thought of tonight's meeting through the eyes of Burrascano. I thought only of what I could get out of it.

"Burrascano knows we're investigating. Why all the guys at the golf club? I'm sure there were more of Burrascano's men on the premises that we didn't see. Something's going on."

"Like what?"

"It's a puzzle," Uncle Mike said, pulling out his lighter. "Burrascano mentioned Ippo. Alessio Ippolito, known as The Hippo, is a mobster who deals drugs. Although Burrascano hates dealing drugs, he had commitments. He was forced to look the other way when it came to drugs. It was common knowledge within the department. If Burrascano passes away, DiNatale will be free of those commitments."

"I get it. Vic will be free to handle things."

"DiNatale and Ippo the Hippo will fight it out. Burrascano sees the inevitable—a battle of succession. Maybe he gave DiNatale orders. Now we know why all those men were posted around the golf club."

I'd heard that The Hippo was just as vicious as DiNatale. Maybe worse. "There will be fireworks?"

Uncle Mike lit his cigar. "Count on it."

13

THE NEXT DAY, I WAS SCHEDULED TO MEET WITH Pieter Van der Walt, the claiming genius and Sal's top owner. Instead, Vandy called me to say he'd meet with me at the track on Friday and do our test on that afternoon's card.

"I'm excited about what you've got to offer, Eddie," Vandy had said.

Yeah, so excited that he canceled our meeting today and would meet me for the first time tomorrow—then dump his little test on me and drop me when I screwed things up. Vandy probably felt obligated to test me out as a favor to Sal, but the test, the audition, might be as far as the Wizard planned to go.

It seemed the plan to place me close to Vandy had begun to unravel before it got out of the gate. Maybe the whole idea was a pipe dream.

I remembered an old racetrack trick—"Call it a bad beat and move on to the next race." Nicole and Uncle Mike were counting on me to work with Vandy and learn more. That was my goal too—not getting into a "head game" with the Wizard of Thornton.

My role had become even more important now that Burrascano had bowed out. When you solve murders for the mob with the agreement that the killer will be turned over to the authorities, it gives you a certain amount of leverage and confidence. Burrascano was a backstop of sorts. Sometimes people learned of our connection, and it made it that much easier for us to question witnesses. The gambling boss had been our trump card in the dangerous game we played. Now, we'd have none of that going for us.

I worked on my laptop, handicapping tomorrow's races in one corner of O'Connell's, while Nicole worked on the upcoming NFL games in another. I set up shop near the kitchen, where I could keep an eye on things while I studied past races.

My old friend Marini walked up to my table. As a former sportswriter, he often brought Nicole invaluable information on the status of players' injuries—info he'd picked up from his old contacts at the Trib's sports department.

"Hey, Eddie, I see you've got the past performances up on the laptop. I was worried about you for a while. I thought you'd given up on the ponies." His sly smile told me that he had never really thought that.

"I'm going to the track tomorrow to help Nicole's dad, so I thought I'd look them over." It was a cover story. I didn't need Marini asking me "who do you like?" I didn't have much time to get up to speed for tomorrow's test with Vandy, and I couldn't afford to waste it arguing with Marini about horses.

"The Backstretch Murder? It has been hard on Nicole," Marini said, shaking his head. Marini pulled up a chair and sat down. He tossed his worn carryall satchel into the midst of my notes.

"Don't mess up my notes," I said.

"Sorry. You know, I should get you on my podcast to talk

horses sometime." His podcast had grown in popularity throughout the Chicago area, providing talk about football and other sports. "Maybe when football season is over and we have some dead air we need to fill."

Dead air and horse racing—that about summed up the sport. "You want a beer?"

"Sure, I could use one."

Was there a time when Marini couldn't? I got up and refilled my coffee mug and got a draft for Marini. Maybe he'd take the hint and go.

Instead, he stroked his beard and said, "You know, what I could really use is your help."

I set my pen down and leaned back in my chair. Another Marini problem was the last thing I needed. My old friend had a whole laundry list of problems.

"I've been writing this book…"

Marini had been writing "this book" ever since he got laid off from his job at the Trib two years ago.

"I don't know nothing about books." It was a lie. I knew plenty. Growing up, I used to sit on the stairs leading from the back of the bar to the basement storeroom, reading books and listening to the barroom chatter. Uncle Mike had a collection of mysteries and spy novels that I'd absorbed.

"I know," Marini said, "but this is your area of expertise."

I could see my fib wouldn't get me off the hook. "What?"

"Well, I was hoping you could read this over." Marini stood and fumbled through the carryall and pulled out a massive stack of papers. He dropped the mess onto my handicapping notes.

"What the hell?"

"Sorry." He fished around on the table in a sorry attempt to organize the mess, shoving some of my notes onto the floor. I picked them up and placed them under the laptop.

"Let me tell you what it's about," he said, talking fast. "My main character is an old guy named Wynton. He has money troubles. His son is a star quarterback."

"Wynton?"

"Yeah, anyway, Wynton's son, Nolan, is breaking all the QB records that Wynton set back when he was playing at the university."

"What college?"

"I don't know. Pick a Big Ten university, if it helps. It's fiction. But these days, Nolan is getting paid big bucks based on that name, image, likeness thing—almost half-a-mil a year. Wynton—all he ever got out of his college career was a bum knee and concussions."

"Poor Wynton."

"That's not all. Nolan has a new Corvette and is dating the hottest chicks on campus, while Wynton gets laid off from his job at the local car dealership. As the fraternity's adult sponsor, Wynton witnesses the parties and fun that Nolan and Nolan's frat brothers are having, while Wynton needs to schedule a knee replacement and doesn't have any medical insurance. What does Wynton do?"

"He gets drunk and gets in a fight," I said.

"No, he starts getting inside information from Nolan and his frat brothers. Wynton starts betting like a machine and winning—in-game parlays, props, all sorts of bets on his son's games. But he's not telling anyone except his wife, and there's conflict with the wife."

"She's no fun?"

"You see, I need your help to review the manuscript. I'd ask Oscar, but he's dead. I mean, Wynton is winning, and all the legal sportsbooks cut him off. Wynton needs another outlet."

Too bad, our old local bookie Oscar Colasso would've been perfect for Marini's shitty job. Oscar had been murdered several years ago, but that was another story. "Ask me about what? Illegal bookies?"

"Yeah. Wynton wants to bet big money—amounts his wife

doesn't know about. Wynton has the fever, you know?"

"I get it. Wynton wants to get even—he didn't make a dime when he played for the old *alma mater*, but his son is filthy rich."

"Right," Marini brightened and gulped the beverage, beer foam hanging on his beard—it hadn't been my best pour. "Wynton bets his ass off and gets in trouble with the illegal bookies. That's where you come in."

"What?"

"Wynton gets in trouble—the way you did that one time."

"I'm what—a specialist on losing?" This Wynton guy was beginning to piss me off.

"No," Marini began to talk even faster. "Not like that at all. Who else can I get? I can't ask these illegal bookies; they won't talk. They'd probably give me a beating. Just read it. Let me know what you think. I'll leave it right here. No rush. Next week is fine. I really appreciate this, Eddie. You and I go way back. And I tell you, I really need this. I'm thinking of making it into a screenplay. You know these podcasts—Joe Rogan makes a bundle, but the rest of us don't make squat."

What could I say? We did go way back. I wondered how much of Wynton's story was Marini's story—he was always betting too much and losing. "I'll take a look. Want another beer?"

14

LATER THAT DAY, AFTER O'CONNELL'S HAPPY HOUR rush, I grabbed takeout from the Dragon Palace and went home. Nicole had returned from the studio and was sitting in front of the TV, watching the NFL Channel.

"I've got the provisions." I carried the bags to the kitchen counter.

She came over, threw an arm around my neck and pulled me down. She gave me a hot kiss, and I began to lose interest in food. She wore one of my Bears T-shirts and not much else, except that perfume I liked.

"Where are your clothes?"

"I'm too tired to put on clothes."

"What would the neighbors say?"

"I don't see any neighbors." She kissed me again and then shoved me away. "I'm starving. Did you get potstickers?"

"I got all your favorites."

"Great." She pulled out the cartons of food. "I guess you

have to study the horses again tonight?"

"Yeah. I'm getting a good feel for Thornton. I'll just watch more replays."

"Good. That gives us plenty of time."

"For what exactly?"

"Guess."

"Give me a hint."

"I just did."

Nicole pulled out plates from the cupboard. "I don't know what you're doing for that attorney, but I don't like it. Not after what happened in Vegas—it's too dangerous."

Nicole knew firsthand how dangerous our cases could be. "Nicole, we've been over this already. The job for St. Clair should be simple."

She pulled back her long, silky black hair and began to fill her plate with food. "I still hate it. You talked about winding down your detective business. I have my dad to worry about—I don't need to worry about you, too."

"Uncle Mike knows the ropes. Just worry about Sal." It was a lame excuse. Just because Uncle Mike was working the case with me didn't mean things couldn't become dangerous.

"Too bad Dad couldn't join us," she said.

"I'm sorry he couldn't make it. We have enough to feed an army."

"He said he needs to clean up loose ends at the office. It's the last thing he needs." Nicole was afraid he might do something drastic. Questions had already come up about Ronnie Orman. Orman wanted to winter at Turfway, a track in Kentucky, while Sal preferred the track in New Orleans, where a judge's injunction, placing the new federal law in legal limbo, would allow Sal to continue to train. "I gave Dad the name of my therapist so he could vent. He thinks a therapist is for suckers."

When Nicole couldn't get the image of Jessie lying in the mud out of her head, she'd gotten in touch with a therapist right away. Thank God, she no longer cried out, "*Who* would *do* this to Jessie?" The anguish still persisted, but she was making progress.

She continued to stay in touch with Isabel and others who worked for Sal. Nicole was concerned about them. A couple of Sal's employees had gotten jobs with Orman.

"Sal needs to move on," I said.

"God, what a nightmare."

I let her comment hang. It seemed everything was part of the nightmare—Sal, the murder, and me.

"Move on? What bullshit." She looked around the kitchen. "One of these days, Eddie, when my white elephant sells, we need to get a place."

Nicole had taped her broadcast earlier that afternoon and was still in "TV Nicole" mode—that meant she was "on her game"—sharp, quick, and insightful. I'd gotten used to it. She could switch subjects and catch me off guard, but I'd learned to roll with the punches.

"The house will sell. It's in a great location." When it did sell, and if my bankroll was in decent shape, it would be nice to get a house with extra room. Right now, we had boxes stacked to the ceiling in the spare bedroom.

"If I have to drop the price again…"

I changed the subject. "How did it go today?"

"The show is in the can. Nothing I can do now but hope and pray the games go my way. At the moment, my picks seem like they're one-hundred percent perfect, but just wait. I picked the Bears to win this week. If they lose, I'll have to keep my head down."

"Against the Rams? I don't know."

"The Rams are coming off a big win against the 49ers. They're due for a letdown."

"What about tonight's game?" The Thursday night game kept NFL fans from over-salivating as they waited for another Sunday beatdown.

"It will be another stinker—Cowboys at the Giants. The Giants are getting five and a half points, which is a lot for a divisional home game. The Cowboys need a win, but the Giants looked decent last week. I went with the under. I'm not sure I'll watch it."

"You'll find something better to do."

"The football gods hate Amazon almost as much as we all do. What did you have in mind?"

"Stay tuned. What NFL team is your Best Bet this week?"

"C'mon, Eddie, don't go there. Remember, I'm the one who just left Vegas. You promised to show me a regular life without action. Don't jinx me by betting on my top pick."

My request for her Best Bet had become a weekly ritual. I argued that we should be winning money from her picks, and she argued that I'd jinx her. She was right, of course. Superstition ruled when it came to gambling.

Her cell rang. She glanced at her phone. "It's Wit."

Like so many others, Wit was reaching out to Nicole to offer support. He must've heard about the Backstretch Murder and, as the unofficial but undisputed dean of the Vegas poker pros, was looking out for Nicole, one of his favorites.

"Good old Wit," I said.

"We've been playing phone tag. I'll call him after I pig-out. Right about now, I'd be on my way to a cash game at Bellagio. It would just be another day at the office."

"I know you miss it." It was a massive understatement.

She dug into the chow mein. "I don't miss those nights when the cards don't come. But that's okay. Compared to the NFL, poker is a sweet, predictable game. I should go back to Vegas for a visit after the season ends. Check in on that damn monstrosity I own. I hear the local delinquents threw a major bash last night. My cameras and security service drive-bys are worthless—I don't know how they get in."

"Forget it. A coat of paint and new flooring and no one will ever know what went on there." Positive, stay positive, I reminded myself.

"You're right. I should think about something else. If I was in Vegas, I know what bets I'd make on tonight's game—"

"Why don't you wager on tonight's game? Maybe then you wouldn't miss the action so much." The minute I uttered these words, I wanted to take them back. She'd left Vegas for a reason. The action was out there, and it could become all-consuming. Making the break would take a lot. We didn't need to be in Vegas—the action was right there on our phones.

"No way. I need to remain objective. Chicagoland is counting on me." She laughed. She always laughed when she said "Chicagoland." "You should think about it."

"Think about what?"

Nicole hesitated and took a sip of her wine. "I know you think I'm crazy not betting on my picks, but you should consider it when you do your test with Vandy tomorrow. Keep your picks purely arm's length and impersonal—"

"Arm's length?"

"You know what I mean. Professional."

"Without any skin in the game, Vandy will think I'm a rookie."

"Or he'll think you're a pro."

"I'll think about it." I couldn't imagine letting a probable winner go off without some action. I had to admit that much of my handicapping was wrapped up in the odds and whether my pick was a value play or not. If I took my wagering out of the equation, it would eliminate that extra variable, and maybe my handicapping would be that much more accurate.

"Something else came up at work today," Nicole said. "WagerEasy wants me to go on the road to play poker with my fans. They want me to start by playing at the casino here on the north side."

"You're going to do it?" I couldn't believe it. Weren't we just talking about how to avoid the action?

"I know—it's déjà vu all over again. You know how much I hate WagerEasy, but I used to love meeting my fans. A game with them at the poker table in a low-low stakes game was the best. They were my fish. Yet with all that's going on with Dad…"

A guy named Evan Tinsley had taken over the management of the local WagerEasy office. He was a go-getter. He was the one who'd spent WagerEasy's money to sponsor the show and was building out the long overdue sportsbook and casino at Thornton Racetrack. I hadn't met him, but Nicole had said he wasn't like the other corporate stiffs at the sports betting conglomerate.

Maybe Nicole needed a diversion, but before long, she'd be drawn to the high-stakes poker table. She needed to break out of the spell Jessie's murder had cast over her. "Poker with the fans might be just what you need," I said.

"You might be right. Damn." She turned silent, her fork chasing a shrimp around the plate.

Nicole was improving. She could talk about her dad's case and Jessie without breaking down.

She studied the TV and then turned to me. "Why don't you forget about those race replays?"

"We could find a movie on the old movie channel."

"Maybe a musical or something," she said. "No crime dramas, nothing heavy. I couldn't take it."

"What musical?"

She got up and came over to me. "How about *South Pacific*?"

I pulled her onto my lap and kissed her. "I could hum a few bars."

"You'd be off-key."

"We can do something else."

"Like what, for instance?"

I stood up with her in my arms and carried her toward the bedroom.

She giggled. "What about Wit?"

"Wit can wait."

15

THE NEXT MORNING AT O'CONNELL'S, I WAS finishing up my managerial duties and packing up my handicapping stuff when Uncle Mike walked out of his office toward me. I assumed he wanted to wish me luck on my meeting with Vandy or perhaps to tell me he'd heard from the professor.

"Everything all set around here?" Uncle Mike asked.

I gave him a quick rundown of the employee schedule. It would be a busy day at the bar, but I planned to be back from the track by happy hour.

"Nothing from the professor?"

"No."

Uncle Mike's gaze focused on my carryall bag. "Mind if I tag along?"

This was a surprise. We'd planned that I'd go alone to meet Vandy. Uncle Mike wouldn't be able to add much, if anything, about the horses, and I wanted to make a good impression. If I was successful with Vandy today and granted entry into his inner circle, it would supercharge our investigation. I'd learn more about Vandy's close relationship with Jessie and their contacts.

Maybe Uncle Mike wanted to accompany me for support. But his strange look—something else was on his mind. "Sure, why not?"

"Good. I'll explain on the drive over."

We hustled up and got into my car. Uncle Mike's truck needed gas after last night's meeting with Burrascano, and I didn't want to be late. A traffic jam was always a possibility, even in the middle of the day with clear skies. I was thankful for the good weather—I'd handicapped for a fast track.

Once we'd settled in and Uncle Mike had promised not to light his cigar, I prodded him for that explanation. "What's up?"

"I got a call from Smiley," he said.

"What about?" Smiley was our contact at the feds. We called him Smiley, but always addressed him as Bertram. He and Uncle Mike went way back. Smiley knew Uncle Mike was retired, so I assumed he must be calling about something related to our investigation.

"He told me there's a guy in town who wants to meet me," Uncle Mike said. "The guy will be at the track today."

This case got stranger by the minute. "Who is this guy?"

"Well, I might as well start from the beginning. One day, a number of years ago when Smiley happened to be in town and I was still working, he asked to meet me. We arranged a place at a busy lunch spot downtown—over the top FBI stuff. I sat down with Smiley and his partner, and then the partner left."

"Smiley needed to tell you something off the record?"

"Exactly. First thing, he starts telling me about this guy that he and his partner have been working with and how helpful the guy has been to their ongoing investigation. Of course, he omits who or what they're investigating, and I don't ask, but I assume it's the mob."

Uncle Mike rolled the unlit cigar between the fingers of his left hand as he talked. Smiley's call could be helpful to us or a hindrance.

He cleared his throat and continued, "I had about a dozen perps in mind and then Smiley tells me the guy's name is Griggs. He's someone we'd questioned in connection with the murder of a political hack. It was sort of a high-profile case at the time— the hack was attempting to pressure a chain of restaurants to use certain video gambling machines in their establishments. He threatened to send in inspectors who 'might' find health code violations. The hack also wanted to get paid by the company supplying the machines; he wanted to make out on both ends of the deal. That kind of greed can get you whacked real fast.

"Anyway, Griggs had been seen with the political hack a couple of times before the murder, and we'd questioned him. We didn't learn anything from Griggs, and he had an alibi. He was a dead end, but we were still holding him. Of course, I didn't tell Smiley what we were thinking about Griggs. I mean, we're friends and all, but I wanted to find out why the feds had taken such an interest in Griggs, a low-life bastard who'd never worked an honest day in his life."

Uncle Mike's past cases always fascinated me. The murder of the political hack wasn't the real story; it was this low-life named Griggs. I was relieved that we had smooth sailing on the Kennedy Expressway.

"Smiley asked me if the department had anything of substance on Griggs."

"You didn't, right?"

"I told him Griggs was a person of interest in the murder of this hack. It was a lie, but you've got to lie in the homicide business, even to your friends. Plus, if Smily wanted a favor, I could cash it in if I ever needed one—and with the feds, I needed about one favor a week. Liz and I had questioned Griggs a couple of times to see if he'd tell us the same story. The lowlife wasn't your typical wise guy—the type who wouldn't talk and demanded a lawyer. Griggs could talk all day, but it turned out he'd tell you nothing. He'd raised it to an art form. I've never heard such a stream of bullshit from anyone before or since."

"And this is the guy who wants to meet you today?"

Uncle Mike ignored my question. "At the meeting with Smiley years ago, Smiley says, 'Can you do me a favor?' It was what I wanted to hear. Smiley says they've been working with Griggs. He's kept them informed on some important matters, and can we please give him a pass? What the fuck—'important matters'—give me a break. If we were going to play dodgeball, I'd toss a few back at him. I told him any favor depended on what was so damn important about these 'matters.' Smiley ducked that one and gave me another line of BS. We kept up the game for a while longer, then I finally squeezed the answer out of him. It turned out this lowlife piece of shit was a big wheel in the mob's gambling operation."

I was dumbfounded. "Why do you think Griggs wants to meet with you today?"

Once again, Uncle Mike ignored my question, stared at an unmarked semi-truck we passed and continued, "After that meeting, and after I'd agreed to do the favor for Smiley and give Griggs a pass, which wasn't much of a favor since we were about to cut Griggs loose anyway, I kept tabs on the guy. Griggs immediately left the country, but I heard stories from Joey L and others. Griggs jumped up the ladder when a large portion of the mob's bookie business moved offshore. He earned a new nickname, Island Willie. The boys told me he was the 'big swinging dick in the Bahamas.'"

"Damn. How did—"

"As time passed, Griggs lost any leverage with the feds and ended up on the Most Wanted List. He'd built an empire out in the islands, I'd heard. I brought this up to Smiley today, and he confirmed that Griggs had been 'wildly successful,' but with legalization, the feds were taking a hands-off policy. Can you believe that?"

"Island Willie, what the—"

"What drove this lowlife out of his safe haven in the islands to Chicago? That's what I want to know. And I want to know why Smiley is still monitoring Griggs. I know you'll be working with Vandy today—"

"Yeah, why is he here now? I want to meet Island Willie."

"We need the Vandy connection for our investigation. I don't want to give you an excuse to fuck things up." Uncle Mike laughed to let me know he was kidding.

"Don't worry." I had a good feel for today's card, but even an expert handicapper could make mistakes, and I wasn't sure I qualified as an expert.

16

UNCLE MIKE AND I TOOK A CHOICE SEAT ON THE first floor of Thornton Racetrack amid a sparse crowd. Many in the crowd were watching races from the East Coast. They could bet on the ongoing races at the track through simulcasting.

We were right on time; almost thirty minutes before the first race. Pieter Van der Walt stood near the bar with a couple of old timers I didn't know. The three of them hovered over a racing program.

I hadn't seen Vandy since that brief encounter in the winner's circle on the day of Winning Spirit's victory. At the bar, Vandy made notes and nodded as his companions pointed at the program.

Uncle Mike opened the program to the first race. "Well, Eddie, we have a nice view of the stretch and the tote board from here."

Once upon a time, a massive crowd would gather on the outside apron between our choice seats and the rail, and from this seat we would've been forced to get up and join them, or watch the race on one of the overhead closed-circuit TVs, but not anymore. A massive crowd these days was about twenty fans strung along the rail.

I spread out my handicapping stuff, including my laptop. "Vandy is up there at the bar."

"Did he see us when we walked in?"

"I think so."

"Well, I hope you're ready. You've studied your whole life for this moment."

"Very funny. You happen to know either of those two guys with Vandy?"

Uncle Mike acted casual and then took a closer look at the guys who were dressed in worn jeans and winter coats. "Nope. They must know their stuff the way they're talking."

"Yeah. Any sign of Island Willie? Anybody with a daiquiri?"

Uncle Mike laughed. "Not yet."

I glanced at my notes. Vandy had only two horses on today's card—one in the first race and one in the third. Both horses were trained for the moment by Sal Nicoletti. Sal's suspension started next week.

Vandy's horse in the first race hovered near the morning line odds of two-to-one. I expected the horse to go off close to even money. Should I consider the fact that Sal might be distracted and therefore these horses weren't up to par? I hadn't contacted Sal about today—I wanted this test to be strictly me versus the horses.

What would Vandy's little test consist of? I'd handicapped the entire card in preparation. If I stood in his shoes and I wanted to enlist a handicapper to provide me with expert advice, what would I be looking for?

It wasn't long before Vandy walked over, the politician's smile again plastered on his face. He was of average height, with a leather carryall bag slung over his shoulder. Under his jacket, he wore green workout clothes with the insignia of Lake Shore University. He again sported the unshaven look, which was almost expected for an afternoon card at the racetrack. The Churchill Downs cap was replaced by a worn Bears cap, perched atop his light gray hair. For a man in his late fifties, he was in pretty good shape.

My haphazard internet research revealed that he once coached football and basketball at a small high school located somewhere between Chicago and Rockford. He'd quit the job after about ten years because of students and parents complaining about physical and verbal abuse. "I'm trying to make men out of crybabies," he told them. His teams had solid winning records, and that had seemed to keep the school board at bay for a while. Vandy had never backed off, at least, until he discovered his love of horse racing.

The horse-racing magazines loved rags to riches stories. Jockeys who came from poverty, trainers who spent years as assistants before going out on their own and, of course, owners who finally stepped into the winner's circle on Derby Day at Churchill. Vandy had gotten the same treatment, despite never having a horse in the Derby—the high school coach now living the rich life with homes in Chicago and Naples, Florida, thanks to a record number of wins chalked up as the Midwestern claiming kingpin.

I stood and greeted him again and gave him a firm handshake, staring him down.

"Eddie, thanks for coming," he said, his intense dark eyes returning the stare.

"You remember my uncle, Mike O'Connell."

"Of course. We met in the winner's circle the other day."

Uncle Mike stood, and they shook hands. "I've heard a lot about you."

"What are you doing here?" Vandy asked. Small talk clearly wasn't on the agenda.

"I thought it might be fun." Uncle Mike shrugged like a man who was retired with nothing to do. "Plus, I don't want to pass up the chance to win a few bucks."

Vandy nodded fast like he hoped this little meeting would end quickly so he could get back to business. "Good luck, Mike. I'm sure you're in for a fun afternoon." He turned to me. "Eddie, as you know, I'm in need of some advice on the gambling end of things. I've heard a lot about you from Sal. He also told me you didn't ask him about the horses I have entered today. I like that."

I couldn't imagine that Sal had given me a glowing recommendation but decided to let it pass.

Vandy lectured me like a coach who expected my full attention with no backtalk. "As you know, from time to time my horses move to other tracks. I look for people like you who can give me an edge. In the claiming game, I need to gamble on my horses to make it all work. It takes constant attention to detail, and that means knowing what other trainers are up to with their horses. Local horseplayers have always been my best allies. Ready?"

"I'm looking forward to it," I said.

Uncle Mike sat back down. He seemed more nervous than I was. I remained standing.

"I have two horses running today—one in the first race and one in the third. You bet a hundred dollars any way you see fit, and we'll see how you do. Any winnings, if there are any, are split fifty-fifty. Deal?"

"I can only bet a hundred?"

"That's right. You need to get your tickets from Roy at the windows. Roy will keep track of your bets. That way, there won't be any questions." He handed me a C-Note. "Give this bill to Roy."

"Okay." There was some writing along the edge of the bill.

"Of course, I usually bet quite a bit more than a hundred

bucks, but this will give me an idea of what you can do. I'll come back after the third race. Okay?"

"I have a question."

Vandy looked puzzled. "What?"

"Who were those guys you were standing with at the bar?"

He planted his hands on his hips and hunched his shoulders. "Why would you want to know that?"

"Anybody with intel about the horses is worth knowing."

He shook his head and smiled. "I like that. That's good. Here I am giving you a test, an opportunity to work with me, and you're using it to find out more. Alright, I'll tell you. They're jockey agents. Those guys are always trying to get their boys on my live mounts. Satisfied?"

"What jocks do they represent?"

Vandy laughed and waggled a finger back and forth in my face as if to say it was too early to ask for the car keys. "Not now, later. I'll see you after the third race. Good luck."

I stepped back to the table and placed the C-Note in my wallet.

"Jeez, Eddie," Uncle Mike said. "You're taking chances, aren't you? What if he got pissed off about you asking him—"

"I'm supposed to take chances, and he needs somebody who will dig for information."

Uncle Mike nodded slowly. "You're right. We need to know more, too. We have a murder to solve. Good work." He hunched over the table and rubbed his hands together. "Now, who do you like?"

17

VANDY'S HORSE IN THE FIRST RACE, A HORSE named Banker's Boy, had been claimed at Santa Anita for twenty grand. It was a substantial investment for a claiming horse meant to run at Thornton Racetrack, a big step down in class from Santa Anita, where the purses far exceeded those offered at Thornton. Today's first race was a Starter Allowance race for horses that had run at a claiming price of ten thousand or less in any race in the last two years. Since Banker's Boy had at one time dropped into such a race last year during a slump, he qualified. The race would allow Banker's Boy to strut his California stuff without the risk of being claimed away. Sal and Vandy had found the perfect spot for the horse.

"Vandy's horse looks like an easy winner to me," Uncle Mike said. "Of course, you're the expert."

It was a sprint race, and the track was fast. Although Thornton had a long stretch, sometimes a front runner could get a lead, slow the pace down through the middle of the race, and then have enough left coming down the stretch. That kind of situation presented itself today. The six-horse Tonka Kat was the speed of the speed. The horse had a decent trainer and was running his third race back off a layoff.

A classy horse like Banker's Boy would be able to stalk Tonka Kat and then whip past the horse in the stretch as Winning Spirit had done the other day, but only if Banker's Boy ran its race and broke well out of the gate. Chances were that Banker's Boy's class would overcome any missteps. Most handicappers would simply pick Banker's Boy as the winner and be done. According to the tote board, that was exactly the case. Banker's Boy was now at three-to-five on the tote board.

If I was Vandy, and I'd just spent twenty grand on a horse, and paid to ship him from California to Chicago, then found a nice soft spot where he couldn't get claimed away, wouldn't I just take the purse and run to the bank? I'd been playing Thornton for a long time, and I knew Vandy and Sal liked to play tricks, especially with a prohibitive favorite. That was why many good handicappers went home broke.

"Don't go up to the windows just yet," I told Uncle Mike.

I moved on to the third race and reviewed Vandy's horse. Out of Truth was another monster. Vandy had claimed the horse a month ago at Churchill Downs, a track that was also a step up from Thornton. Sal was listed as the trainer on both Out of Truth and another horse in the same race, Zombie Gold, which was not owned by Vandy. It was typical for a trainer to have more than one horse in a race. If the horses had different owners, as a general rule, they could run in the same race without being coupled.

Zombie Gold, Sal's other horse in the third, was coming off a three-month layoff, and Sal had good numbers off a layoff. Zombie Gold also had a nice string of workouts in the last month. The horse seemed to be following the same path as Alto Blue.

Since Vandy's horses were in the first and third races, if I could find a probable winner in the second race, I could consider betting a Pick 3. I also had to consider how to bet the first and third races. Betting on two prohibitive favorites wasn't the kind of value play I liked. A handicapper might find the most likely winner, but the horseplayer, the gambler, always scrambled to find the best bet.

Unlike sports betting, with the horses, the odds of a bet were not fixed at the time the bet was placed. They could change, sometimes drastically, depending upon the parimutuel pool. The odds would not be final until the bell rang, and the horses left the gate.

"Time is running out," Uncle Mike said. "What's the verdict?"

"Bet the six horse in the first race."

"What? Shouldn't I go up and bet on Vandy's horse, Banker's Boy? The horse is at really low odds. Everybody likes him."

How could I explain that the track didn't work that way? Favorites only won a third of the time. If a horseplayer bet chalks all day, they'd go broke.

"I plan to bet on the six, Tonka Kat." I also planned to bet the exacta with Tonka Kat and Banker's Boy. For an owner who liked to play the horses, coming in second, and having the exacta, could prove more lucrative than simply winning the race.

"You're not betting on Banker's Boy? I thought that was the whole idea?"

I placed an index finger to my lips to tell Uncle Mike to keep his voice down.

"All right, you're the expert. I like the odds on the six. Jeez, eleven to one." Uncle Mike got up and lumbered toward the windows.

I'd wait for Uncle Mike to come back. I would watch Tonka Kat and Banker's Boy closely in the Post Parade. Then I'd go up and say hello to Roy at the windows.

18

A SIX-FURLONG SPRINT FOR A FIELD OF LOW-LEVEL starter allowance horses at Thornton was typically about one minute and ten seconds, but so much could happen in that time frame. Horses could battle for position out of the gate, allowing a stalker from an outside post to gauge the pace and wait to pounce in the stretch. If the pace got extremely heated on the front end, a closer from far behind could surprise the fans.

Maybe the race would depend on how the track was playing. The track was listed as "fast," but maybe it had rained the night before and hadn't fully dried out. Or maybe the track's maintenance crew had graded the track in such a way that horses running along the rail had an advantage, or the horses running wide could hold the advantage. The track could favor speed or favor closers, sometimes changing day-to-day. A track bias, if there was one, wouldn't reveal itself until after the first couple of races. It could help me on the third race, but not the opener.

Bankers Boy, a musclebound chestnut, continued to get

pounded at the windows. The six, Tonka Kat, a high-strung gray, dropped down to ten to one. Both horses passed my inspection as they strutted past in the Post Parade. Uncle Mike returned to the table, chewing on his cigar and looking like a nervous schoolboy. It was time for the walk up to the windows.

There were only a few fans in line at Roy's window. I didn't know Roy, but I spotted his name tag. He wore a wrinkled white shirt with a frayed collar and thin black tie. He chewed gum like a guy who was in dire need of a cigarette break.

When I reached the head of the line, I had Vandy's C-Note in hand. He'd scribbled on the edge of the bill, "To Roy— Vandy." I handed the bill to him.

After he glanced at the note, Roy said, "You must be Vandy's new guy." He reached out his hand, and we shook. "Good luck, Eddie. I'll make a note of your bets and initial the tickets— okay?"

I could bet my own money by going to another window or using one of the betting apps on my phone, then I decided against it. I'd go arm's length like Nicole suggested. I had to show Vandy I was a pro. It was a matter of focus and perspective.

"Sure." I gave him my bets for a total of seventy-five dollars. In case I bombed, I'd still have twenty-five dollars to play on the third race. I sure hoped I'd read things right on the first race. If not, I wasn't sure Uncle Mike would let me live it down.

I went back to the table. The horses were being loaded into the gate for the six-furlong race. The gate was located across the infield in the direction of the barns and dorms, at the start of the backstretch, giving the horses a long run before they'd enter into the far turn and then into the top of the stretch. The sun reflected off the glass. I would've gone outside to watch them from the rail, but I had my laptop at the table and other materials. I couldn't leave them or they'd disappear, and even though they were, for the most part, just props, I'd hate to lose them.

The announcer brought everyone to attention. "They're off in today's opener from Thornton Racetrack."

Tonka Kat popped out of the gate as if he had a head start on the rest of the horses. When the jock forged a comfortable two to three length lead, he took hold of the colt and settled him down.

Bankers Boy stumbled out of the gate and into last place. One misstep and all that money on the favorite was in jeopardy. Fate always worked overtime at the track.

Uncle Mike was cheering on Tonka Kat, the six horse, as if his very life and economic well-being depended on the horse to "keep going," and "don't stop," and "you've got this race—go, go, go."

Although I had the six horse to win, I also had the six with Bankers Boy in the exacta. The jock on Bankers Boy had moved up to mid-pack by the turn and seemed to have momentum. Still, the big favorite was making me sweat—I needed the horse to finish second, not win.

At the top of the stretch, Tonka Kat had a comfortable three-to four-length lead over the pack. The horse was running confidently. Bankers Boy, hanging in mid-pack, got the wake-up call from his jock, weaved around a couple of horses going nowhere and then began to charge toward the leader. Now with second place a done deal, I was sweating bullets about Bankers Boy beating my six horse to the wire.

I joined Uncle Mike. "C'mon, six—run!" Tonka Kat was now five lengths in front, but Bankers Boy was running out in the middle of the track like a freight train, eating up ground on poor Tonka Kat with every stride.

At the sixteenth pole, Bankers Boy was breathing down the neck of Tonka Kat, who began to wobble—or maybe it was my imagination. Everyone around us was cheering for the favorite, and our cheers for the six bounced against the glass and back into our faces.

"C'mon, damnit." So much for my cool exterior. Forget about asking questions, gathering information and giving advice—I needed oxygen.

We strained to see the last few jumps to the wire. Did the six hold on? The announcer called Tonka Kat and then Bankers Boy. Tonka Kat won by a head or so. I could breathe again.

Uncle Mike was shaking.

Sometimes when you win, you feel like you shook the hand of God, and then you quickly realize winning could be nothing more than business as usual. I'd recognized the speed of Tonka Kat and the lack of another speed horse in the race. In his last three races, Tonka Kat had been bumped out of the starting gate; shipped to the Indiana track to run on turf; and, in his third prior race, before a layoff, got caught in a speed duel fading to fifth. Those last three races caused horseplayers to think Tonka Kat had lost his form when, in fact, he had valid excuses.

"What the hell?" Uncle Mike yelled out. "Look at the six on the tote board. He was at ten to one before post-time, I swear. Now he's at three to one."

Uncle Mike probably bet his standard ten bucks. At ten to one, it meant he'd clear a hundred bucks, but at three to one, he'd clear about thirty-five bucks. I always hated to see a guy lose a fortune.

"It's the late money," I said. "It came in on the six horse."

"The what? I know it's been a while since I've been out here, but what the hell?"

"They call it computer-assisted wagering or 'CAWs.' These groups make their wager right when the horses leave the gate."

"That isn't legal."

"Go ahead, call up the precinct and get a few detectives on it," I laughed. "The racetracks make up the rules as they go along."

The color of Uncle Mike's face had blossomed into an overripe tomato. "These Late Money Boys must bet a lot for the odds to drop like a rock."

"They bet a ton. That's why the tracks love them. Small-time horseplayers are quitting the game in droves."

"The tracks and these guys are in cahoots?"

"The tracks even give them rebates on the takeout." A percentage of the parimutuel pool went to the track to help fund purses.

Uncle Mike looked like he might pick a fight with somebody. "Why are you still playing? I didn't raise a dumbass nephew."

"Thanks. It's the way things are." You could play the horses and submit to theft or quit. Talk to any horseplayer; they'd call it theft.

"I used to know some guys who played the tote."

Watching the tote to see which horse was "live," and getting a bet down in the final minute, had been an ancient tradition at the track. The tote board, a structure in the infield facing the grandstands, approximately thirty yards long and about twenty feet high, had always been the center of attention. Closed-circuit TVs placed around the track monitored the tote board. The odds were lit in neon and changed every ten-or-fifteen seconds, reflecting changes in the odds based on money flowing into the parimutuel pools. It had kept the playing field somewhat level— the sharp money moves on a horse could be detected by those who could patiently "read" the tote.

"The tote board is useless these days," I said. "In fact, the Late Money Boys, as you called them, move money around to make other horseplayers think a horse is getting sharp money, and then they pull their money back at the last possible second and bet it on another horse. Did you notice that the odds went up on Banker's Boy?"

Uncle Mike stared at his ticket. I thought he might rip it up. Then he placed it in his shirt pocket. "Late Money? I'd call it Crooked Money. We need to talk to Arlene about this."

Uncle Mike and I had developed a close relationship with

Arlene after handling an investigation for her. I wouldn't mind hearing a track owner's tale of woe and how their hands were tied. "Let's do that one of these days. See if she can bullshit us. Now I have to work on the third race."

"Damn. You're right. Vandy and his little test…"

I searched the bar to see if Vandy was in attendance; perhaps watching me for signs of stress. I didn't see him, but I did notice a familiar face at the bar. "Hey, isn't that Lou by the bar?" Lou was one of DiNatale's boys. We'd seen him at the country club the other night when we met with Burrascano.

Uncle Mike glanced over. "Yeah, that's him. I didn't know Lou played the horses. Why don't you tell him about the Late Money Boys? He'd probably have enough sense to run out of here. Wait a minute. How about that? Well, look who else is at the bar—it's my old friend, Island Willie. Here he comes. You're in for a treat."

19

A MAN WALKED TOWARD US WITH SMALL BABY steps, his shoulders hunched forward as if each step caused him pain. His long white hair with streaks of gray and black that hung down his back was pulled back into a loose ponytail. The long hair matched the look of his long scraggly beard. He wore faded jeans, a dark vest over a Levi's work shirt, rimless glasses, and an old black leather newsboy hat perched on the top of his head.

Uncle Mike stood up to greet him. "Hello, Mr. Griggs."

Griggs laughed and reached out with both hands and took Uncle Mike's hand in a warm handshake that made them look like old army buddies. "Mike O'Connell, the man who made it all possible. Thanks for being here." His voice was rough. Each word was emitted with great effort.

"What's that? Made what possible?"

"You were the one—"

"This is my nephew, Eddie." Uncle Mike steered Island Willie toward our table.

It seemed my uncle also wanted to steer the conversation. He'd told me how Island Willie had raised bullshit to an art form.

"Hello, Eddie. Nice to meet you," he said, taking aim at the seat we'd placed at the end of the table. The transformation from a bent-over old man to an old man in a chair required a superhuman effort.

Seated, he gasped for breath, taking in the view through the window. "How about this? Your nephew. My prior inquisitor. All of us at Thornton on a beautiful day to take in the ponies. It's been a long time. This couldn't be better. It's so good to be back in the States."

Uncle Mike had watched the descent of Island Willie with amusement. "You're moving slow these days."

"My feet hurt like hell. It travels up my back and into my neck and sets my nerves on fire."

"Damn."

I said nothing, allowing the two old friends to get reacquainted. Were they really old friends—Uncle Mike had questioned Island Willie as a suspect in a murder many years ago.

"When did you get out here?" Uncle Mike asked.

"I don't know—I lost track of time. It's better in the islands. I float like a butterfly down there compared to Chicago."

Uncle Mike laughed. "You haven't been back in the States since—"

"That's right. You gave me the opportunity of a lifetime." Island Willie turned his head gingerly in my direction and smiled. "Eddie, everything in life is timing. Mike was a square shooter and let me go. I'd been falsely accused before, you understand, and that typically entailed days of interrogation, beatings, and deprivation, but your uncle is a man of honor. He did not resort to such tactics and did me a favor, and now I'm here."

"Let me get this straight, Willie," Uncle Mike said. "You're here to see me?"

Island Willie turned his head back toward Uncle Mike and

took a deep breath before launching into an explanation. "Not totally, but sort of. You see, when you let me go, I had something lined up in the islands. It was a startup, and they needed me to manage the workers. I spoke their language, you know? You can't hire somebody from the States to manage folks who grew up working for peanuts and picking bananas. They simply can't relate."

"What do you mean?" I asked. I should've sat out this old-timer's reunion. I had that third race to work on. There were two parts to Vandy's test, and I had to ace them both.

Island Willie nodded. "I grew up on the islands of Hawaii. But islands are still islands to some people. I'm in the Caribbean. You adjust to the circumstances. Hold on." He placed his finger on the earpiece in his left ear and listened. He cleared his throat and talked into a cell phone he pulled from his vest. "He's a friend, right? No, limit him to half per game for now. Bleed him slow."

"How much? Half?" Uncle Mike asked.

"Now where was I? Oh yeah. My dad had a job at a hotel on Kauai. We lived in a beat-up, tired old town, which had at one time been known for its crime and opium. Time had passed it by, and the vegetation was taking over. Can you believe that?"

I'd become captivated. What kind of operation did Island Willie run, and why was he here to talk with Uncle Mike? Any minute he might find his way through the bullshit and say something meaningful.

"No, I can't believe it," Uncle Mike said. "How much?"

"They have to clear the bigger bets with me personally. This was about a new customer. I'm always on call. I don't do much anymore, except with the big players. I tend to be more hands-on with them. Can you believe it? One moment I'm in handcuffs and the next I'm in the Caribbean making money. Of course, there was a long stretch where I couldn't step one foot in the States without being jailed. Most Wanted List—some guys really respect a guy who makes the List. Thank you, Federales. Now where was I? Oh yeah, Kauai. Beautiful place—the garden island—but hell for somebody like me who didn't fit in. You do what you have to do."

"How much? How much was the bet?" Uncle Mike had reverted to the detective who wouldn't take bullshit for an answer. Maybe he wasn't all that happy about letting Island Willie go or having done a favor for Smiley. Maybe Island Willie had slipped through Uncle Mike's fingers, and that wasn't something that would sit well with my uncle.

Island Willie smiled and stroked his long beard. "A hundred thousand. He wanted to bet two hundred grand. It pays to play hard to get." He watched our reaction.

"That's per game?" Uncle Mike asked.

Uncle Mike's mouth dropped open, and I suppose my face hung between dumbfounded and utter disbelief. How was this man, this guy who looked like a bum—dealing in this amount of money? A hundred grand per game and how many games per weekend? How many customers? And what did he mean by "bleed him slow"?

Island Willie grimaced and rubbed the back of his neck as if it'd just caught fire, ignited from the bottom of his feet. He took a deep breath and spoke through gritted teeth. "My place is where you go when you graduate from the WagerEasys of the world and local black market. When no one will take your action, you turn to me. No taxes and a line of credit. I've learned to take it all in stride—there are just more zeroes. Here in Chicago, people treat me like royalty. It's cool."

"They do?" Uncle Mike asked.

"You do what you have to do. Somebody has to do it. In Kauai, you got a dog and a knife. When the sweet potatoes are ripe for picking, the pigs come. You have to go. Thousands of pigs roam the island. The dogs—Hawaiian pig hunting dogs— part pit bull, part bull-terrier—are needed because the damn boar can be right next to you in the bush and you wouldn't know it. The dogs work the thickets. They bite and hold the hog, then you go in with your knife and battle the pig. Your adrenaline shoots through you. You're getting scraped up by thorns and gashed and bit, and you lose it. You absolutely lose it."

Island Willie grimaced again and stretched his right arm. "You stick it and then sling the pig over your shoulder and carry it out, the blood dripping down your chest. Damn."

I wondered what it'd be like to take a wild boar and thrash around in a thicket. You do what you have to do, Island Willie had said.

"Why did you want to see me?" Uncle Mike asked in a flat voice.

Island Willie looked out the window and hesitated, then stroked his beard again. "I never know if some official will decide whether today is a good day to bring Island Willie in for questioning. I need time. It's all good. All good. A slight bump in the road."

"Like what?" Uncle Mike asked.

"Let me tell you—"

Uncle Mike shook his head. "Not again —"

"It's okay, Mike." Island Willie talked fast. "It will only take a minute. I'm golden, don't worry. I employ hundreds of people on a couple of different islands. Despite what you may've heard, not the Bahamas. But the rest is true. The women there—they don't mind doing it with an old broken-down husk of a man like me. They're wonderful."

"Right," Uncle Mike said. "A big swinging dick—we heard."

"But here's the good part. I got so big now I'm golden in the eyes of the good old USA. It's diplomacy, which we all know can make heroes out of villains. Me, Island Willie, the hero. The US has to respect the country's biggest employer or the diplomats create a hornet's nest, and they don't need another Cuba."

"Okay. I'm figuring this out," Uncle Mike shrugged. "Let me

pretend there aren't any pigs out there in the infield—why are you here?"

"That's a good one, Mike. Pigs in the infield." He laughed and then turned grim. "Something's rotten out there. Jessie shot dead outside her dorm. That's sacred ground. In my world, you get pissed. People like Jessie aren't just migrants; they're a major cog in the machine. I got somebody placing a big bet on a Thornton horse or other track—who do I call? Who is working the horses? Who talks every day to the other exercise riders? I need contacts. If it's a football game, do I call ESPN? No. I got sources. C'mon."

"What?"

Uncle Mike was right. Island Willie could talk all day and not say a thing.

"Here comes the two horse," Island Willie said with a nod toward the track.

I looked up. The two horse in the second race swept right past me. I had him in my Pick 3, but I'd been distracted. I needed to watch that race in real time and pick up pieces of information about how the track was playing. I was getting sidetracked by a carnival showman.

Island Willie pulled a ticket out of his vest and flashed it at me and Uncle Mike. It was a ticket on the two horse and the amount was seventeen hundred and fourteen dollars. There were also other miscellaneous bets on the ticket, for a total wager of two thousand dollars.

He waited for our reaction and then tucked the ticket back. "I used to be out here at Thornton every afternoon. I couldn't wait for this day. A chance to go up to the windows and watch them count out real cash. A stack of crisp bills—no crypto shit. I love it."

I had to sweat to find the two horse, now reduced to odds of three to one, and I had to use the pick with two other horses in the Pick 3, and here was Island Willie flashing a ticket around like everybody in the place knew the two horse would be a winner.

Island Willie began the slow process of standing up. "I've got to run, gentlemen. But before I go, Mike, let me shake your hand once more. I owe you. You wanted to know why I'm here. I'll be seeing you around, but first let me share with you two words."

"What?" Uncle Mike asked.

He leaned over and whispered to Uncle Mike, but loud enough for me to hear. "The Hippo."

He raised himself up and groaned, then began walking away using those baby steps. Lou, a giant, came over and gave him his forearm as a balance beam. Other guys near the bar moved in tandem with the pair. I figured they were more of DiNatale's guys.

Another guy stood at the bar and watched Island Willie's exit and studied me. It was Vandy.

20

THE "HIPPO" WAS THE LOCAL MOBSTER ALLESSI Ippolito, who had been mentioned the other night by Burrascano. I'd learned the origin of his nickname from Mr. Urbanski, a regular at O'Connell's. According to Mr. Urbanski, the origin of the nickname began in his brother's courtroom in criminal court. The Hippo was in his early twenties and had pled guilty on assorted charges, including loan sharking and possession of narcotics. More serious charges, including conspiracy to commit murder and the sale of narcotics, had been thrown out as part of the plea deal. His lawyer had turned a twenty-year stretch into five years.

At the sentencing, Judge Urbanski was making his findings and coming to the sentence when he stopped.

"Are you yawning, Mr. Ippolito?" the judge had asked.

"Yeah, Judge."

"Am I boring you?"

"Just tired." Ippolito smiled—a smug smile according to Mr.

Urbanski.

"You must be very tired."

Ippolito shrugged.

"It was a very wide yawn," the judge said. "Like that of a hippo. Have you ever seen a hippo yawn? They have a big mouth like you."

Now, Ippolito began to squirm in his seat

"Let me tell you what I can do for you, Mr. Ippo, The Hippo. I'll add another two years to your sentence so you can get a little rest. Think that will be enough?"

Ippolito's smug smile had vanished, and he slid to the edge of his seat. "You can't do that, Judge."

"Watch me."

Mr. Urbanski loved the story and used to tell it around the bar often. "My brother, the judge, doesn't take any of their crap in his courtroom. To this day, Ippolito is known as The Hippo. All the mob guys call him The Hippo."

I loved the story; a wise guy getting showed up by a judge.

After Island Willie had dropped his Hippo bomb and left, I asked Uncle Mike, "What did you make of that?"

"It confirms what we talked about. We're going to see fireworks," Uncle Mike said, shaking his head.

"If Burrascano dies—"

"Exactly. If Island Willie is in league with DiNatale, and from what we saw with Lou and the boys following him around, I'd say that's the case, then Island Willie will be in the middle of any fight between The Hippo and DiNatale for Burrascano's spot."

"Now we know why Island Willie left his safe haven. It might not be so safe anymore."

"They're anticipating trouble. The island operation is a moneymaker."

"I'll say. A hundred grand limit for a new player. What amounts are being bet by the veteran customers?" I wouldn't be surprised if Island Willie's operation took individual bets in the amount of a million or more.

Uncle Mike pulled out a cigar and stuck it in the corner of his mouth. He'd need to go outside to smoke it. "Maybe Burrascano did us a favor when he didn't hire us. Don't believe anything Island Willie says. Bodies turn up around the guy—I've seen that time and time again."

"I wonder what Vandy thought of our little visit from Island Willie? He was standing at the bar."

"I guess we'll find out. What have you got on this third race? You said there were two horses trained by Sal?" Uncle Mike fished around in his coat pocket for his lighter.

"It's going to be complicated. I want to check out a couple of things."

"Well, I'm going outside to smoke and smell the horse manure. Whatever you decide, place a wager on it for me."

"I can't."

"Oops. Sorry about that. I forgot—you're playing the professional horseplayer today. Maybe that's why you're winning. I'll come back when the post parade starts."

I wouldn't mind a whiff of horse manure myself, but I had work to do. In the next race, I had Sal's two horses to consider— Out of Truth, a recent claim by Vandy, and Zombie Gold, coming off a three-month layoff. Both of the horses held my interest, but there was another horse with good speed, the one horse, a long shot, by the name of ClassicMasterD, trained by Ronnie Orman.

I opened my laptop and reviewed the video replay of the second race that I'd missed. Although the winner had won by coming from behind, two long shots had maintained a prominent position from the start to the end of the race. Speed had also held up in the first race. I concluded that the track was favoring speed, and therefore, ClassicMasterD had a good chance in today's third race.

When Sal had two horses in a race, he typically tried to get his horses to finish first and second. The horse at higher odds would win, giving him a better-paying exacta. If that usual scenario played out today, then Zombie Gold would win and Out of Truth would finish second.

One would think that horseplayers would be in-step with Sal's winning ways when he entered two horses in a race, but horseplayers would be fooled again. They would bet Vandy's Out of Truth down to low odds, evaluating the horse based on its record at Churchill and the probability of winning against today's field, without viewing the race based on Sal's past strategies. The fact that Vandy's favorite had just disappointed in the first race would be excused due to the stumble from the gate. Horseplayers would think that the connections—Sal and Vandy—would want to make amends for that first race stumble, and that Out of Truth would win this race for sure.

Instead of taking into account Sal's past strategies and trends, horseplayers, a forgiving lot, would fall into the same trap. It was easy to do. I'd done it for years.

If I was wrong, Vandy would think I was a chump. Maybe Sal wouldn't employ his time-tested tactics and opt to begin his two-year suspension by "running honest" for once. No, I had to follow my original analysis of the race. Rethinking things and casting doubt sent horseplayers to the pawnshop.

I had plenty of money from my winnings on the first race, and I'd need to put it to work. I'd bet Sal's horses in an exacta box and bet each horse to win, with the majority of my money to win on the long shot horse Zombie Gold. Then I thought again—the speed-favoring track worked into the hands of ClassicMasterD.

The race had other speed horses, but ClassicMasterD was the speed of the speed and was reaching the top of his form cycle. The horse had run well in its last race and was moving up in class. It was a move that Orman liked to make when his horses were "live."

Didn't I just talk about "casting doubt?"? What was wrong with me?

Horse racing always looked so easy in hindsight, but in these moments before the wager, second-guessing could drive a horseplayer mad. Another factor I needed to consider—what about Ronnie Orman? He was about to be the beneficiary of Sal's stable. His reputation would be enhanced by taking over Sal's horses. Other owners like Vandy might decide to give Orman a try, if he was able to prove himself.

Nicole had mentioned that Sal and Orman were arguing about where to winter—in Kentucky or New Orleans. Maybe it was a power struggle, and maybe Orman would flex his muscle in this race. It was too late for Sal to arrange for another trainer to take his stable during the suspension.

I decided to change my wagering strategy. I had to be cold-blooded and use every bit of information I had. I'd have to fit ClassicMasterD into my bets on the third race.

During the post parade, I inspected each of the horses. Were any horses showing signs of sweating or acting unruly? Did my horses appear to be on their toes, alert, their ears pricked up and a sheen to their coats? I didn't know how to describe my examination of the horses. Horses that seemed to be "all business," was the one I wanted.

Uncle Mike walked back inside. He'd left his cigar in one of the ashtrays outside.

"What have you got, Einstein?"

"Let me make it simple for you." I handed him a piece of paper with my suggested wager.

Uncle Mike nodded. "I'll burn this after I place my bet, Mr. Bond."

"Hilarious."

When the post parade ended, I continued to watch the overhead video that televised the horses during their warmups. Orman's horse was allowed to gallop, a sign that he'd utilize his speed out of the gate today.

With a few minutes before post, I walked up to the windows.

21

OUT OF THE GATE, CLASSICMASTERD BATTLED with two other speed horses through the first quarter mile and edged away in front. Then the heavy favorite, Vandy's horse, Out of Truth, made a move around the far turn in the six-furlong sprint. At the top of the stretch, Out of Truth and ClassicMasterD were neck and neck. Zombie Gold had followed Out of Truth around the turn and was in third place, gaining on the leaders. The other horses in the race seemed to be dropping back.

Uncle Mike was yelling, but I couldn't hear which horse he was yelling about.

I was yelling too, just to keep my lungs in shape.

By the sixteenth pole, Out of Truth was out of gas. ClassicMasterD kept on, but now would need to fend off the late charge of Zombie Gold. The long duel with Out of Truth had taken its toll on ClassicMasterD, and Zombie Gold took full advantage, nailing the Orman horse by a half-length at the wire.

The top three horses were flashed up on the tote board—the numbers three-one-four. Zombie Gold was first, ClassicMasterD second, and Out of Truth held on for third.

Uncle Mike came around the table and slapped me on the back. "You nailed that race. I don't know how you did it, but you nailed it."

On that piece of paper, I'd given Uncle Mike the following bets—an exacta box of the one, three, and four, and a trifecta box of the one, three, and four.

Vandy, who I'd noticed standing by the bar when the race began, slipped through the crowd and joined us. He held a piece of paper.

He glanced down at it. "Damn, Eddie. I don't know how you did it. You bet only a small amount to win on each of my horses? What do you know that I don't know?" He laughed.

I assumed he'd gotten a printout of my wagers from Roy.

At the moment, I was still feeling the adrenaline rush of seeing my three horses coming down the stretch in a tight bunch, separated from the field. Zombie Gold and ClassicMasterD were at four to one and eleven to one, respectively. I took a deep breath and dug down deep to play my role as the "expert" by remaining serene and businesslike.

"Speed is holding up today," I said in a measured tone, similar to the cop voice Uncle Mike employed at a crime scene.

Vandy shook my hand. "Damn, this is something. Let's go down to the winner's circle with Sal. I have a few things to talk over. I wonder what the trifecta will pay?"

Uncle Mike flashed a broad smile. "What do you think, Eddie? You think it will pay a hundred bucks?"

We walked outside, through security, to the winner's circle near the finish line, where Sal and his grooms were out on the track welcoming the triumphant jock on Zombie Gold and then greeting the jock on Out of Truth. Alejandro took Out of Truth back to the stables, while Zombie Gold and his jock paced about in a tight semicircle waiting for the results to be declared official.

We stood off to the side while Zombie Gold's owners stepped into the winner's circle. Isabel took hold of a loose rein on Zombie Gold. The race was declared official. The fifty-cent trifecta paid $87.50. I had twenty one-dollar box tickets on the three-horse combination for a total wager of $180, resulting in a payoff of thirty-five hundred dollars. I also won a thousand dollars on the exacta, based on a more conservative wager. Altogether, including the first race, I'd cleared almost five grand.

I wouldn't have impressed a sharp player like Vandy by winning only a couple hundred dollars.

Vandy elbowed me and shot me a coach's intense look. "You talked to Orman about that horse of his?"

"Nope." I wanted to ask him how much he'd bet on the exacta with Out of Truth and Zombie Gold, and lost, but decided to be nice.

He did a double-take. "Then you've got a talent for picking them. I think we can do business. Going forward, I'll email you the races where I need a second set of eyes. On a commission basis, of course."

"I'll look forward to it." It was official—I would once again play the imposter.

"I have a meeting to attend next week—owners and others who meet once a month or so. There is a small reception afterward. I'll send you the info. I'd like you to meet some people. Why don't you bring your better half along? Hell, bring your uncle, if you want. Bring your buddy with the beard, too."

"That would be fine," I said, trying not to sound too eager. The "buddy with the beard" was Island Willie. It told me that Vandy knew of Island Willie.

Uncle Mike, Vandy, and I stood off to the side while the Zombie Gold owners had their picture taken with Sal and the winning horse and jockey. After the photo, Vandy talked with Sal, and then they both went over and talked with Orman, who was there probably in hopes of getting his picture taken with ClassicMasterD. Orman was close to Sal's height, although younger and stockier. The discussion became heated. Vandy turned at one point and gestured toward me. I assumed he was asking Orman if he'd talked with me about ClassicMasterD before the race. I could see Orman verified my story that he hadn't.

Uncle Mike whispered to me. "It seems you made quite the impression. Congratulations."

"It looks like Sal has a few things to say to Orman." The two trainers seemed to be arguing, although they tried to appear civil.

"Yeah. We've got to meet Orman. He has a lot to gain from Sal's trouble, and that makes him a good suspect."

I was thinking the same thing. "I'll see what I can do."

22

THINGS BEGAN TO HEAT UP WITH THE PROFESSOR'S case. The thief had called, and the professor refused to talk to her, referring her to Uncle Mike. A number of calls ensued, and it was agreed that the professor would make a down payment as a show of good faith.

On the night of the drop, the thief called at the last minute to cancel. After a heated argument, where negotiations seemed to be at the breaking point, cooler heads prevailed and the following night was chosen.

That night, Uncle Mike and I drove to the drop location. The thief had given us detailed instructions—instructions that spoke volumes—she had picked Thornton Racetrack as the drop location.

"Why the track?" I asked.

Uncle Mike was all-business, puffing away on his cigar. "The track is one thing—the cash is another. Why cash? I keep asking myself that. Surveillance cameras make it almost impossible to pick up cash and get away clean. Why not crypto? And yes, why the track?"

I kept my eyes on the rearview, expecting a tail by the thief, but so far nothing. "Is the thief trying to tell us something?"

"I keep thinking about the amount—seventy-five hundred down and then twelve thousand five hundred for a total of twenty grand. That kind of money isn't worth the risk. The thief could be facing charges for theft and extortion. It would make sense that the thief has another motive behind all this other than the money."

"If it's about the horses and blood tests, why not just turn the lab book over to the feds?"

Uncle Mike zipped up his coat. It was a typical October fall night in Chicago—the temperature in the mid to upper forties. "It must be our connection to Burrascano and gambling, so why didn't St. Clair tell us more?"

"I don't know. Is the thief waving a red flag to get our attention?" I asked. "Are the lab book and Jessie's murder related somehow?"

Uncle Mike laughed. "Now that would be something."

I liked long shots. "Maybe Sal did juice his horses, and maybe there's evidence of it in the lab book."

"And the professor hasn't turned the incriminating results over to the authorities?"

"Something like that."

"Damn. I'm not sure I can buy that Sal is mixed up in the professor's lab book theft. Let's focus on tonight's drop."

"How do you do it? How do you switch from one case to the next?"

"You mean, how do I obsess about Jessie's murder one minute and the professor's lab book the next? Years of working as a homicide detective. The department could never afford for us to work on one case at a time. You get used to it."

The thief had told us to come alone and demanded that one

of us walk around the perimeter of Thornton Racetrack and await their call for further instruction. It was typical, Uncle Mike had said. The thief would be watching to make sure we hadn't alerted the police and then would contact us by cell phone about where to drop the cash.

Uncle Mike would wait in the truck, parked at the very edge of the parking lot. We'd discussed the option of calling some of Uncle Mike's buddies on the force, then decided to handle it on our own. Uncle Mike knew Extortion 101 and had filled me in. "The thief might call to give you further instructions. I doubt that they'll tell you to drop the cash tonight. I think this is just a dry run—a test."

That sounded reasonable, but now that we were going through the actual drop, I had my doubts. "You still think tonight is a dry run?" I asked.

"The thief doesn't trust us. Right now, they've got all the power. They've got the lab book, and they want to see how willing we are to follow orders. If we slip up and show we're over-anxious to get the item back, then they'll raise the ransom."

"It's a tricky situation."

"You'll be a target. It's a shitty neighborhood too. Don't forget to dive for cover if one of those muscle cars speeds past with the hip hop blaring—they might decide to use you for target practice."

This was turning into more than a dry run; it was an obstacle course.

We parked, waited until the exact time set by the thief, and then I got out and began walking along the prescribed route—a rectangular route along the streets bordering the track. It would take me south past the parking lot and the backstretch area—about ten or fifteen blocks, then east behind the track complex, and then back around to our parked vehicle.

Armed with my cell phone and a gun, I walked down the street outside the track. I assumed there were track guards around, but I didn't see any sign of them. A lone streetlight illuminated my path.

The treeless neighborhood across from the track consisted of rows of small tract homes built for factory workers. A couple of decades later, after the jobs were gone, and the neighborhood had changed over, public housing projects were added. It wasn't a quiet suburban enclave anymore.

Loud voices emanated from the neighborhood—a couple fighting. Others screamed back, and the neighborhood erupted into a war zone. Dogs started barking. No gunshots, but car engines revved and tires screeched. Somebody turned up the music on their stereo.

I kept going. If the thief was watching me, I had no idea where they might be hiding.

A noise echoed behind me to my left—near the clubhouse. Maybe it was a firecracker. I ducked down and turned to look across the dark infield toward the empty grandstands. The few track lights did little more than cast shadows. The old grandstands on the eastern end of the complex were encased by a vast network of scaffolding—the sportsbook/casino under construction.

I kept walking, my senses on overdrive.

After a block or two, I approached the backstretch area, where Jessie had died.

Her murder seemed to demand that I match wits with trainers and owners. How could I do that? I never worked horses into shape or owned horses. I envied Nicole and her experience working for her dad. She knew more about a trainer's skills than I would ever know.

As a horseplayer walking past the track, I couldn't help but think of the sport. What must it be like to gallop out a horse at the break of day? The thrill of watching a young horse mature into a champion runner?

How much didn't I know? What did it take for somebody like

Sal to orchestrate more than sixty horses?

A car sped around the corner and came right at me. I dove onto the broken cement. Music and laughter swept over me as the car passed. I got up and shook off the pain in my knee.

A couple of blocks ahead, a car was parked on the wrong side of the street. The track property ended at the cross street, and I'd been instructed to turn east to continue my walk around the perimeter. My cell buzzed. I pulled out my cell and noted the "unknown" number.

I answered.

"Drop the cash by the streetlight on the corner and keep going," a man's voice instructed. We'd always heard a woman's voice before.

"Don't turn around. Just walk. If you want the fucking book in one piece, do it."

The wrong-way car turned on its headlights. I walked toward it. I left my hands free to show I wasn't planning anything. I walked as slowly as if I approached a bull that might charge. I was fully exposed. I assumed the vehicle had been stolen. My long walk seemed like a death march.

At the streetlight, I pulled out the paper bag containing the cash and dropped it like it was trash. Then, I turned to my left and kept walking. I maintained the same slow pace, sweat dripping down from under my arms. Did they know the real value of the lab book?

I resisted the urge to call Uncle Mike and tell him it wasn't a dry run after all. When I was more than a block away, I heard a car stop at the streetlight behind me and then drive away.

I didn't turn around. The idea was to develop trust. My uncle's sage advice echoed—don't be a hero. The money was no big deal, and they probably didn't have the lab book on them. One more thing to think about, he'd said—there might be somebody waiting in the shadows watching you.

23

RONNIE ORMAN FINALLY CALLED ME BACK AND left a message on my cell phone. He was anxious to meet. It's amazing what can happen when you win five grand at the track.

I called him back, and we arranged a time and place to meet the next day. I told him I wanted to meet with him at Elena's.

"What exactly do you need?" Orman asked, his voice betraying a case of nerves. Orman was worried. I assumed that Vandy could always take his business to another trainer or split his horses between trainers if he wanted. It told me I had a certain degree of clout. I'd give Orman the impression that my role as one of Vandy's advisors included helping him decide which trainer he should use.

"We'll talk more. I don't have the time right now," I said. "But I'll need a list of your owners and their horses."

"What do you need that for?" Orman whined.

"We'll talk more. I have to go." I wanted to leave Orman in a state of anxiety.

The next day, Uncle Mike and I showed up ten minutes late to Elena's.

Orman stood up as soon as we walked in. He was about five years older than me, with a stout middle and horn-rimmed glasses. He wore a faded Turfway cap. "Eddie, I'm glad you could make time to meet."

"Vandy thought we should talk," I said. "This is my uncle, Mike O'Connell."

"Nice to meet you, Mike," Orman said, shaking hands with each of us. "I got a booth over here."

The server came over, and we ordered coffee. The establishment served a few workers who looked like they'd been up before dawn. We asked about the lunch special, introduced ourselves, asked the waitress how long she'd been working at Elena's, and essentially made a nuisance of ourselves.

Orman tried to move things along. "Vandy told me about Eddie, but what do you do, Mike? Are you a handicapper too?"

I liked Orman's folksy approach, but I didn't buy it. I could see his ambition bubbling beneath the surface.

"I'm retired," Uncle Mike said. "The nephew has me doing research."

Orman seemed excited and interested. "What kind of research?"

"Did you bring that list of owners?" I asked.

"Yeah." He grabbed a file from his backpack. "You can check with the office."

"I wanted one that's up to date with the names of each owner's horse in your barn."

"Sure." He slid the report across the table to me. "Eddie, how did you get this job with Vandy? He isn't easy to work for."

"I have connections."

Our coffee arrived, and Uncle Mike went through a long-winded discussion with the waitress about what type of sweeteners they had in stock versus what his doctor had recommended. I almost broke up.

"How did you pick my horse yesterday?" Orman asked in an off-hand way as if he was talking about the weather. "I mean ClassicMasterD even surprised me."

I evaluated his demeanor. Could a trainer still be surprised by his horse? Maybe he was just trying to flatter me. "It takes research, Ronnie. That's why I need a researcher. You might see my uncle drop by to talk with an exercise rider or one of the owners from time to time. You don't have any objections to that, do you?"

Orman hesitated, then said, "No, why would I?"

"I didn't think so. You see, we're all working together—me, Mike, and you. If Vandy's bottom-line increases, it'll be good for all of us. Vandy can claim more horses here at Thornton and other tracks. You would then need to think about adding more staff. With expansion, other benefits will follow. Ultimately, you'll be able to pick and choose from the best owners. We all benefit."

Orman nodded. He licked his cracked lips and leaned forward in a sign of eagerness. "Tell Mr. Van der Walt that I'm ready to do that. Some guys worry about expanding, but not me. Well, if you're able to sniff out a horse like—"

"Like ClassicMasterD? Yes, Vandy will consult with me and Mike on what horses to claim. Vandy doesn't have unlimited resources. He has to make the most from every claim. He has claimed a number of horses from your barn over the years, I understand?" I hadn't learned this from Vandy; I knew it from my handicapping. I had no idea if Vandy would want my advice on what horses to claim.

Orman's upper lip curled. "Yeah. Vandy and Sal have targeted me."

"Maybe I can help. You need to do a better job of disguising your horse's form." I couldn't believe these words were coming out of my mouth. I didn't look at Uncle Mike or his expected what-the-fuck expression—it would make me snicker. As a handicapper, my job had always been to unravel all the moves a trainer made to disguise a horse's form; now here I was advising a trainer how to do it. A trainer couldn't simply tell a jock to "stiff" their horse when they ran a race, or they could get in trouble with the stewards, or incur the wrath of the owner. The jocks found other means to solve this dilemma—they ran their horses into traffic trouble or stumbled out of the gate.

Orman shrugged as if he no longer had to worry about Sal claiming horses. "Now that Sal's suspended—"

"Someone else will step into Sal's shoes and start claiming your horses. I'm sure your owners won't be happy either when their horses are claimed," I said.

Orman rubbed the back of his neck, but didn't argue.

I asked, "Were you surprised about Sal's positive test?"

"If it can happen to Sal, it can happen to any one of us," Orman said. "Sal had this game figured out. He learned from his old man and his brother. I was an assistant for years before I went out on my own, but it always looks a lot easier from the outside. Then I tried it myself. The bettors love Sal. That's the reason ClassicMasterD went off at such long odds. Sal is a tough act to follow."

Nicole had told me that Orman had been an assistant for Sal a number of years ago. That was why Sal had picked Orman to look after his stable. I liked the fact that Orman was feeling the pressure. "Why are you two arguing over Turfway or the Fairgrounds for the winter months?"

Orman's face reflected the "no-win" situation. He shook his head as if he was reluctant to discuss the winter move. "Turfway has synthetic. I like the surface."

"They have fuller fields, and then your horses need to switch to dirt when they come back to Thornton," I countered.

"A different surface will only make us better. I should know—the north side track was synthetic," Orman said.

"I plan to be on site at either track," I said. "Let us know if your decision is final."

Orman studied me. Maybe he was wondering if I was his adversary or his ally. One minute I was talking about working together to expand his operation and the next questioning his motives. He'd sweat even more if he knew Uncle Mike and I were also judging him to determine if he'd drugged Sal's horse and covered it up by murdering Jessie.

Orman stood and pulled the backpack over his shoulder, then leaned down over the table. "Look, I didn't want things to happen this way. But that's what happened, and I'm going to make the most of it. When I do, I'm not taking any shit from you, understand?" He started to walk off and then rushed back to the table. "Let me talk to a few people about Turfway or New Orleans. I have to get back to the barn. I'll be in touch."

Our sandwiches came. Uncle Mike asked the waitress, "Do you have any of that hot sauce?"

I wasn't convinced by Orman's little speech. But we'd rattled him, and that was the point.

24

I WASN'T GOING TO WASTE MY FREE PASS TO THE backstretch. As the recently crowned handicapping guru extraordinaire, I'd play the role to the hilt and stroll among my subjects. At least, until the inevitable implosion, when the races failed to cooperate.

After lunch, Uncle Mike and I took a slow walk to the stables and back as if we owned the place.

A steady stream of people was coming and going from the parking lot to the stables. Golf carts taxied wealthy owners back and forth. Workers crisscrossed from the stables to the dorms and to the parking lot. We were able to get lost in the crowd.

We stopped outside the stables. "We've got a few minutes before our meeting." Through Nicole, Isabel had asked to meet with me. We were scheduled to meet her in the dorms shortly. "What did you think of Orman?"

"Seems kind of soft. No wonder Sal picked him to handle the stable."

"He knows horses. He must also know how to inject a horse, but then lots of workers on the backstretch need to inject horses for therapeutic purposes. Did you see the way he reacted when I brought up the fact that Sal and Vandy had claimed a number of his horses?"

"Yeah, he said he'd been targeted. People fight back when they're being targeted by someone."

"He wants success so bad he can almost taste it," I said.

"Orman can't wait to cozy up to Vandy, and you didn't help things—talking about how he can expand with you and Vandy by claiming lots of horses. I almost choked on my coffee."

"He ate it up, didn't he? He hopes Vandy will forget about Sal," I said.

"Yeah, Vandy is the key. Jockey agents are schmoozing him. Trainers treat him like royalty. And you're his Thornton expert. If there's all this intrigue with claiming horses, what must it be like for those high-priced horses the Saudi crown princes buy?"

"Fortunately or unfortunately, Thornton can't afford to run those kinds of stakes races. Orman had motive, opportunity and knowledge," I said.

We walked back toward Elena's and turned the corner of the first dorm. It was a similar path to the one Jessie must've taken. Uncle Mike and I examined the scene closely, each of us playing and replaying the scenario—the pounding rain, Jessie's anger, and the murderer meeting up with her. The parked cars and bike rack blocked the view of those who might have stood in the doorway.

When we knocked on Isabel's apartment door, she was waiting for us.

"Eddie, Mike, thank you for coming." Isabel looked out into the hallway and then shut the door. "I'm so glad you're here."

She directed us to take a seat on the lone bed, but we opted to stand. She sat in the desk chair, her hair unkempt and her eyes bloodshot. As an exercise rider, she must've been up since dawn.

We were probably interrupting her well-earned naptime while her daughter was in school.

I'd prepared Uncle Mike for the dorms and the small rooms where the workers resided. Isabel's space was crammed with possessions, stacked in neat piles, unlike some of the other rooms we'd passed. Several doors had been ajar, and we'd gotten a peek inside—clothes stacked in piles and trash cans overflowing.

I said, "Nicole told me you wanted to talk—"

"You said you could help. I prayed to the Virgin Mary. Sometimes we feel forgotten." She faced Uncle Mike. "Without Jessie around, it's bad. Mr. O'Connell, I saw you with the policemen that night. Are you a policeman?"

"No, I'm retired," he said. "Don't worry. I'm helping Eddie."

"Thank you, sir. The police are no good. If you call for help, and if they do come, you'll get arrested or turned over to ICE. They won't find the ones who killed my Jessie. I don't know where to begin. Much has changed." Her hands and fingers were knotted in her lap.

"You can tell us," I said. "I'll tell Nicole as well."

She hesitated, studying me and then Uncle Mike. "Hugo has disappeared."

"What?" I'd hoped Hugo had recovered from my knockout punch.

"None of his men are around."

I expected her to be relieved. "Will they come back?"

"We don't know. Another man sells pills instead. Two people overdosed. They went to the hospital and now they're back. The pills are poison."

I assumed it was fentanyl. Overdoses from the pills had been reported throughout the city. The backstretch was not immune from the trouble that plagued the streets.

"Who is this 'man'?" I asked. "Is he one of Ramon's friends?"

"No. We don't know who he is or who is in charge. Maybe another cartel. Ramon's friends still come around. People owe money to them. It's bad to borrow from them, but sometimes people have no choice."

"We'll ask around," I said. "How is Juanita?"

Isabel took a deep breath. "She is getting in fights. I will need to look for another school."

"I'm sorry to hear that. Sal will start serving his suspension. Will you have a job?"

"I don't know. Right now, everything is fine. Who knows about tomorrow? We hope things will stay the same."

"I'll see what I can find out. I assume you know that Mr. Orman will take over Sal's stable?" She nodded. "What do you know about Mr. Orman?" I asked.

"What?"

"What kind of trainer is Ronnie Orman—compared to Sal?"

She shook her head. "Mr. Ronnie thinks he's a great trainer. He cuts corners and lies to his owners. High vet bills. I don't want to work for him, but I will have no choice."

"Cuts corners?"

"Yes. A trainer has to get the horse feeling good—full of themselves. Their teeth need to feel good. Their body and legs. The right feed, the right care. Sal's barn does this over and over. Sal is the best here. I was proud to work…" Tears came to her eyes, and she grabbed a tissue from a box on the corner of the desk next to the king-size box of cornflakes.

"Did Jesse and Orman get along?"

Isabel shook her head. "Never. Mr. Ronnie blamed her whenever Vandy claimed one of his horses."

"Have owners left Mr. Ronnie?"

"Yes, they are not happy. Mr. Vasquez can tell you."

"Who is Mr. Vasquez?"

"He's a jockey agent. He's smart. He represents Arrellano."

"Arellano gets a lot of live mounts," I said. Every year

Arrellano was at the top of Thornton's jockey standings. "I'll talk to Mr. Vasquez. I might need to ask you about 'live' horses you've ridden or heard about. I'm working with Vandy."

Isabel's face lit up. "I can help. I helped Jessie with those horses, and she'd talk with Mr. Vandy. Everything worked. Jessie made it work for us."

"Thanks. I'll talk to Orman about a job for you. If you get a name for this man selling the pills, let me know."

She nodded. "Thank you so much. I will let you know about the man. It may take time. If I ask too much, people will think I want to buy the pills. My daughter might hear and not understand."

"That's okay. Get in touch with me if Hugo or his men come back."

"Each day I worry."

Uncle Mike told Isabel how much we appreciated her help and assured her again that he wouldn't talk to the police.

She listened closely and nodded along. "I know Nicole and Eddie are lovers. I'm so glad. You should know how happy it made Jessie to see Nicole so happy. I can trust you both because I trust Nicole. I will pray for you both."

25

OUR NEXT STOP WOULD BE SAL'S OFFICE. IT WAS moving day. Nicole wanted to be here to help her father pack up, but he'd told her in no uncertain terms that he didn't need her help.

"Sal has been more of an asshole than usual lately," I said.

"Thanks for the warning. He's under a lot of pressure, Eddie," my uncle said in response. "Sal has murder charges hanging over his head. The last time I talked to Saboski, I didn't like his attitude. The guy can play the arrogant shithead, and that's how he talked to me. Like I was a piece of shit and that he didn't owe me a thing. If he arrests Sal, I'm going to try damn hard to prove Saboski wrong. You'd think he would've learned something from Liz, but he didn't."

"Saboski needs a big dish of humble pie jammed down his throat? I'd be glad to do that," I said.

"Let's hope it doesn't come to that."

We walked to the end of the shedrow and knocked on Sal's

office door.

"It's open," Sal yelled out.

We walked in. The walls were now blank, with rows of eight-by-eleven-inch squares where the winner circle photos had once resided. The paint behind the photos hadn't faded. The desk had been cleared. We had to maneuver around stacks of boxes piled up to eye-level. Somehow the room looked bigger.

"Hello, Eddie, Mike," Sal said. "You're here for moving day."

The old trainer sounded upbeat, as if a great burden had been lifted.

We said hello and uttered awkward comments about how sorry we were.

"Well, it is what it is, gentlemen. The way I see it—I'm paying for other trainers' sins of the past. Those guys who got caught juicing, or those who got away scot-free. The bill for all that rotten shit had to become due sometime, and that time is now. We owe it to the horses and to the fans, and most of all to the grand old horsemen of the past like my father."

I'd prepared myself and Uncle Mike for Sal's mood swings, but I didn't expect this—rationalization, sentiment, and contentment. It hit me like a fastball I couldn't dodge. I was speechless.

Sal came around the stack of boxes and clapped me on the back. "Good job with your wagers the other day. I have to hand it to you. If you can make Vandy happy, you've done well. I didn't see that Orman horse—ClassicMasterD. Even on his best day, I didn't think he was that kind of horse."

"What do you mean?" I asked.

Sal smiled. "I didn't think the horse would be able to duel with our horse, Out of Truth. Usually, class comes to the forefront in the stretch. Nobody can guarantee anything out here though." He hesitated as if trying to decide if that was good or bad, then said, "Wouldn't it be something if ClassicMasterD came back positive? Then what would I do?"

I let that question hang. "How are things going with Orman?"

"Here to check up on me?" He laughed a short, bitter laugh. "Smooth so far. All the papers have been signed. The horses are his worry. When the meet closes, we agreed he'll ship a string of horses to New Orleans for me to train, and Orman will keep the rest at Turfway."

"It doesn't sound like you approve," Uncle Mike said.

"I don't approve of much these days, Mike. I'm hanging in there, but I don't know why. I used to think I was a caretaker—keeping things going for Nicole as a way to honor the Nicoletti name. Today could be the end of a long run. It all came crashing down on my watch. I got to admit, I'm almost relieved that Nicole doesn't want any part of it. Can't say I blame her."

"You going to take up fishing?" Uncle Mike asked.

"Maybe I will. Maybe I had to be forced into retirement."

Uncle Mike rubbed the back of his neck. "That's what happened to me."

"From what Nicole tells me, you two still do detective work." Sal studied me and then Uncle Mike. "I suppose it's different from being on the police force, though."

"No comparison," he said.

That was an understatement if I ever heard one. We couldn't confront witnesses with the authority of a homicide detective, so we had to find ways around it. We had to find witnesses like Isabel, who would only cooperate with somebody who was not with the police, or question somebody like Orman only after we'd gained a position of leverage. It wasn't easy, but it allowed us to dig deeper. Witnesses could be guarded when they were questioned by police detectives, or maybe they'd get a lawyer, and say nothing at all.

"Why did you go with Orman and not some other trainer?" I asked.

Sal shook his head. "He approached me. Maybe I was having

a bad day. I told him, 'You can have them.' If I had to do it all over again, I'd probably talk with other guys as well. I hoped Orman would be somebody I could work with because he used to be one of my assistant trainers. Shit, I don't know. If it doesn't work out, what can I do? It's out of my hands."

I was sorry I'd asked the question. I'd ruined Sal's good mood.

"Do you know a guy named Island Willie?" Uncle Mike asked.

The question surprised me. But it was a good one.

"Yeah. I heard he's roaming around the track. Something must be happening. I never bet with Island Willie. Some guys get in debt real bad doing that. You owe big money to somebody like him, and you never know where it will lead."

"Last year there was talk about the manipulation of the exacta pools," I said. "Was Island Willie one of those who got scammed?" Pools could be manipulated by making bets at the track on other horses or other exacta combinations, resulting in an inflated payoff for a target horse or exacta. The instigator would then bet on the horse or exacta with illegal bookies or off-shore, and get paid the inflated on-track odds.

Sal laughed. "Island Willie got his ass burned on more than one of those schemes. Maybe he's here to nail somebody for that. It goes on more than people know. One of these damn CAWs or somebody like them."

The Late Money Boys seemed to be involved in all sorts of schemes. "How about Vandy?" I asked.

"I guess it could be him. He bets big money and hates to lose. You got a tiger by the tail with your job, Eddie. Don't start planning retirement anytime soon."

This time Uncle Mike laughed with Sal. I knew my imposter job for Vandy would be short term, but I'd like to think it'd last for a while. "Very funny."

Sal wiped a tear away from his eye. When he managed to

regain control, he said. "Sorry, Eddie. I'm sure you and Vandy will have a long and happy association." He started laughing again. Or maybe Uncle Mike started, and Sal couldn't help himself.

"You guys are a lot of help," I said, starting to get pissed off.

Sal composed himself again. "Like I said, there are no guarantees. If I told you the number of times Vandy fired my ass, you'd go looking for another gig. Ask around about Vandy, they'll tell you. We're dealing with horses. Sometimes they do what they want to do. It's not like the old days, either. Lots of new faces. Some people are barely making it, sleeping in shit hotels or on somebody's couch. I've seen stuff."

"You mean shady stuff like what Eddie's talking about?" Uncle Mike asked.

"That's the nature of the business. But now it's gotten out of control. The crackdown by the feds on drug use is sort of like spraying for cockroaches—they just run somewhere else. Or they find one of those designer drugs that's untestable. It's sad. I hear that there's a lab book out there."

Uncle Mike and I looked at each other. This was the first we'd heard of this. It had to be the professor's lab book.

"Where did you hear about this lab book?" Uncle Mike asked.

"Vandy, I guess. He's all shook up about it. He told me in confidence, so don't say anything. A lab book—that's the icing on the cake, isn't it?"

"Did Vandy say anything else?" I asked.

Sal shook his head. He shut his eyes tight, and his breath came in short bursts. "Another thing that's sad—something I try not to…"

This time Sal stared at the blank walls, and his breathing grew short as if he was hyperventilating. He reached out one hand and steadied himself on one of the stacks. We waited. Then Uncle Mike took a step toward Sal, and Sal responded by extending one arm to stay away.

"I'm okay. I'll be okay," he said. "I was going to tell you something important." He took a deep breath. The transformation from belly laughs to utter despair caught me by surprise.

Sal cleared his throat. "Try not to let your anger get the best of you. Try not to get angry with somebody who might not deserve it. You'll regret it. And you'll hate yourself forever if you never see that person again."

Jessie.

26

THAT NIGHT I SPENT A GOOD PORTION OF MY TIME working the next day's races. Vandy didn't have a horse running, but he might ask me what I thought about a certain horse that he wanted to claim.

My old friend Marini had asked me earlier that evening at O'Connell's if I'd had a chance to read his manuscript. I got off the hook by telling him I hadn't had time, but planned to start reading it later that night. It might take my mind off the stolen lab book.

The professor had called Uncle Mike and me earlier. It wasn't an easy call. It had only been a few days since the drop, but we thought that once the thieves got a taste of the easy currency, they'd want to cash in again fast.

"I take it by your silence that we haven't heard from the thief or thieves?" she asked.

"I'm afraid that's right," I said.

She sighed. "I can't let that lab book fall into the wrong

hands."

"We could question some of the people at the school," Uncle Mike suggested. "You were going to give us the names of the IT people you were sparring with."

"God, no," she said. "My worst nightmare at this point. The first thing they'd ask is *when* the theft occurred. My failure to report would put me in a terrible position."

We told her we understood.

"The thieves could do anything. They could sell it or burn it. Damn it. I don't care. It won't stop me." She hung up.

Uncle Mike and I had looked at each other. What did the professor mean by "it won't stop me"? What was in that lab book? It must be more than her "notes." We'd been riding high on the backstretch after Vandy's test, and now we crashed back to earth.

I was beginning to understand what Uncle Mike lived with— those cold cases that still haunted him. The detective business had its ups and downs and the downs could cut deep.

Sal had been a no-show at dinner. Nicole had tried to get in touch with him, but he wouldn't answer.

I'd told her about our meeting and the stacks of boxes. "We could drive over—"

"I'm not driving over to his house. If he doesn't answer my calls, why should I?"

I ate like a guy who hadn't eaten in a week, but Nicole barely touched her fancy meal. After dinner, she played internet poker to prepare for her first night of poker with her fans at the local casino, which was scheduled a few days out, and then she watched a movie, while I spent my time watching videos of past races.

After our meeting with Sal, Uncle Mike and I had discussed Sal's news about a lab book. Track gossip and rumors could spread like wildfire. It could be that the thief had spread the rumor to increase the ransom or start a bidding war.

That night, after Nicole fell asleep with the aid of a prescription sleeping pill, I started in on Marini's manuscript.

Both Wynton and his son, Nolan the star QB, were unlikeable. Wynton was sitting in the frat house trying to chat with coeds who found him "icky," while Nolan had one coed under each arm. I tried not to laugh out loud to avoid waking Nicole.

The football games were described meticulously right down to Jimbo, the starting left tackle, strapping on his shoulder pads. Jimbo had made it his sworn duty to protect Nolan's blind side. The detailed description of the games, quarter by quarter, and play-by-play, to score a come-from-behind victory, was a chance for Marini to show off his sportswriter talents, but it put me to sleep.

27

WE DROVE OUT WEST TO THE OLD SHAGBARK
Country Club for Vandy's "reception" on Friday night. I
wondered why the reception was scheduled at the same golf club
where we'd met Burrascano the other night, and Uncle Mike
filled me in.

"I've been out here a number of times over the years. Our
police union had its annual golf outing and dinner here back in
the day. The club is on the west side—a perfect meeting place for
those traveling from opposite ends of the city. It was also the
only place that could handle a crowd that size. It has a huge
dining room and two golf courses."

Uncle Mike, Nicole, and I made it to the country club shortly
before five thirty. In the parking lot, we saw people leaving and
rechecked the time—it was the time given to us by Vandy. After
we left our coats with the coat-check person and walked into the
Hickory Pub, we could smell the wonderful aroma of roasting
meat. People walked around with drinks and plates of food from

the buffet, set up along the far wall, near the stained-glass windows. A chef carved slices from a three-foot slab of beef. Others congregated at the dark oak bar, involved in animated, alcohol-fueled conversation.

"Looks like we're late to the party," Uncle Mike said.

My bartender background told me the crowd had been at the trough for at least an hour.

"What did Vandy say this party was about?" Nicole asked above the din.

A woman with straight blonde hair and a perfect smile approached us with an iPad in hand. "Hi there, I'm Haley. I'm with Mr. Van der Walt."

We gave her our names and apologized for being late. Even though we fit right in with our sports coats and Nicole's businesslike pantsuit, we must've looked like newbies, because Haley had singled us out.

"Here you are—on the guest list." She typed away on the iPad. "No, you're fine." She handed each of us a guest name tag to pin to our lapels. "Help yourself to the open bar and appetizers. Everyone's raving about the nacho cheese dip." She slid past me and Uncle Mike to Nicole. "And you're Nicole?"

Nicole nodded. "That's me."

"It's a pleasure to finally meet you. I've heard so much about you. I'd like to introduce you to some people who are anxious to meet you." She turned to me and my uncle. "Do you mind if I borrow Nicole for a moment, gentlemen?"

Nicole was the celebrity poker pro who was picking football games at an unheard-of win percentage. No wonder she was being singled out. We both shrugged and watched as Haley led Nicole away to a large group at the far end of the bar. We made our way to the opposite end and waited for a bartender to come over.

"See any familiar faces?" Uncle Mike asked.

I glanced across the room. Nicole had been surrounded by

six or seven people and had them laughing. She accepted a glass of white wine from a waiter buzzing around the "in" crowd.

"Vandy is in the crowd around Nicole. It doesn't look like Nicole had any trouble being served," I said.

"Maybe you can get a bartender's attention if you tell them you're Nicole's boyfriend."

"Very funny. Hey, I recognize that guy standing alone talking on his cell. The guy by the windows." He was a man in a dark suit and one of the few attendees wearing a tie.

"Who is he?"

"I never did learn his name. He works with Arlene." Quite often she'd brought the man in the suit along. He was most likely her lawyer or one of the managing officers of the track.

"Oh, yeah," Uncle Mike said. "I remember him."

We managed to get a couple of seats. When the bartender finally got to us, we each ordered a dark microbrew that we were eager to check out and possibly include on the beer roster at O'Connell's.

A man behind us, waiting to be served, was talking in a low voice with his buddy. "I'm telling you I saw him just last night. He's here in Chicago."

"C'mon. Where did you see him?" the buddy with a New York accent asked.

Uncle Mike and I tried to act casual and made small talk. You'd think our lives revolved around microbrews.

"A Greek place downtown," the man replied.

"Shit. What's he doing here?"

"I don't know. It can't be good. We fucked him over good on that exacta."

"That was Vandy's idea. He better come through on football." The New Yorker's anger almost made me feel sorry for Vandy.

"Yeah. I see he made good on the invite of Nicole Nicoletti."

"We should've stayed with our original way of doing

business—grinding it out race after race."

"Horse racing is drying up."

The two ordered their drinks—a gin and tonic for the guy who was partial to Greek restaurants and a martini for the New Yorker.

"They could've hired another bartender," the New Yorker griped.

"What did you think of the speaker?"

"She could turn the backstretch upside down."

"Yeah. Just when all our algorithms are working..."

The two fast talkers got their drinks and drifted off. They eventually ended up at the end of the bar, where Nicole was being peppered with questions. She was in her element, her laughter echoing across the room.

"What did you think of those two?" I asked, looking around to be sure no one could overhear us.

"Damn. We learn more sitting on our duff than we do asking questions," Uncle Mike said. "I guess ninety percent of life is showing up. Let's sample another microbrew."

I signaled to the bartender. "Were they talking about our friend?"

"The big swinging dick? I think so."

It had to be Island Willie. The manipulation of the exacta pools had been discussed on social media and in racetrack newsletters, but the practice had been going on for some time. Only a dedicated horseplayer studies fun stuff like exacta pools and payoffs.

"This must be a CAW—The Late Money Boys," I said. "Anonymous rich guys who bet the late money."

"Fuckers. I'm beginning to think you were right about something else—the connection between our little meeting the other night with Burrascano and today's scheduled reception. Both held at Old Shagbark."

"Those guys sounded scared."

"Maybe they should be." Uncle sipped from his fresh beer. "When you take money out of the mouth of the mob, you better hope you're anonymous."

An older woman in a red pantsuit with a jeweled brooch the size of a baseball on her lapel stood behind us trying to get the bartender's attention. Her hair was beauty-salon perfect. She nodded to me. "I don't believe we've been properly introduced. My name is Gloria Willingham."

We introduced ourselves, drawing a blank stare from the woman. I tried a new tack. "We're with Nicole."

"Oh, that's wonderful. Thank you for coming. Nicole will be perfect for this group. I'll need to introduce you to my husband, Richard, when I can tear him away."

"You and your husband own quite a few top horses." I refrained from any mention of Sal and the promising three-year-old Freedom Rider that the Willinghams had recalled.

She perked up. "Why, yes, we do. It isn't often we're recognized for ownership here in Chicago anymore. Thornton Racetrack simply isn't what it once was, and the north side track has been demolished. It's a mud field—have you seen it? Terrible."

We nodded. She was on a roll.

"When we're at Oaklawn or Saratoga, in the club suites, we feel like celebrities. Sometimes it gets to be too much. Before we know it, it's post-time." She talked fast as if post-time was coming up.

"You had Jazz Sax in the Derby last year."

"Yes, he won the Rebel, but didn't take to the Churchill surface. It was a shame. Jazzy boy is getting a rest after his big win in the Travers. We've been to the Derby for the last fifteen years, and it's getting more and more crowded. We wonder if it's worth it anymore. What horses do you own? Will we see you at Hot Springs?"

"No, we don't own any horses. We're sorry we missed the

meeting earlier. How did it go?" I asked.

"Oh my, you weren't at the meeting earlier?" She began searching through the crowd again. "They say it's about insurance, but that's something I leave to my husband. I'm here to touch base with old friends, you understand." She waved to another woman, who had snagged a bartender.

After she left, Uncle Mike asked in a low voice, "What is this? The owners are part of the Late Money Boys. You know what? I think we need to get Irv working for us. We had that list of owners from Sal and Orman—"

"Most were shell corporations."

"Right. I bet some of those owners are here, and we don't even know it. A meeting about insurance—I don't believe that. Fine detectives we are. We walk into a party and we don't know what it's about."

"I've never seen people party so hard over insurance."

"Look over there," Uncle Mike said. "By the entrance."

I saw a woman in an expensive coat waving to several people. She then turned to walk back into the clubhouse, which would lead to the exits. "It's the professor."

"What the hell? Did she see us?"

"I don't know. Why don't I try to catch up with her?" Was she the speaker—the one who would "turn the backstretch upside down"? I was dying to ask her what she knew about the meeting.

"We need to be careful. Remember, we're supposed to maintain confidentiality."

"You're right. What if I kept my distance and caught up with her in the parking lot?"

Uncle Mike agreed.

Our moment of uncertainty cost me. I'd lost sight of the professor. I snaked my way through the crowd. Once I got into the clubhouse lobby, I had to choose between a stairway that led down to a small lot to my left or a much larger lot in front of the clubhouse. I chose the bigger lot.

Due to the outbuildings, I couldn't see the smaller parking lot as I walked out front. Her chauffeured limo could be tucked away anywhere in the tree-lined lots. I heard screams from the other lot. I circled back, but a crowd had already congregated along the stairway.

I pushed my way through, afraid I'd find the professor. A body was wedged between parked cars. I squeezed past the onlookers and Good Samaritans who tried to administer first aid. The victim was a man and for that I felt a moment of relief. I didn't recognize him.

His throat had been slashed to the bone.

28

EARLY THE NEXT MORNING, UNCLE MIKE AND I stood by the rail at Thornton Racetrack to watch the workouts.

"Damnit, Eddie, I can see my breath." Uncle Mike sipped from his coffee and squinted into the sun.

"We have to put on a good front to show Vandy we're doing all we can." It was a cold, crisp fall morning. A slight crowd stood nearby. Many had stopwatches and binoculars.

"You never did this, did you?"

"I should've. Horseplayers stop by once or twice, then they get lazy."

"Damn, Eddie. They publish the workout times and stuff. Isn't that enough?"

"That's only part of the story. You watch enough workouts and you'll be able to tell things. Sometimes horses work 'in company'—running with another horse in the stable. A frontrunner learns to stalk and pass horses. Sometimes they gallop. You'll hear things. Isabel said she'd tell us—"

"Okay, okay." Uncle Mike took out a small notebook.

I glanced back at the grandstands. "Look who's coming over to join us. See if it's important enough for him—"

"Good morning," Uncle Mike called out.

It was Island Willie. He took careful baby steps, measuring each step as if he traversed a steep mountain path instead of the slight slope of the track apron. He wore a down jacket and a wool Bears stocking hat, his long flowing beard ruffled in the breeze. "I didn't think I'd see you two. I'm impressed."

Four of DiNatale's boys, including Lou, wore overcoats and stood near the glass doors, dancing around to stay warm. A short man, another of DiNatale's crew, exited and hustled down with a cup of coffee in hand.

He handed it to Island Willie. "Cream and sugar. Can I get you anything else, sir?"

"That's fine, just fine."

"Let us know, sir." He raced back to join the others.

Island Willie took a quick sip. "There's nothing like taking in the early morning parade of horses. You two must be serious horseplayers. You'll have to give me some tips."

"Anytime," I said.

"Appreciate it. Myself, I'm not a morning person. I blame Vegas. You see, when my family relocated from Kauai to Vegas, I naturally gravitated to the nightlife. I'd gotten into some trouble back home, and my father, bless his heart, thought it best if I got away from the old gang for a fresh start. They call Vegas the Ninth Island, you know. Lots of Hawaiians move to Vegas, so I just took up where I left off."

"We heard about a murder yesterday at the Old Shagbark Country Club," Uncle Mike said.

Uncle Mike and I had talked about the murder on the way to the track. The dead man's name was Donnie Egan. He was known for being the father of a current star college football quarterback named Darien Egan. Darien had led his team into the college playoffs and then signed a contract for big-money to transfer. It sounded an awful lot like Marini's shitty manuscript.

"No kidding? Old Shagbark? I've played both courses at that club. I prefer the number two course, the one where you hit your second shot over the lake on the eighteenth hole—"

"You know anything about the murder, Willie? His throat was slashed," Uncle Mike said.

Island Willie held his binoculars up to his eyes. "A terrible way to die. I suppose one suffocates if the cuts are deep enough? Look. Out there. It's Isabel. She knows how to ride."

I had my binoculars and followed her white horse along the backstretch. Isabel must be working for Orman. Why didn't she tell us?

"Isabel's the one I need. She reminds me of Jessie," Island Willie said.

I recalled what Island Willie had said about Jessie. When he needed information about a horse at Thornton, she had been his source.

"You're going to sign up Isabel?" I asked.

"I'm trying. I pay a nice monthly stipend, too, but she's reluctant."

I wondered whether Isabel knew something. Maybe things hadn't gone well between Island Willie and Jessie. Before I could follow up, we heard loud voices behind us.

"All I want to do is talk," a voice called out.

I was ready to pull my gun. After yesterday, I wasn't going to leave home without it.

The guy who delivered the coffee ran up to Island Willie. "Sir, it's two men. One of them is The Hippo."

"Frisk them and then escort them down here," Island Willie said.

He ran back. Lou supervised the frisk, and the entire group walked up to us.

What was The Hippo doing here? Uncle Mike took a step or

two to the side. We expected a succession battle between The Hippo and DiNatale, but we'd hoped that would happen in some dark, uninhabited corner of the city.

"Hey, Griggs," The Hippo called out. "You don't call to let me know you're in town. Island trouble? What the fuck?" The Hippo was five foot-five inches tall and wasn't hippo-sized around the middle, but he was getting there. He did have a wicked, elongated jawline and a wide, gaping mouth.

Island Willie stiffened. "Mr. Ippolitto, what a pleasant surprise."

"You think this is a surprise? Well, fuck you."

Lou took a step toward The Hippo and his men, his fists clenched.

"Sorry, big guy," The Hippo said, holding up a hand as a sign of truce. "I'll be good."

Island Willie relaxed somewhat. "Let me introduce you to my friends. This is Mike O'Connell and his nephew, Eddie. This gentleman is Alessio Ippolitto. And the other gentleman—I haven't had the pleasure—"

"He's nobody," The Hippo said. His underling kept his focus on Lou.

The tension in the air made me feel as if a race was about to start and I had a big bet on a live long shot.

The Hippo looked us over, his upper lip curled into a sneer. "Mr. O'Connell, the copper. Hey, Eddie," he reached out his hand. "Nice to meet you. You're the kid with the big right hand. Thanks for taking care of Hugo."

I shook his hand so I could tell my grandkids about it.

Island Willie tried a less formal approach. "What brings you to Thornton—"

"Shut up, Griggs. I don't need any of your bullshit. What I want to know is why the degenerate fuck got whacked yesterday, and why wasn't I told about it. The fucker owes my books a shitload. He told my guys he won big and not to worry."

Island Willie cleared his throat. "You aren't supposed to be here. Take your fentanyl—"

"You'll be paying me what I'm owed," The Hippo said, his face turning red.

Island Willie grimaced in pain. His feet must've been acting up because The Hippo's threats didn't seem to faze him. "I'm afraid you'd have to ask other—"

"Like the big prick sucking up to Burrascano? Tell DiNatale we're going to have a showdown before anybody does anything." The Hippo spat a glob of phlegm at the feet of Island Willie and walked off, his "nobody man" watching Lou closely. Two of DiNatale's boys followed.

Lou smiled through clenched teeth. "See you soon, Mister Ippo—lito."

At the glass doors, The Hippo and DiNatale's men talked with a track security guard. After a heated argument, it was agreed that the guard would turn over the guns once The Hippo got outside.

"Damn." Island Willie sipped his coffee, watching The Hippo gripe about his guns. "I can't even enjoy my Morning Joe in peace."

29

AFTER THE MORNING WORKOUTS, I GOT A CALL from the Thornton Racetrack executive office. Arlene Adams asked to meet with us. It wasn't exactly a request.

Uncle Mike and I took the elevator up to the executive offices on the fourth floor and were led into a small meeting room overlooking the track. I took in the view while we waited for Arlene. Beyond the backstretch, where people hustled to prep for today's racing, lay the cityscape. A couple of abandoned factories to the east were in the throes of being demolished— their smokestacks chipped away by the wrecking ball. To the west, the reliable refinery continued to chug hydrocarbons into the atmosphere.

A brief knock on the open door brought us to attention.

"Hello, gentlemen," Arlene called.

I walked over to greet her, and Uncle Mike stood up from his chair. She seemed so much younger and vibrant than at our last meeting several years ago. Her confident smile exuded warmth and gratitude. The last time we'd met, Uncle Mike and I had taken a case on her behalf in Vegas, and it had been concluded to her satisfaction.

Unlike at our last meeting, her hair had been colored again and done up by a beauty salon architect. Gone were the sweatpants and baggy sweater. Back was the high fashion her fans had grown accustomed to admiring. A dark green wool pantsuit, accented by a string of pearls, would put even Gloria Willingham in her place. Arlene was known for being chic, dressed to the hilt like one of those characters she'd played in her old movies—the cosmopolitan divorcee always on the hunt for a handsome, bedazzled man with money. It was good to see, and I almost felt partly responsible for her transformation back to her old self.

"How are my favorite detectives?" She cooed.

"It has been a while," I said.

"I had to get away. I've been staying with family in Arizona."

We played the role of the bewitched men from her old movies—complimenting her on her accomplished style, pulling out her chair, thanking her for setting up this meeting, and generally treating her like the last in the line of Chicago racetrack royalty, which she was.

Having exhausted the long list of social inquiries, Arlene hesitated for a moment and brought the meeting to order by placing her palms on the table and hunching her shoulders. Her movie-star eyes focused first on me and then on Uncle Mike. We waited.

"I'm sure you know why I asked you to meet," she said, taking a deep breath. "What the hell was going on out there? Guys with guns at the morning workouts?"

"Some rough characters had a difference of opinion," Uncle Mike said.

"Difference of opinion?" She shook her head slowly as if she wasn't buying it. "Okay, I'll give you a pass on that. Let's try to be more forthcoming, shall we? I hear you two are prowling about my backstretch." A hint of a smile told us she was willing to forgive us. "What have you boys been up to?"

The absence of her legal advisor confirmed that today was an informal meeting. "We heard about the coffee at Elena's," I said.

She chuckled. "I wish we could match it here. Why upgrade the coffee or the food? I mean, who gives five cents about the races anymore? We're the only track in town and no one is coming—what does that tell you?"

She studied me, and I remained silent. "I know what you'd say about the deserted grandstands. You'd say that your generation deserves a second chance. Well, I say that they're too damn busy on their phones to do anything. When I see them, they are so focused on their phones, they nearly run into me on the sidewalk. I'm surprised they don't simply wander out into traffic and get run over by distracted motorists."

"They have an app that tells them when to look up to avoid highways and high cliffs," I said.

"You're kidding. Does this app also tell them when to fall in love, when to eat? It's nuts. We're building this goliath casino in the east grandstands with WagerEasy and I don't even know why. I feel like I'm running a museum."

She fingered her pearls and looked out the window at a lineup of puffy clouds. "Do you know how it feels to be a museum piece? All your old co-stars are dead and buried. Photos of people who you think you knew don't matter because you can't remember their names. Well, I'm not under glass yet, gentlemen."

We waited while she held the floor.

"I know what you two are up to and, to tell you the truth, I am concerned about Jessie's murder. I had grave misgivings when Burrascano told me he wouldn't pursue the matter."

Uncle Mike leaned forward. "We thought—"

She waved a hand in dismissal. "I need to find out who murdered poor Jessie Rivera. She excelled for years on behalf of the best barn on the grounds. If this track can't protect its own, we're in even deeper trouble than I thought. Look, I understand I can't be expected to build and manage a perfect world, and that the world's problems are going to seep inside through the cracks, but, by God, I can't have a murder. I won't stand for it."

"Burrascano gave us the green light," Uncle Mike said.

"Perhaps we should've cleared it with you," I said with a note of apology.

"Thank God you've been looking into it. Any suspects?" She hesitated, but we simply shrugged. "No, I didn't expect you'd share that with me. Oh, hell, Burrascano isn't himself anymore. Any day we'll be mourning his passing, and I don't know what that'll mean. Damn."

"I'm working with Pieter Van der Walt," I said.

She gave me a slight nod. "You are? Vandy is so full of himself, he won't have a clue."

Arlene was right. Vandy was so focused on the races, he didn't have time to fully evaluate me and my uncle.

"I'm Eddie's research assistant," Uncle Mike said.

She laughed and slapped the table. "Perfect. I know what's going on. I remember when Eddie worked at WagerEasy. You can't fool me twice. Good. You'll learn a lot. Vandy keeps the claiming game honest around here."

An honest claiming game meant one thing to Vandy and another to the horseplayer, although now wasn't the time to raise such issues.

"Vandy invited us to the reception yesterday at the Old Shagbark Country Club," Uncle Mike said.

"We saw your man there—the guy in the suit. I can't remember his name," I said.

"No one can remember his name. Nor do they want to. Did you go to the meeting?"

"No, just the reception after. They told us it was about insurance," Uncle Mike said.

"Insurance? Phooey." She pulled at her collar, and her lips grew taut. "It's the damn devil, is what it is."

She shifted in her chair, her head bowed and her voice low. "Those people are what we used to lovingly call a 'syndicate.' Today, I think of their little band of anonymous venture capitalists as cannibals."

She shook her head. "The worst of it? The absolute horror of it? I'm part of it. They have a smartass from Australia to run it and hide behind. It's a CAW operation—computer assisted wagering. Thornton—me—gives them special rebates on the takeout. I don't run the show anymore; they do."

"The Late Money Boys?" Uncle Mike asked. "They owe me fifty bucks."

She nodded toward my uncle and hesitated. Her lips quivered. If she was playing one of her old movie roles, the director would call for a closeup. "They're the devil, and I'm forced to give them concessions. If they pull back, Thornton is dead. All the real horseplayers, the folks who played the horses and churned their bankroll through our handle, allowing us to take our cut to pay expenses—they're long gone. They know when they're being robbed. Thank God for the simulcast dollars. The CAW manipulates the pools and places its wagers at the last second. Killed the tote board. They see all the odds and pools in real time and then send in a massive number of bets at the last second. The wagers are based on advanced software. How can the horseplayers compete? It's theft. A terrible scandal. And I'm at the heart of it."

It was gut wrenching. Arlene couldn't stand what had happened to her beloved track. She painted herself as the helpless victim, although I still held out hope that something could be done. "They seemed interested in Nicole," I said.

"They would use anyone in the name of good, clean profit—

a way to mask their treachery."

"I saw Island Willie the other day," Uncle Mike said.

She let out a short laugh. "I heard he was here. In the old days, we'd have thrown him out."

Before mobile phones, the track protected its turf with an iron hand. It wouldn't allow pay phones for fear people would place bets with their bookie instead of at the windows.

"Now, the joint is infested," she said. "All we're left with are the rats. Sal Nicoletti, a solid operation and one of the last, is forced out because he has no right to a defense. Migrants overrun the dorms, but we couldn't run the place without them. I do what I can for them and provide services. When was the last time anyone made a show bet besides the Late Money Boys as you call them? Families haven't been here for years. I've got a ghost track."

She pulled a lace handkerchief from her sleeve and dabbed at one eye. "Burrascano was my white knight. The Hippo would never step foot in the track when he was healthy. I hang on, gentlemen, and I don't know why."

30

AFTER OUR MEETING WITH ARLENE, WE WALKED past the grill to the first-floor bar to meet with Vandy.

Uncle Mike shook his head. "That was uplifting."

"I'm beginning to worry about the track. With all that Arlene has to worry about, I'm sorry she has to worry about The Hippo."

"She's a terrific lady. She said that all the horseplayers have left. What are you doing out here?"

"I don't know. The horseplayers can't compete with the Late Money Boys on ROI. I guess they can bat cleanup by working with a guy like Vandy."

"That's true. You've got the advantage—working for a card-carrying member of the track's notorious Late Money Boys. I think we've stumbled onto something."

"Don't forget, you're supposed to be the researcher. I need to get Vandy's approval. Be ready to tell him something about this morning's workout."

"Holy shit. Let me look at my notes. You're a slave driver."

We got up to the bar, where Vandy was waiting. I turned to Uncle Mike. "Just stand to the side and listen in."

We would play our roles and avoid any mention of our meeting with Arlene Adams. I did want to learn more about yesterday's meeting. Maybe if I mentioned the murder in the parking lot, Vandy would open up.

He nodded in my direction but was surprised by Uncle Mike's presence. "Mike, you're back?

"Eddie says I can do some research. You know, be an extra set of eyes?" Uncle Mike said.

I thought I'd told my uncle to shut up and listen—that went well.

"That's a great idea," Vandy said. "As long as Eddie pays you out of his share."

I laughed. "I planned on it."

Since it was more than an hour before post-time, there were only a few simulcasters at the bar. The TVs planted at strategic locations above televised races from the east coast.

"I hope Nicole had a good time yesterday," Vandy said.

"Are you kidding? She loved it. She gets tired of talking football to me, and I get tired of talking about the horses to her, because neither of us listens to the other." Actually, Nicole had complained all the way home about being peppered with endless questions from the cocktail gang.

"I'm in the same situation," Vandy said. "The wife and I divorced a long time ago. I live and breathe the horses. I love football, don't get me wrong, but I'm not a student of the game. Not yet."

"Nicole said your colleagues wanted to know more about Same Game Parlays, Props, and stuff like that?"

"Well, we're all horse racing fans, but we feel like we're missing out. A few of us are considering participation in a collective on behalf of Lake Shore University. A school can build its own team through the portal. Did you see where that quarterback from last year's top college team will transfer and get four million from his new team? That's for one year."

"I read about his father being murdered yesterday in the club parking lot."

Vandy's lips grew tight. "I invited him, and then that has to happen. They stole his watch and his wallet."

"We didn't hear that it was a robbery," Uncle Mike said.

Vandy nodded and shrugged. "Life goes on. The tax deductions with the collective are so inviting, it's a no-brainer. Everything we could ever want. If you add the NFL to the mix, there is a lot of potential. Unlike horse racing, which is dying on the vine. We wondered if Nicole would be willing to do something similar to what you're doing?"

"Consulting on a percentage basis?"

"Yes. It's still in the talking stages, and it won't come to pass until next year—"

"I'm sure she'd be interested." Why not? Nicole wasn't happy with WagerEasy's meddling. They wanted Nicole and her fellow on-air prognosticators to back certain teams that would balance their book, and it didn't sit well with her. It wouldn't hurt to find out what Vandy and his group were up to. If they planned to bet on sports the way they'd bet on the horses—and obtained similar sweetheart advantages with a sportsbook that they'd gotten from the race tracks—it would be a win-win both for Nicole and Vandy's Late Money Boys.

"Good to hear," Vandy said.

Maybe I could find out more about yesterday's meeting. "Nicole said she heard that a professor gave a talk—"

"Yes." Vandy studied me. "She runs the labs and says she has a new test. It's going to change everything."

The professor had told us that the theft of the lab book wouldn't stop her.

"How?" Uncle Mike asked.

"I don't know about the scientific stuff. It's a wake-up call." Vandy opened his racing program on the bar. "Let's get started on today. Unfortunately, I won't have Orman's horses to claim anymore."

"You don't want to piss him off. I get it. We talked with Orman yesterday," I said.

"I heard. Orman was excited about the prospects. He was impressed with you, and he was especially impressed by the fact that you have a retired homicide detective on your team as a research assistant."

Was Orman really "impressed" or nervous? Was Vandy becoming suspicious? I tried to downplay things. "It's good to have family connections. My uncle knows how to listen," I said.

"That's something you learn to do," Uncle Mike said.

I tried not to laugh.

"Well, I'm not an idiot, guys. I know you've been asking questions. I also know you had a run-in with some drug dealers in the backstretch."

He meant Hugo and the cartel. My fight had risen to "rumble in the jungle" fame.

"You're right," Uncle Mike said. "We're helping out. The detective in charge is an old friend."

I liked Uncle Mike's ready-made explanation. I hoped Vandy wouldn't check up on it—Saboski wasn't exactly asking for our help.

"I'll let the police do their job," Vandy said.

I decided to change the subject. "Orman says he's headed to Turfway for the winter instead of New Orleans."

"We'll have horses at both Turfway and the Fairgrounds. You might need to travel from one to the other," Vandy said. "I was looking at the six horse in the fourth race. The barn treats the horse like its pet, and they're dropping it into a claim for the first time in two years. They have to win a purse with the horse sometime."

Vandy had few scruples. He would claim another trainer's "pet"? He still refused to send Winning Spirit off to his planned retirement, although he hadn't yet found a race for the horse. You had to be ruthless in the claiming game to stay on top.

"I'm not crazy about the last workout of that horse in the fourth. What do you think of the nine horse, Mint Jewel, in the sixth race?" I asked. "The claiming price is higher, but the horse loves the synthetic. You can run him here in Starter Allowances, pick up a slice of some purses, and then run him at Turfway and win real money."

Vandy studied the horse. I couldn't gauge whether he was irritated by my choice of another horse or not.

Uncle Mike's cell phone played an ancient rock song by Bachman-Turner Overdrive—*Taking Care of Business.* "I have to take this." He stepped away.

Finally, or more accurately, reluctantly, Vandy started to nod. "I see what you mean, Eddie. You know, sometimes I get caught up in the current meeting and the owner standings. I don't look ahead to my next stop. Good point. Let's go with Mint Jewel. I'll have my people prepare the paperwork." He stopped and then touched my arm. "Another thing—another reason I work with people like you, people who can be 'cool,' and remain objective. Sometimes I 'run hot.' It's the action, you know? Like I'm at a buffet and I can't stop getting this and getting that. My plate's full, but I need more. One bet after the next."

I knew what he meant. I'd had my days. In Vegas, Nicole and I could go on-tilt and play table games through the night.

"It happens to a lot of guys," I said in an off-handed way, making it sound like one of the typical pitfalls of our trade, and nothing to worry about.

"Yeah. I've seen others go down. You'll watch me. Remind me."

"Sure."

My cell pinged with a text. Uncle Mike returned, the cell still in his hand, his face set in that stone cop face that meant trouble. I glanced at the text I had from Nicole—it stopped me. My mind went blank. "They arrested Dad. They found the gun."

31

I STEPPED OVER TO UNCLE MIKE. "WHAT THE FUCK?"

Uncle Mike rubbed his chin and shrugged. "Let's get to Sal and make sure he doesn't do something stupid."

"Like what?" I'd asked.

"Like talk."

Vandy looked up from his racing program. "What happened? Did somebody die?"

It seemed like it. "Sal got arrested for murder."

"What? You've got to be kidding me."

"Nope. I guess they found the gun." I tried to gather my thoughts. The news hit me like a sledgehammer. I knew Sal could be arrested, but I didn't think there was enough evidence. Sure, Sal and Jessie had words, but there wasn't any evidence of past abuse or domestic assault.

How did the cops find the gun? Was it from their search of Sal's house or workplace—no, that search had been done a day or two after the murder—we would've heard.

"Look," Uncle Mike said to Vandy. "Eddie and I have some calls to make. I guess we'll have to cut things short today."

"Of course," Vandy nodded. "Let me know what you find out." He seemed just as flummoxed as we were.

Uncle Mike and I began walking toward the exit. I called Nicole. "How are you doing?"

"How am I doing? Who cares? What does that have to do with it? I don't matter. We have to think about Dad and getting him help."

"Sal never talked to a lawyer, did he?"

"Hell, no. He wouldn't listen. Dad just said, 'Why should I? I've got nothing to hide.' Damn." She mimicked Sal's response to the lawyer question we'd raised multiple times. "Now that the shit has hit the fan, he's left to face those cops alone. I knew it. How many times did you tell him?"

I tried to squeeze in a few words that might constitute a plan of action. "Why don't—"

"What the hell?" she yelled in my ear. "They found Dad's gun at the track? Where the hell was the gun? Why didn't we know about it?"

Uncle Mike nudged me. "I got the precinct where they're holding Sal," he whispered.

I nodded and returned to my cell and Nicole as we walked past the empty admission stand. "Look, Nicole—"

"I've got that 'Poker with the Fans' tonight. That should be a good one. Ask the poker pro about murder. Go ahead. She's full of advice. She'll tell you that she's holding a full house—a house full of shit."

"You'll have to cancel."

"Damnit, damnit—"

"Settle down. Take a deep breath. We're going to the precinct where they're holding Sal."

"Tell them to throw the key away. What the hell is going on? I can't fucking believe—"

"Take it easy." Where was the composed poker pro with the aluminum alloy nerves? "I'll give you the address when you're ready."

I turned to Uncle Mike. "Nicole is losing her shit."

"I don't blame her. I'm pissed off, too." Uncle Mike shouted. His words echoed down the hallway toward the parking lot. "Saboski must've kept the gun under wraps—the fucker."

"Eddie, what the hell?" Nicole shouted from the cell.

I didn't need a pair of screamers. I didn't do well as the only stable adult in the room. I was on the verge of losing my shit as well.

"I need to call St. Clair," I told Nicole and Uncle Mike simultaneously. "Sal needs a lawyer at his side immediately."

"Tell Mike thanks for everything he's doing," Nicole said.

"I'll find out what's going on," Uncle Mike said, pulling out his cell. "I've got a better source."

Nicole's voice came in an octave lower, trembling. "Do you think Dad could do it? He was sort of crazy due to the suspension. But that crazy? No way. Maybe. So sick, he would break up with Jessie and tell her to go out on her own. God, could he have done it?"

She was desperate. "Don't even go down that road," I said. "You know your dad better than that."

"Do I?" She took another gasp for air. She was already a mile down the forbidden road. "He gave us that fixed harness race to bet on in Vegas. He gave me other bets to place. Did he juice his horses? Is this suspension only the tip of the iceberg? The drug culture is so embedded in horse racing. What do I know? I've been in Vegas playing poker with my head stuck up my ass."

"None of this is your fault, and you know it," I said. "He heard stuff. He took advantage. That happens every day at the track. You know that. It doesn't mean he was juicing."

Uncle Mike stopped to talk on his cell. He had contacts throughout the department.

I talked to Nicole in a low, calm voice. "I have to drive. Uncle Mike will learn more. As soon as he does, I'll let you know. We'll get St. Clair on the line. That's the first thing—get Sal an attorney."

"Please, Eddie. I know you and Mike are doing all you can, but please make this go away."

"We're working on it."

32

A DAY LATER, WE FOUND OURSELVES SITTING IN St. Clair's conference room. The window with the closed blinds still had those two slats turned the wrong way. The ashtray was empty. Sal had retained St. Clair to defend him on a charge of first-degree murder.

St. Clair once again came into the office on the arm of her junior partner, Pam Ferguson. After St. Clair was seated, Ferguson switched on the fans.

St. Clair lit a cigarette, examined first me, and then Uncle Mike, and back again. She was hunched over the desk, coiled like a defense attorney about to pounce on the prosecution's key witness. I'd prepared Uncle Mike in advance, although I thought about asking St. Clair if I could bum a smoke. My nerves were a jangled mess.

"I have another case for you. You're doing so well on the professor's lab book exchange…"

It was not praise. We each received her cold, icy stare, waiting for us—daring us—to argue. We were in no position to argue. It had been more than a week since our initial drop of the down payment of seventy-five hundred dollars to the thief. Then, no contact whatsoever. Why? We had no answers. What had appeared to be an easy case had gone south.

St. Clair cleared her throat as Ferguson kept her head down, reading a file. No doubt Ferguson was accustomed to these verbal tongue-lashings. On my first case for St. Clair, I'd been tested by the experienced criminal lawyer. She'd wanted to see if I could stomach her kind of law—representing scum or representing those who'd been wrongly accused but couldn't pay.

After the long theatrical pause, she said, "I expect to find the professor's lab book on the shelf at Barnes & Noble any day—"

Her satirical comment was not meant to be funny. It might be closer to the truth than either the professor or St. Clair imagined. People around the track had heard about the lab book, and rumors about its contents had given them the jitters.

I swore I'd find the thief and make them pay. The delay was a way to inflate the ransom price, and it made me all the more determined to catch them. The delay had cost me. I wanted to prove myself to St. Clair as the top investigator in her stable, and what had I accomplished—nothing more than a long list of more and more creative excuses and bullshit.

What did the professor have to say to St. Clair in private about our long, drawn-out mess? St. Clair had painted us as the A-Team, but so far we were a D minus.

Uncle Mike didn't seem perturbed in the least, tapping his pen on the blank pad of lined paper he'd brought along. When was the last time he'd taken a note about anything? He simply absorbed everything like a savant. The next thing I knew, my uncle would start doing my handicapping for me.

But why should Uncle Mike mind abuse from St. Clair? He wasn't building a PI business from scratch or trying to compete with Nicole, a freak in the world of picking winners. He was retired, collecting a pension to augment his profits from O'Connell's.

Everyone was looking for that damn lab book. Maybe it was on the dark web's version of eBay.

St. Clair continued to smoke as if waiting for me to offer some lame excuse about the lab book. We were here about Sal, damn it. If Uncle Mike could wait and Ferguson could wait, I could wait, too.

Finally, St. Clair muttered something under her breath, and said, "Okay. Let's move on. Eddie has told me a few things." She dug into a legal pad, flipping pages, as if each page and the entire meeting had brought a great weight down upon her shoulders. She licked the tip of an index finger and flipped another page. "Fine. You have made some good contacts at the track. You've developed a relationship with Ronnie Orman, the trainer taking over for Sal. I agree he's a person of interest to us. You've also developed an interesting contact with an exercise rider who knows about the mysterious 'friends of Ramon.' Those friends include a man named Quintela, and a man named Campos. You are working with Sal's major horse owner, Pieter Van der Walt or Vandy. Eddie is playing the role of gambling consultant, and Mike is his researcher."

She looked up and studied us as if to confirm these notes. When we said nothing, she licked the tip of her index finger again and turned the page. I began to wonder what else was included on that legal pad. Maybe Sal had discussed things with his attorney that he hadn't divulged to us.

"I applaud your efforts." Her praise rang false. She picked up her cigarette from the ashtray—the butt now about an inch long—took a deep drag, then stamped it out over and over as if everything about it pissed her off. "It overcomes some of the reservations I have about hiring you two. You have a connection to the client and the client's daughter that could be considered a conflict. However, the client has been advised and signed off."

After another waiting period to let the necessary talk of a conflict sink in, she said, "Let's talk about this damn gun."

St. Clair stared at Ferguson, who was smart enough to keep her head buried in the file.

Again, we didn't say anything.

"The weapon is registered to our client, and, according to forensics, was used to murder the victim," St. Clair said. "A victim, I might add, who happened to be the lover and top assistant of our client. A victim who had worked for years for our client and lived with our client. A victim who just had a days-long argument with our client." She checked the legal pad. "Our client had told the victim to 'leave his employ' and 'go out on her own.' How charitable of our client."

She pulled out a cigarette and tapped it on the conference table.

She took a deep breath, her lungs wheezing, and continued. "How can I explain this to my objective, constitutionally challenged jury, who have read every juicy little thing about this tawdry affair in the newspapers or heard about it on the national news or simply picked up their phone and discovered a news feed? Maybe I can plead insanity, gentlemen. Insanity on my part for taking this piece of shit case."

She lit the cigarette and took another deep drag. "All these wonderful facts laid out one by one as if our hapless client was eager to spend life behind bars."

She studied each of us again. We followed Ferguson's lead and stayed silent.

"You see, this is why I hire investigators—so I can lay out my strategy or lack thereof—and throw all these wonderful facts at your feet and then you can come up with a witness or an act of God or perhaps a supernatural event, to explain what the hell happened. A phantom home invasion won't cut it."

She flipped another page of the legal pad and turned to Ferguson. "What have we got?" she growled.

Ferguson looked up for the first time and glanced our way and smiled as if we'd done well so far. "I always like that last part. Supernatural. The vampire defense hasn't worked for some time."

St. Clair nodded astutely as if the vampire defense remained in her stockpile of plausible defenses.

Ferguson said, "We got a break-in at the client's home, and he alleges that's when the gun was stolen, although he didn't know it at the time. In fact, he hadn't used the gun in some time. The client said, 'I don't go out to the range anymore.' The break-in was not reported to the police." She sighed. "Nothing else was stolen."

"A nightmare for us, a lollipop for the DA," St. Clair said.

The way St. Clair spit out the word "lollipop" showcased her "fuck you, too" attitude toward her adversary. She was a fighter, and that made me want to fight just as hard for our client.

"What we need to know," Ferguson continued without any recognition of St. Clair. "We need to focus on that gun so we can file a motion to exclude. The gun wasn't locked up because there weren't any children living in the house. Sal pointed a finger at Ramon's friends for the break-in. What do we know about them? Jessie is the wildcard. Did she take the gun? She lived with Sal and would have access. Sal was under pressure due to the suspension. Had Jessie and Sal invited anyone over lately? If so, what motivation would they have to steal a gun?"

Ferguson stopped and glanced at St. Clair as if she were passing the ball back.

"Gentlemen," St. Clair said, "the gun was found by the boy who discovered the body—"

"The Lopez boy?" I asked.

"Yes," St. Clair said. "I guess the twelve-year-old boy thought the gun would make a fine grown-up toy. Like any twelve-year-old boy, he isn't talking. After being severely disciplined, he probably thinks talking will only make matters worse for him.

Some anonymous tip to the police broke this case wide open. Thank God, the boy didn't shoot anyone, but its discovery has led to the arrest of our client. I ask you, gentlemen, if you murdered someone with your own gun, would you toss it near the body?"

She puffed away. "The DA wants a narrow little murder with convenient facts. Sal drives up in his golf cart, knowing Jessie is on her way to the dorms, shoots her in a rage, throws the gun away in another unexplained emotional outburst, and then drives away in a heavy rain back to his office. Clean and simple."

St. Clair leaned forward, smoke billowing around her angry, wrinkled face, transforming her into a demon soothsayer. "I want to paint a vista of possible suspects, one of the racetrack, of the backstretch where the buffalo roam, filled with mystery and intrigue—horses and gamblers, where anything can happen—drugging horses, suspensions, and people with hidden agendas. The backstretch murder sells papers. Why? Because it's a world people don't know about. We want to draw people into that world—a world of intrigue and reasonable doubt."

33

UNCLE MIKE AND I WENT TO SAL'S HOUSE WITH Nicole. Sal was still in jail awaiting his bond hearing. Based on our meeting with St. Clair and Ferguson, we needed to find something, anything, to bolster Sal's claim that his gun had been stolen during a break-in at his house the month before Jessie's murder.

The house was in a leafy, comfortable suburb four or five exits west down the interstate from Thornton Racetrack. I could envision Sal zipping east on the interstate prior to dawn to work his horses at the track.

The house was located at the end of a cul-de-sac, a modest four-bedroom two-story with attached garage. Nicole had told us that she'd never lived in the house. Sal and Nicole's mother had gotten divorced when Nicole was twelve, and she'd lived with her mom. Sal had bought this house about ten or twelve years ago. It was at the same time Nicole was still attending college, and the financial stress caused friction all around. At the same time, Sal had started dating Jessie. It was Jessie who had been the driving force behind buying the house. Lucky for us, that mess was in the past, and all we had to worry about was murder in the first degree.

Nicole had gotten the house keys from Sal. We parked in the driveway. It was one of those sunny, crisp October days meant for football.

"Look at this lawn," Nicole said.

The grass had grown to a foot, and the leaves had started to fall. It reminded me how your life can change in a very short span of time and that sometimes those changes are out of your control.

We opened the door and were confronted by a disaster. Except for the couch and a chair, every possible surface was crammed with junk. A stack of mail, maybe a month's worth, covered the table in the entryway.

Stacks of books from a bookshelf littered the floor. Every cupboard in the kitchen had been stripped bare. Pancake mix, cereal boxes, canned soup, and dozens of other items were stacked or, more accurately, tossed on the counters and kitchen table. Pots and pans were scattered beneath the table.

A small area of one counter had been cleared. That one spot held a number of liquor bottles, including several handles of whiskey.

"What the hell is all this?" I asked.

"It's not Dad," Nicole said.

"This is what the cops do when they search your house," Uncle Mike said. "They're especially destructive when it's the residence of the main suspect to a murder. I guess Sal left it as is." He pulled out his cell. "I'll take pictures. It won't do any good, but I'll complain."

"He had so much on his mind," Nicole said. "The suspension was hard enough for him. It ate him up inside. Sometimes I wonder if Jessie took the gun."

"You think Sal might've considered ending his life?" Uncle Mike asked. "I'm sorry to ask, but is there any family history?"

"Dad has his dark moments, and yes, there is a history. My uncle. But that's another thing we don't talk about."

This was a shock. I knew Sal's brother, Nick Nicoletti, Jr., had passed away, but I had no idea he'd taken his own life. I thought Nicole had said her uncle had been hospitalized for an operation and complications had set in, or something like that. Maybe I should've asked more about it.

"That's not good—not talking. But entirely understandable," Uncle Mike said.

"Tell me about it," Nicole said. "When you grow up, you look for answers. All I got from my parents was one of them blaming the other."

Nicole had the courage to walk through the house, the willingness to follow the path of the police tornado that had upended mattresses, rifled through closets, bookshelves, and drawers, and ripped up carpeting, without uttering a complaint. The storm had even swirled into the attic; all in hopes of finding the weapon—a weapon that had been in the hands of the Lopez boy the entire time.

In the garage, we found the stacks of boxes from Sal's office that he must've brought home only a couple of days ago. There were also piles of tools, lawn implements, and auto parts strewn about like junk.

"I'm not sure I want to go into the basement," Nicole said.

She was a strong woman, and I admired her and loved her even more at this moment. What must she be going through? This had been Jessie's house, too. Jessie was Nicole's "big sister." Nicole and I had been here several times for dinner, and Sal and Jessie had always made us feel at home in their comfortable house.

The destruction rose to the level of a criminal act, but Nicole continued to hold steady, despite the extensive damage. She'd wanted to come along with us. She'd told me bitterly that she needed to face it. She was going to see this through for her father and get justice for Jessie, no matter what it took. Her poker persona had risen to the forefront, and she seemed to use it as a sword and a shield.

Nicole walked back in from the garage and stopped. "Dad told us about his house being ransacked. He said it was Ramon's friends, but had no proof. Do you think any of this destruction is from that break-in, instead of the cops?"

"Good question," Uncle Mike said. "That's what we need—proof of the break-in. The search by the police may've covered up some of that."

"Maybe the police took pictures of the house before the search," I said.

"I doubt it. It's not a crime scene," Uncle Mike said. "Let's check the rest."

We stumbled through the crap in the basement and then went outside. Because the house was located on a Cul-de-sac, the backyard was wider than normal. The perimeter was bordered by a high wooden privacy fence. There were a couple of trees in need of pruning and more weeds growing up through the long grass. A tool shed sat in the far corner of the yard, partially hidden by a row of overgrown junipers.

"We might as well take a look at that," Uncle Mike said, walking off toward the shed.

Nicole and I followed. I put my arm around her shoulders. I'd told her we were investigating, but I hadn't told her much about it. What could I tell her about Orman, Island Willie, Vandy, The Hippo, or Ramon's friends that could give her hope? We had nothing concrete. The current thoroughbred meeting would run out of days in a few more weeks, and we'd be left holding a pair of deuces.

The tool shed held more boxes of junk—tools, a lawnmower, and some old rusted bicycles. An old harness was tacked up on the wall. The boxes had been torn open, and a jumble of trophies spilled out of them. Uncle Mike took another photo with his cell. It was sad to see the evidence of lives and memories intentionally ripped apart and laid waste.

Why hadn't Sal restacked and reshelved his possessions? The trophies weren't broken. I knew the answer. It was the suspension. He'd kept cool on the outside, but inside, he must've been falling apart.

—

Uncle Mike and I walked down the sidewalk outside Sal's house. Nicole had stayed behind, insisting that she needed to get started on the cleanup.

"I hate doing grunt work," Uncle Mike said. "On the force, we had uniforms for this."

A few doors down, an elderly man was doing yard work. According to St. Clair, Sal had neglected to make a police report or an insurance claim. Even a photo or emails at the time would've helped, but Sal had failed to do any of this. Why should he? An insurance claim probably wouldn't exceed the deductible. The police couldn't do anything. Sal's belief that Ramon's friends were responsible had no basis in fact. He'd had a threatening phone call about Jessie, but couldn't identify the caller. He couldn't tell the police a thing. No email or cell phone photo of the damage. Who would he email about it? He was naturally tight-lipped and didn't have a social media presence. We'd even checked a neighborhood watch website, but no luck.

The neighbor looked up from his raking as we approached, seemingly eager to take a break from his work. He pulled out a tobacco pipe as we approached.

"Hello, sir," Uncle Mike said. "We're looking into a break-in over at that house." He pointed toward Sal's house. "It was about a couple of months ago. We're working on his behalf and wondered if you knew anything about it." Uncle Mike flashed his old badge. I had my detective license ready as well.

He glanced at Uncle Mike's badge and took a deep breath. "A break-in? Oh, my God. Is everyone okay?"

"Yeah. Everyone's fine. They just tore up the place. The owner didn't call the police at the time—"

"I heard the police were there recently." He held the bowl of the pipe in his left hand and pointed the stem toward us.

We couldn't talk about the recent search by the police or go too far into details. It seemed the neighbor didn't know about Jessie's murder. So far, it hadn't made its way to CNN. "He didn't want to make a big deal about it at the time, you know," Uncle Mike said.

The man grasped the bowl of the pipe with one hand and tamped down the tobacco with his index finger. "I'm afraid I don't know him. I see him come home late, and I hear he trains horses. He revs up that truck of his in the middle of the night. Goes to work before dawn. Usually, things are always quiet at his place otherwise. The lawn service hasn't been by in a while." He hesitated as if trying to come up with something useful. "I'm afraid he didn't talk to me. We might've waved to each other, but we don't talk. Did they get anything?"

"Not much. Not enough to even make an insurance claim—"

"He must be well-off. They're gone all winter, the both of them. I guess they're lucky enough to have a house in Florida. That's where everyone goes in the winter, if they can afford it. I'm afraid I'm not much help."

"No," Uncle Mike said, "you've been very helpful. If you hear anything from anyone else, will you let us know? Here's my card."

I gave him my card as well.

He read it intently. "Damn. A private detective. You're both private detectives?"

"Yes, sir. We've already put a call into the lawn service," I said.

"Good. The place could use it. He used to keep it looking sharp."

34

IRV'S FIRM WAS LOCATED ON THE TOP THREE floors of one of the tallest buildings in the Loop. Uncle Mike and I took the elevator up to the 86th floor. It was eight o'clock in the evening, well past working hours.

Irv's firm now had offices in New York, Washington, Los Angles, Atlanta, Houston, and Denver.

Inside the office, the receptionist stood beside her desk and greeted us as if she'd been waiting for our arrival. I was glad we were on time.

"He's ready for you," she said in a French accent.

I couldn't help but be a little awestruck by the lobby even though I'd been here before. They had gallery-quality paintings on the walls, thick throw rugs, and leather couches. If I had enough cash on hand to need a major-league accountant, I'd feel like I'd come to the right place.

I looked through the expansive glass windows that encased the conference room and its thirty-foot-long desk, where fifteen to twenty people stood. Some held their phones, but many were clapping, and some appeared to be cheering. The room was soundproof. I looked behind me to see if a celebrity had walked in.

"Wave, dummy," Uncle Mike said.

Then I realized what the cheering was about—they were cheering us. We were a team of sorts, although I hadn't thought of that before. They'd gotten us what we'd needed, and we never talked one on one, but I assumed Irv had told them that we'd been successful. They deserved our gratitude. In each case, we needed to follow the money, and we needed to know the possible suspects who had risked all, and would commit murder because of it.

I stopped and raised a hand and mouthed the words, "Yes. Way to go! Let's get them!"

The crowd inside the glass case erupted.

Uncle Mike joined in, pumping his fist and giving a silent cheer. "Go, go, go!"

That really churned up the accountants, who cheered back in a mad frenzy.

I probably would've felt a little better about the wild celebration if I'd already zeroed in on a suspect or felt a little more comfortable about where we stood, but that's how these investigations went. I reminded myself to be patient. What the hell. I gave it one more cheer for the A-Team as we walked down the hall.

They probably cheered more for Uncle Mike than me. It was Uncle Mike and his old partner in homicide, Liz Zelinski, who were responsible for Irv's generosity. Irv did accounting legwork for our investigations on a gratis basis, and it wasn't your traditional accounting stuff. No tax returns or tax planning. Irv's work for us was about as unconventional as accounting could get.

The firm went the extra mile for us because of Irv's son.

Tommy Turnquist had gotten into serious trouble when he was twenty-one. This was about twenty years ago. He'd been charged as an accessory to murder and armed robbery. Uncle Mike and his partner, Liz, had found the guilty parties just as Tommy was being led to prison. Much later, in a scandal that rocked the department, it was revealed that the original detectives in Tommy's case had forced confessions and extorted money from the suspects, and they had done so for many years.

Once Tommy was freed, he'd finished med school and left the good old USA, practicing general medicine for the Red Cross in Nigeria. Tommy and his wife had a son, and it was Irv's custom to show us pictures or videos of his grandson.

Irv met us at his office door. We would give him an outline of our current investigation and what we needed.

"Mike, Eddie, how are you?" Irv asked. He always talked fast as if he never had enough time in the day. "C'mon in. I know your time is valuable. But first, there is someone here who wants to say hello."

Uncle Mike whooped, "Well, hello, doctor."

A thin, bald, middle-aged man with a full, trimmed beard hopped up from his chair. "Detective O'Connell, so good to see you."

Irv's son was swallowed up in Uncle Mike's bear hug. Then it was my turn to hug the doctor. Tommy had become like family.

After Tommy gave us an update on how well his son was doing, he said to my uncle, "I can't tell you how much I appreciate what you and Detective Zelinski did for me, Mr. O'Connell. My fellow inmates and my lawyer told me at the time that you and your partner worked a miracle."

What must it have been like to undergo the stress of a trial and conviction before a jury of your peers and be powerless to prove your innocence? Then, as if you were in a movie, on your way to prison, two other police detectives, disguised as earthbound angels, save you at the last minute. I only hoped we could do the same for Sal.

We talked about Tommy's work for the Red Cross. He was in Chicago for a scientific conference. He'd taken a new position with the Red Cross that would start next year, allowing him and his family to take time off back in his hometown.

"Tommy is moving up the ladder," Irv said proudly, looking at his watch, and giving special emphasis to the word "moving."

His doctor-son took the hint and said, "I know you all have urgent business to get done, so I'll be going. Please give my best to Detective Zelinski as well."

We promised to do so, and once he left, we got down to business. Uncle Mike gave Irv a brief outline of what we had.

"Holy mackerel, guys. The Backstretch Murder? How do you do it? That's big time. Everybody's talking about that case. We have people here in the office going to the track this weekend because of it. Wait till I tell the team. What do you need? How can I help?"

I loved Irv's enthusiasm. It always gave me a boost.

Uncle Mike looked at me.

I pulled out my notes from my carryall bag. "We need to know the names of the owners behind some of these various shell companies listed as owners of horses at Thornton." I handed the list over.

Although we knew certain companies and LLCs weren't required to disclose the names of actual owners, quite often Irv and his team had certain connections. Or maybe they knew members of the law firm that filed the corporate docs and they were owed a favor. All kinds of backroom risks were taken on our behalf. It seemed that Uncle Mike's willingness to cross into a gray area motivated others to do the same.

"We also need financial info on some folks," I said, handing over another list. It included Ronnie Orman, Sal, the owners on the prior list, Willie Griggs, any members of the Late Money Boys we'd been able to identify at the reception or obtained from Arlene Adams, Pieter Van der Walt, Professor Kovalenko, and her lab,

The Hippo, and other major trainers at Thornton.

Irv, still standing, glanced at each list. "I've heard of these Late Money Boys. They make an effort to remain anonymous." Then he looked down at us over his black-framed glasses and said, "Who is Willie Griggs?"

Uncle Mike laughed. "That's a long story."

35

THE NEXT DAY AT THE TRACK, WE DROVE TO THE backstretch. We had everything arranged for ten in the morning.

Our investigation had Arlene's approval. We were therefore able to obtain the full backing of track security.

We needed to question Ramon's boys. We'd learned from Isabel that Quintela, one of Ramon's collectors, came by each Tuesday morning at ten o'clock, after the morning workouts, to make loans and collect from backstretch employees. Typically, he set up shop in a back room of Elena's with the approval of Security, who Quintela paid to look the other way. However, these token payments by Quintela meant nothing to security personnel when it came to Arlene's orders or the murder of Jessie.

Quintela was escorted by security to a vacant equipment shed where Uncle Mike and I waited. His last name reminded me of "Quinella"—a bet that required the bettor to pick the first and second place horses. Unlike the Exacta, the "Q" didn't require the horses to finish in exact order. Most racetracks no longer offered the Quinella wager, and Thornton was one of those that had deleted it from its wagering menu.

"What do you want? I don't know nothing," Quintela said when we confronted him.

A little guy with a bald head and a nasty sneer, he was a loan shark, preying on backstretch employees who were barely making ends meet. He had a couple of front teeth missing, and I fought the urge to loosen a few more. Patience, I told myself, stay patient.

"We already talked to Campos," I said.

Quintella took a step forward, his chest out. "What did that fucker say? He lies."

Campos was Ramon's other collector. He griped about Quintela the whole time. He said Quintela got all the good accounts, while he got the past-due accounts. "I always got to use my fists to get payments," he'd told us. "Little Q just smiles and gets paid and sometimes gets laid."

"He told us the shitty interest rate you charge," I said. It wasn't something Campos told us, but we assumed that was the case.

"That's Ramon's doing," Quintela said. "He makes the loans."

"Campos told us lots of stuff," Uncle Mike said. "Like the money you keep and how you cheat Ramon." Campos hadn't told us this either, but we assumed larceny was part of the job.

"I don't keep anything. Shit, Ramon gets his money for cigarettes and drugs inside. He sells to those convicts and makes three times what I do."

"Tell us about the day you broke into Sal and Jessie's house," I said. "Campos said you were the mastermind."

"What? I didn't break into any house. I'm legit," Quintela said.

I tried another tack. "Ramon hated Sal—"

"Ramon hates a lot of gringos." Quintela reached for something in his coat pocket.

"What's that? In your coat?" I took a couple of quick steps and pulled a gun from his coat. In the process, I shoved him to the ground.

"You think you'll shoot your way out of here?" Uncle Mike asked.

"After you shot Jessie, you needed another gun? Where did you get this?" I asked.

Quintela stayed prone on the ground, rubbing his shoulder. "Fuck. I landed on my bad shoulder."

"You want me to even things out with your other shoulder?" I asked. The guy was too small to beat on without a good reason, but I could threaten him.

"No," he held out an open hand in a plea for mercy. "I get crazy. I'm around meth-heads all day. I have to kiss ass to get paid. Ramon wants to pull all of his accounts. Campos wants to break my neck. I can't take it no more."

"You and Campos take care of Hugo?" Hugo had been the cartel meth connection, but nobody had seen him lately. I'd begun to worry if my knockout of Hugo had severely injured the drug dealer. The cartel would come after me.

"No."

"Tell us about the cartel," Uncle Mike said.

"I don't know nothing," Quintela said.

"You want me to read Ramon's court transcript? You guys know a lot," Uncle Mike said.

"Yes, yes, okay," Quintela said. "I don't fool with the cartel. The money we loan goes to them. They get paid for their product, so they leave me alone."

"Where is Hugo?"

"He's gone. Nobody tells me nothing. I don't ask." Quintela's fear of the cartel was clear.

"What do you mean 'he's gone'?"

"Dead. That's what I heard, anyway."

What the hell? Did my knockout punch do it? Did Hugo hit his head on that tractor? The Hippo shook my hand—he thought I was responsible.

"What about The Hippo?" We surmised that The Hippo had begun dealing fentanyl after the cartel left.

"I never fool with The Hippo. Let them kill each other."

"The Hippo's men sell the pills?" I asked.

Quintela shrugged. "It's bad. No one pays when they overdose. It makes no fucking sense."

"With The Hippo around, you need a gun, right?" I asked.

"Like the one you stole from Sal's house?" Uncle Mike asked.

"That gun is mine. I bought it," Quintela said.

"Let's go over it again," Uncle Mike said.

We kept it up, but he wouldn't admit to ransacking Sal's house or stealing Sal's gun. It was the same story we'd gotten from Campos.

36

ONCE WE WERE DONE WITH QUINTELA, WE STOPPED at Elena's for coffee. We hadn't expected much from Quintela. The guy was a hardened criminal who carried a gun, and when that didn't work, he knew how to squirm and plead and not admit a thing. It was no surprise that he was no help, but in the investigative business you try to touch all the bases.

We sat in a vacant corner of the place. The lunch rush had come and gone.

"Very educational," Uncle Mike said, stirring sweetener into his coffee.

"Why don't you drink it black like every other detective?" I asked.

"I would if I had donuts."

"I can see if they have any."

He held up a hand. "Don't tempt me with pastries. Your aunt will kill me."

"What do you think? Hugo is dead?" It's what Quintela had

said. "You don't think I killed him?" It had been one of my better punches. Years ago, that Golden Gloves I won had almost gotten me prison time because of a bar fight, and now this.

"That was a shock." Uncle Mike swirled the coffee. "He did hit his head pretty hard when he fell against the tractor."

"I swear I didn't hit him hard enough—"

"No way. The cartel would've come after us by now if your punch killed Hugo. No, I don't think it was a freak accident. My money is on The Hippo."

It made sense. The Hippo had taken over the drug trade at the backstretch.

A couple of men in overcoats entered. One of them saw us and came over. It was Detective Saboski. Beneath the overcoat, he wore a sports coat and starched shirt. He was all-business.

"Hi guys." He sounded like somebody who was having a great day. He took a seat. "I hear you're beating the bushes for St. Clair on the Sal Nicoletti case. How's that going?"

"Not bad," Uncle Mike said. "It won't be the first time we do your work for you."

Saboski grinned. "I don't mind taking some shit. Go ahead. You guys got lucky last time. That was back when I was a beginner. Since then, Liz taught me all I needed to know."

Uncle Mike sipped his coffee. "You've made your arrest. But how do you explain it? A guy kills his lover and then leaves the gun at the scene?"

Saboski leaned back in his chair and hesitated, as if he needed to relish this moment. "I'll tell you. Why not? There's nothing you can do about it. A killer leaves the gun if he's got a death wish. We see strange stuff these days. It's gotten bad out there. Real bad."

"A death wish?" I asked. "Because of Sal's suspension? It's just a couple of years. It happens to a number of trainers."

"I don't want to talk out of school, but as a professional courtesy, I'll share it with you guys. For old time's sake." He checked around us to be sure he couldn't be overheard and said, "We got Sal's med records. He's on drugs for depression. It's a family thing. You know—suicide?"

"You got proof of an attempt?" Uncle Mike asked.

Saboski shook his head. "No, but we've got Jessie and Sal arguing. Sal told the victim to go out on her own. We got witnesses—they tossed some ugly stuff back and forth. You might want to back off this one, Mike. You've got a major conflict. Eddie here is living with Sal's daughter."

"That doesn't mean shit," I said, trying to sound calm and objective.

Saboski grinned. "I agree you got lucky before on the Blowtorch Murders, but this Backstretch Murder has been blown out of proportion in the media. It's a simple case. Ninety-five percent of the time, the killer is somebody close to the victim. We see it all the time."

"I guess you don't play the horses," I said. "Things can be complicated."

"What?" Saboski laughed. "The crowd out here on race days could barely fill a city bus. Give me a break."

Saboski had written off the track. He didn't know about the extent of simulcasting and the Late Money Boys. Online, things were still humming. The simulcast handle was ten times the amount bet through the windows.

"What you guys need to do is relax. Enjoy retirement. I know you've talked to people in the dorms. Why waste your time? They don't know nothing. Except for the Lopez brat playing around with the gun. Too bad you didn't talk to him."

According to St. Clair, the police reports stated that the Lopez boy and the gun were discovered through an anonymous tip. It had probably been someone in the dorms and, as Isabel had said, no one wanted to get involved and garner the attention of the cops or the cartel.

"If we'd learned he had the gun, we would've turned it over," Uncle Mike said.

Saboski nodded with a smug smile.

"What about that disaster area in Sal's house? Were you there?" Uncle Mike demanded.

"C'mon, you want to read my warrant? Give me a break." The detective said, leaning back. "How's the coffee in here? You guys want pie? I'm buying."

"No, we don't want any pie," Uncle Mike said.

"I heard you were talking to Ramon's lackey—the guy who picks up the monthly payments—Quintela? I talked to Ramon. Yep, I schlepped out to the prison and sat across from the rat. He's got more tats than skin. I think he's found his feminine side, if you know what I mean. Anyway, the scumbag squealer loves to talk—but only when he can get a deal on a reduced sentence—and that ain't in the cards. But he did say this—he said, 'Why would I kill my sister to frame Sal? I'd just kill Sal.' That's one bright boy."

It was always nice to have your opposition explain why you were fucked. I squirmed in my chair.

"Ramon is a piece of shit scumbag running a pharmacy at the prison," Saboski continued. "But he ratted out the cartel and could have a nasty fall anytime. He might even slip in the shower or have his bowels fall out while he's exercising in the prison yard. He's a casualty waiting to happen. You guys should talk to him before it's too late. He's full of shit and accident-prone. He's also the lowest life form on the planet, but he's got a fucking point. Why not just kill Sal? Makes sense to me."

"I can see you've developed a detective's instincts," Uncle Mike said. "Good for you. Another closed case will help your ratings within the department and move you up the ladder. Your father must be so proud."

Saboski's smug smile disappeared. He stood up. "You guys need to go back to that little bar you own and sponsor a bowling team or something." He walked off.

Uncle Mike stared down at his coffee and then looked up. "Maybe I will have that fucking donut."

37

A FEW DAYS LATER AT THE TRACK, WE HAD A meeting set up with Island Willie. I had researched him and his offshore operation. There were photos of the old buzzard with heads of state as if he was a guru dispensing holiness upon the flock. Uncle Mike had a buddy check his Interpol databases. It seemed that murders followed Maharishi Willie wherever he went.

"Are you sure you want to do this?" Uncle Mike asked.

"It's the only way I'm going to really get inside Vandy's operation," I said.

Uncle Mike and I had been over it a couple of times. Vandy wanted me to make wagers on his behalf because he had a habit of what he called "running hot." It meant that sometimes he couldn't quite control himself and he'd either over-bet or under-bet. I knew what he meant, because I'd gone "on-tilt" in Vegas too many nights to count. You either bet too much because you needed to get back to even, or because you had fallen in love with the wager and convinced yourself it was the best bet ever, or you stood on the ledge with doubts and second thoughts and didn't adequately bet—one more combination or one more horse and you would've hit a big one—but instead you stood there with your hands in your pockets, instead of reaching for that bankroll. I was an expert on all of it.

If Vandy put me at the controls, he could remain cold and objective and convey smart and coherent wagers to me with no chance of gumming up the works by over-betting. The only problem? These wagers wouldn't take place at the Thornton windows, where I normally placed wagers when I was in attendance, no, these wagers were of the sophisticated, high-rent variety. A wise bettor would not want these hefty wagers to find their way into the parimutuel pool, where the odds would be affected and correspondingly drop like a rock, making the whole bet a waste of time and manpower. Instead, Vandy planned to bet in another market entirely.

The wagers would need to migrate to the black market. It would be the chance for me and Island Willie to get up close and personal and, although there was a degree of risk, it was the next logical step in our investigation. At first, Uncle Mike thought I was out of my mind, especially when he heard what my "next logical step" involved, and then, after thinking about it some more, he'd proclaimed it "pure genius."

Now, all we had to do was execute it.

We walked toward the old grandstands, bypassed the warning signs and walked up several flights of stairs into the construction area beneath the grandstands. WagerEasy's fancy sportsbook and casino remained a dream project. A sign in block letters advised, "Construction Area—Danger." Island Willie sat at a table amid the sawhorses, drills, ladders, and stacks of lumber.

He waved to us. "Over here, gentlemen."

We waved back. I looked up toward the high ceiling where the beams beneath the stands extended upward at a forty-five-degree angle. The ticket seller booths that once lined the far wall had been torn down. The bar along the east side was gone. Even the shiny checkerboard floor tiles had been ripped up, exposing the original, scuffed hardwood floorboards.

"Hell, Willie, is it safe in here?" Uncle Mike called out.

"It's a shit show, isn't it?" Island Willie looked around from his table located at the edge of the chaos. "We're okay here. I think that far wall is about to come down, and they tell me it's load-bearing. I'm listening for any strange creaking or cracking, but the joint is holding up, at least for now."

Uncle Mike cussed under his breath and shook his head.

Why were we even here? It made no sense. There were plenty of other empty suites above the clubhouse. Then, I took a closer look around. Wires hung down. The closed-circuit TVs hung sideways off brackets. Work had been done on the beams. It meant there wasn't any track surveillance here.

"The architect has been advised, and that's the reason for the work stoppage," Island Willie said. His voice caught once or twice, forcing another cough. "Of course, money is now an issue as well."

We sat down and joined him at the table. I had a good view of the top of the stairs. Island Willie had an even better angle, allowing him to see down the stairs. Unlike the clubhouse suites, there wasn't any chance that someone could "accidentally" witness or overhear our upcoming transaction.

Island Willie cleared his throat and then leaned in close. "Mike, I want you to know that Eddie came to me. None of this was my idea."

"What is this?" I asked. "I'm not a teenager buying his first car."

"Let the man talk," Uncle Mike said, putting on his glasses.

Maybe my uncle was worried about the fine print. I crossed my arms.

Island Willie studied each of us separately and then pulled

out a sheaf of paperwork from his bag. "I don't usually give anybody paperwork. I'm doing you two a favor because I like you and because of my solid relationship with Mike. I don't forget a guy who gives me a break when I needed it most, so I'm going to lay things out for you."

Island Willie's hoarse voice strangled some of the words, but the force of his emotion came through. He meant to discourage us from going down this road.

"Remember how I said that I'm the place bettors go when they've burned through the WagerEasys of the world—when the so-called legit billion-dollar conglomerates won't take your action anymore because they're searching out quick and easy prey? When these same bettors have tried a few illegal bookies and gotten shut out, they turn to me because there's no one else. Everything gets funneled down to me, and I'm happy to take it."

Island Willie laughed. "Some of my customers cheat and win. Then they bet more and lose it all back. Then they bet more. I get rich, my partners get rich, and we let bygones be bygones. Those that cheat and win and try to screw me over and over like I'm a cheap whore will face consequences—understand?"

He studied each of us closely. "You hear what I'm telling you, Eddie? You bet for Vandy and cheat, okay, I will tolerate some larceny. Do it too much without losing and there can be serious consequences."

"What consequences?" Uncle Mike asked.

But he ignored the question. "Tell you what," Island Willie said. "I'll even give you another benefit besides this little pep talk, which I don't give nobody. If I think you've gone too far and you're on dangerous ground—I'll let Mike know. How's that?"

We nodded.

"I have a simple rule. You play fair, I'll pay. Bettors are drawn to the horses and sports. They want something for nothing, but they want something else too. Each race, each game, and prior thereto, looks like chaos. Like this fucked-up construction behind me. It's human nature to demand order out of chaos. They get nervous in the head when things 'don't seem right.' It's maddening. You see what I'm telling you?"

Island Willie cleared his throat again. "I'm telling you, people can't help themselves. It doesn't matter if they're the bartender or the board chairman. Order out of chaos. It's as old as the oldest profession."

"I think you've made your point," I said.

Island Willie stroked his long, stringy beard. "Maybe I have or maybe I haven't. When I was a young guy working as a valet at those fancy hotels on the island, the tourists always wanted action and came to me. They'd run up a debt with me betting ball games. Then they'd try to fly home without paying up. It made me cynical."

Uncle Mike stifled a yawn. "What did you do?"

"We got their itinerary from the front desk. If they owed money, we slipped into their room at night and swiped their driver's license or passport."

You couldn't catch your plane without any ID. "Nice."

Island Willie nodded an acknowledgment. "Now, I have here a piece of paper that shows the credit line we discussed—one hundred grand. The credit line can be raised as I see fit. Here's another piece of paper for Mike to sign, pledging assets. Since Eddie has nothing to pledge, I'm afraid that's how it is. Usually, I don't require paperwork, but I'm doing this for Mike. I had these drawn up special."

He leaned back, stretched his neck in obvious pain, and picked up his water bottle while we reviewed the paperwork. It looked like something a lawyer would've drawn up.

Island Willie stood and groaned. It seemed to help his neck pain or his foot pain, or other radiating nerve pain shooting through him. "The paperwork is not legal. I know that. All I wanted was something I could wave around if we get in sideways. I like Chicago. God knows I got enough places where I can't show my face."

"Understandable," Uncle Mike said, signing it.

There was a signature line for me as well, although it had already been made clear that I was the one at the table who didn't have a pot to piss in when it came to assets. I was allowed to add my signature for posterity.

"You'll get a code," Island Willie said. "Use it when you go online. Don't give it to nobody. Okay? Nobody."

Uncle Mike rubbed his eyes as if the legal jargon had seared his eyelids. "Damnit, Willie," he said. "You've got a hell of a thing going down there, don't you?"

"That it is, Mike. Come down anytime for a visit. One thing you guys can do for me…"

"What's that?" I asked, feeling like I was already a hundred grand in the hole.

Island Willie, still standing, pulled down his leather hat. "I've heard about this lab book."

"Oh, yeah?" I said, playing dumb.

"What lab book?" Uncle Mike asked.

"I heard about a professor who runs the Lake Shore Labs who gave a talk the other day. Something about a new way to analyze for prohibited substances." Island Willie began coughing and sat back down, taking another swig from his water bottle. "All these chemicals floating in the blood. Science can zero in on them if they look hard enough. Remember what I said—all I ask is that people play fair. I suspect that hasn't been happening here at good old Thornton, and if I get proof—"

"You think this lab book—"

"Exactly," Island Willie said. "There will be consequences."

38

UNCLE MIKE AND I SAT IN HIS OFFICE AT O'Connell's the next morning. An anonymous delivery person dropped a package off at nine a.m. It was a banker's box crammed with documents. Irv had gone overboard as usual.

We began to dig into the mountain of information Irv's team had provided. It seemed our workload was increasing with each passing day—check this company's background, question this witness and, at the same time, keep up to speed on the horses. Reviewing the true owners of the corporate shells listed as owners for the horses might yield results, or it might be a waste of time.

We'd received a call from one of Sal's owners who wanted to meet today. Uncle Mike called back and left a message, but it seemed odd that they'd call us instead of calling Sal's office, which would refer them to Orman.

"It's probably somebody who wants to complain, and I can't say I blame them," Uncle Mike said. "Your trainer gets suspended for drugging horses and then gets arrested for murder, and now your horses are turned over to Ronnie Orman, a low-percentage trainer. Maybe they don't like Orman, or maybe they're just pissed. Hopefully, they'll call Orman. Let him straighten it out."

I'd agreed. I was getting worried that I wouldn't have sufficient time to handicap this weekend's races. It would be my first real chance to get in tight with Vandy and the Late Money Boys. Were they up to something as Island Wille seemed to think? If so, it might explain a lot of things, like the positive drug test that resulted in Sal's suspension.

Uncle Mike and I had again impressed Vandy. I considered it test number two. At the track yesterday, we recommended a horse to Vandy. Uncle Mike had come up with some input on the horse from Isabel and I liked the horse as well. Vandy agreed with us and told me to bet five hundred to win on the horse.

"It's just a test run, Eddie," Vandy had said, as if five hundred was the equivalent of five bucks.

Island Willie had previously given me a quickie tutorial on his offshore website and had set up my account. I used my personal code when I logged in. In response, another code was sent to my cell. Island Willie ran a sophisticated operation.

I'd placed the five-hundred-dollar wager on my Island Willie account for Vandy, and the horse won at three to one odds. My offshore account now showed a positive balance of twenty-six hundred dollars, and fifty percent of it was mine, based on my agreement with Vandy. Part of my winnings would be paid to Uncle Mike. Maybe we weren't imposters after all. Maybe Uncle Mike and I were the real thing.

No, I couldn't in good conscience go that far. I had been a longtime horseplayer, but now I'd graduated to another level; something I could've only dreamed about. Here I was working with the track's claiming wizard and giving him advice on what horses to claim. I placed our joint wager from my offshore account. When you live a dream, you can't help but feel like an imposter.

Vandy had been impressed not only by the fact we picked a winner, but by my relationship with Island Willie. "We're going to really go to town now, Eddie," Vandy had said.

I didn't mind winning money, but I didn't want to end up on Island Willie's shit list either. The offshore guru roamed around the track with Burrascano's boys, including Lou, who was the size of an upright appliance. I searched through the box for stuff on Island Willie.

"We can add Island Willie to the list of people who know about the professor's lab book," I said.

"Yeah. They seem to know it's out there floating around. I guess the thief is trying to auction it to the highest bidder."

"Damn. That will make me look like a complete fool." I thought of what St. Clair had said—how she expected to find the professor's lab book at the library.

Uncle Mike pulled another Irv file from the stack. "I wish we could get the professor to tell us what she knows about the Late Money Boys and her little talk at the reception."

"She's going through St. Clair's paralegal. She's tired of us asking her for more information about school personnel." I couldn't blame the professor. She'd hired us to obtain the lab book, and all she had to show for it was a loss of seventy-five hundred dollars, plus our fees to date.

Uncle Mike's cell buzzed. "It's that same owner who called earlier—the one who wants to meet today."

He answered and put the phone on speaker.

"Hello, is this Mike O'Connell?" a woman's voice asked.

"Yeah," Uncle Mike said.

"Thank you so much for answering my call." She sounded young and apologetic. "I work for an owner of horses trained by Sal Nicoletti at Thornton Racetrack. My employer asked me to call you. They need to talk with you today in person if you don't mind."

Uncle Mike shrugged. "What's it about?"

"They told me to tell you that they insist—"

"And you don't know what it's about, is that right, young lady?" Uncle Mike asked.

"Yes, sir, I'm afraid I don't."

"Okay, what's the address?"

I wasn't happy. The last thing we needed at the moment was to run off on some wild goose chase. I needed time to get through Irv's docs. I mouthed my complaint to Uncle Mike.

Uncle Mike shrugged. "And the name of your employer?"

She gave us the name and an address near downtown. At least we could arrange to stop by on the way to the track so the trip wouldn't be a major waste.

"What time?" Uncle Mike asked.

"The sooner the better, they told me. If it's not too much trouble."

"Alright, young lady. I have some things to do first, but we can be there by…" Uncle Mike looked at me. I said twelve o'clock. "We'll be there at noon."

She thanked us profusely and hung up.

"Why did you agree to meet? Why not just give them Orman's number?" I asked.

Uncle Mike shook his head and picked up his cigar. He lit it and puffed away. "Eddie, you need a few more of these investigations under your belt. When you got a murder case and people insist on meeting, you complain and bitch, but you go."

39

WE CHECKED THE DEMANDING OWNER, WHO JUST called us, against the list in Irv's docs, but unlike many other shell companies, Irv's team listed this one as "owner unknown." Whoever this person was, they'd gone to a lot of trouble to hide behind their corporate shield.

We drove to the place of business of the mysterious owner and pulled up to an older, compact, two-story office building perched at the edge of a rundown shopping center. The asphalt and curbs in the parking lot were broken, and several storefronts were boarded up. Beside the office building stood a row of old, mud-covered dump trucks, bulldozers and snow-plow blades behind a chain-link fence. A dollar chain store at the opposite end was the only place showing signs of life.

"The place looks vacant," I said. "Are you sure this is the right address?"

"Yeah, this is it," Uncle Mike said. "C'mon, let's get this over with. If nobody's home, that's their problem. We're here on time."

We walked into a cramped lobby and checked the directory. Except for an attorney's office in the basement, the entire building was devoted to companies related to Diamond V Stables. The list of companies included Diamond V Steaks, Diamond V Financial Advisors, Diamond V Sports, Diamond V Real Estate, Diamond V Solar Systems, Diamond V Construction, Diamond V Concrete, Diamond V Auto Sales and Diamond V Bitcoin.

"I guess they've got all the bases covered," I said.

"Maybe we can get some steaks cheap," Uncle Mike said.

We walked through the main entrance into an eight-by-ten-foot lobby. The walls were dirt-beige, with an old plaid couch slumped against one wall. A young woman sat behind a desk. She tore herself away from her computer screen. "Are you Mr. O'Connell?" she asked, getting up to greet us. She almost tripped coming around the desk.

She had short, brown, unkempt hair and wore a loose-fitting dress that hung to her ankles. What was she doing in this dank, ugly joint?

Uncle Mike nodded to her as if he made house calls like this every day. "What's this all about, young lady?"

"Please wait. I'll get my employer. Would you like coffee or water? I can brew some."

"No, we're fine," I said. "We're in a hurry."

"A shot of Jack?"

"No, we're fine."

"It will just be a minute. I know he's anxious to see you." She turned around before she left and said, "Don't go away."

Uncle Mike leaned over to me and whispered. "I don't think she's had any visitors before."

"What the hell? A shot of Jack? It's only noon."

I stared at the blank walls. They were in need of paint. The carpet was threadbare. If this was Diamond V headquarters, the business must be nothing more than a shell company. At least Diamond V got a great deal on the rent.

A few minutes later, the receptionist, out of breath, walked back in. "He'll see you now."

She showed us into a large room that was vacant except for one desk and a dozen folding chairs. Wiring hung down from the ceiling. A man in a dark pinstripe suit stood behind the desk, his arms crossed.

"Eddie, Mike," he said.

It was DiNatale.

I didn't like being in an abandoned building with the mobster. He'd have his boys nearby. Uncle Mike glanced toward the door behind the desk. It was ajar.

Burrascano would've called us to set up a meeting.

Uncle Mike placed his hands on his hips. "Why all the mystery, Vic?"

"You've been hanging around the backstretch."

"Burrascano gave us the greenlight. You were there," Uncle Mike said.

I'd let my uncle do the talking. I was pissed. Why hide behind Diamond V?

"You're investigating the murder of that exercise rider—"

"Jessie Rivera, assistant trainer."

I couldn't keep my mouth shut. "What is this? You know Sal Nicoletti and Jessie were close. I live with Sal's daughter, Nicole. Don't tell me—"

"I'm not telling you nothing—yet." DiNatale's face remained expressionless. My outburst ignored.

Uncle Mike took a small step forward, taking charge once more. "You better have a good reason—"

"Burrascano is dead."

"What?"

"That's what I'm telling you."

"We didn't hear—"

"You expect a parade down State Street, for fuck sake?"

"Shit."

I cussed as well. We knew it was coming, but still it caught us by surprise. "He passed away from his illness?"

"No, he got run over by a bus." DiNatale shot us a sour look. His shoulders tensed, and he took a couple of steps like a caged lion. The Burrascano empire was all on him. "Now look, you know what I think of you two. I don't approve of outsiders—"

"Tell us something we don't know." Uncle Mike was ready to match him.

"Burrascano said I would handle it. Now I'm handling it."

"If your guys go around asking questions, you'll fuck things up."

"Quiet. I've got lots of stuff to handle. I never liked Burrascano's deal with you guys—turning the killer over to the cops. Fucking bullshit."

"Non-negotiable."

"The track is my place of business. No one fucks with me there."

What was Uncle Mike doing? We couldn't trust DiNatale. We should turn around and get the hell out of there. I smelled a trap.

"I know what's going on. Guys dealing drugs." DiNatale continued to pace like a man confined by invisible walls. He'd been in jail before. "I don't have commitments. People know it. Shit will fly."

"You don't want drugs on your backstretch?"

"When the time is right. You two will—"

"You want to hire us?"

"I've owned horses for a lot of years. Sal has been my man out there. Jessie was the best."

"C'mon, Vic, why should we work with you?"

"Because I'll pay."

"That's not enough."

"I'll protect your ass—"

"From who? The Hippo?"

"Don't tell anyone you work for me."

"This doesn't make sense."

DiNatale's voice rose. "It doesn't make sense for me either. Fucking Burrascano. Smart as hell. He even planned on dying."

"I don't know—"

"Your shit-eating deal," DiNatale growled.

"Wait a minute. Eddie and I are doing fine on our own."

"I got something you need."

"What?"

"The fucking lab book."

40

AFTER WE LEFT DINATALE'S TEMPORARY OFFICE, we drove to the track.

Everything had changed in an instant. We had the professor's fucking lab book in our possession and would now get paid top dollar by DiNatale to find Jessie's killer. Our investigation had done a 180. So why did I have a queasy feeling in the pit of my stomach?

We'd made a deal with DiNatale, a guy we couldn't trust.

Uncle Mike puffed on his cigar and thought great thoughts while I drove and battled heavy traffic.

"Well, Eddie," Uncle Mike pontificated, "we got the hottest commodity. Everybody at the track wants the damn lab book and its secrets. Too bad we can't decipher what it says."

We'd taken a quick look at the pages of notations and scribbling. Each page was filled with dense notes, scientific jargon and even drawings, as if the professor had been worried about not having enough room on the page.

The scribblings were in a foreign language, probably Ukrainian, and the chemistry stuff was another foreign language. That "F" in chemistry had come back to haunt me.

"You think we can get this translated?" I asked.

"You think there are clues in these races?"

There were references to races at various tracks. "I'll research the races listed in the lab book. That's why Island Willie wants the lab book so bad. He feels he's been getting screwed."

"Why do you think he suspects foul play? Sal got nailed for juicing, but everybody swears they don't juice their horses."

I didn't know exactly how to explain it to somebody like Uncle Mike, who wasn't a track regular. "I'll know it when I see it."

"What?"

"Let me explain. If a certain barn has historically been a low percentage barn, and then, all of a sudden, this racing season, they are winning thirty percent of their races, there is reason to be suspicious."

Uncle Mike nodded. "I'm beginning to see what you mean."

"I see specific examples as well. A suspicious barn claims a horse, and then the horse runs better than it has for the last year and a half for the new barn. There are no reported workouts, no major changes in equipment, or other factors that would explain such a big turnaround in performance."

"Does that happen often?"

"Often enough. I try to incorporate it. Handicapping becomes a chore. A lot can go wrong. Sometimes, if I'm betting a Pick Five, I might add a horse from a suspicious barn just to be on the safe side." If I could integrate my strategy with the results in the lab book, I might find a pattern.

"Damn. How do you plan to keep Vandy happy?"

"I won't. I've only got so much time. I'm bound to hit a slump soon, and Vandy will terminate our relationship."

"Vandy has a lot of emotion boiling under the surface. I can see it," Uncle Mike said. "What about the Late Money Boys? From what you tell me and what Arlene told us, they are here to stay, and there's nothing anybody can do about it."

"That really sucks." I wanted to blow up the Late Money Boys and Vandy with it, but that was another one of my silly pipe dreams. "You're right. We get rid of one group, and another will pop up and take its place."

"Island Willie suspects cheating here at Thornton. He said he would get in contact with Jessie prior to accepting certain bets. If Jessie knew so much, then the person or persons involved in cheating Island Willie might've killed Jessie."

I liked this logic. "That would be Vandy. Wait a minute— others could be betting with Island Willie. The Late Money Boys or others."

"Are the Late Money Boys and Vandy one and the same, or do you think Vandy also bets on his own?"

"Vandy definitely bets on his own as well," I said. "The Late Money Boys look for steady returns. They are known to manipulate the pools and the tote board, but Vandy has gambling in his blood. I can tell."

"I keep thinking about that reception and Vandy's efforts to exclude us from the festivities. It pissed me off. Taking Nicole to one end of the bar to question her about sports…"

"Nicole told me that her presence at the reception earned Vandy lots of brownie points with those high rollers. She said they were excited about the prospect of investing heavily in sports betting."

"What does that tell us?"

"It makes me wonder why Vandy felt he had to win brownie points from the Late Money Boys in the first place. He's the main man in the Midwest. Vandy says he "runs hot" and over-bets. Maybe he caused the Late Money Boys some losses with his claimers."

Uncle Mike took a sip from his water bottle. "Nice analysis.

When guys feel like they're in a tight spot, murder can result."

"Maybe Jessie learned that Vandy had drugged one of his horses. He told me the other day how the claiming game is an ongoing battle, if not a war, and sacrifices must be made. He treats me like one of those high school players he used to coach. He always wants more. No matter how much we win, he's rarely happy."

"If you're one of his players, what does that make me? The equipment manager?" Uncle Mike laughed.

"It's also odd for a guy like Vandy—the Wizard of Thornton—to admit to me that he runs hot."

"When it comes to gambling, he respects you. I always knew your gambling would come in handy."

"Stop it." My uncle had high expectations for his nephew. He'd raised me. The murder happened at the track, on my turf. I was the horseplayer. The pressure was on.

Uncle Mike puffed away. "If we look at Island Willie—Jessie—Vandy—and an unknown person, say X, as our love triangle or quadrangle or whatever—"

"That's good. Winning lots of money or losing lots of money and cheating can get people killed."

"Right. The question is—is there a person X to add or not? Orman comes to mind—he had the most to gain due to what's happened to Sal."

"I don't see Vandy drugging horses himself. If he did, he must've had someone helping him. Maybe he got Orman to help him."

"Vandy and Orman working together? Interesting," Uncle Mike said. "Does that mean Orman slipped into Sal's stalls?"

"I'm not sure of that. It seems too risky. What are we going to do with the lab book now that we've got the damn thing? I can't believe DiNatale got it, and I can't believe we're working for that guy. I feel like we're being set up." I tried not to think about what DiNatale might do if we failed to solve Jessie's murder.

"Yeah, DiNatale set us up. He had the lab book as his trump card. And DiNatale has the name of the thief—Otis Horan. I'll see if he has a rap sheet. We have to visit Otis right after the track. I don't want to waste time. I've got questions for that scumbag."

I had questions as well. At first, we were contacted by a woman about doing a deal for the return of the stolen lab book, and then Otis turned up.

DiNatale had contacts in the underworld. When he put out the word, people made it their business to help. They knew what doing a favor for DiNatale and the mob could mean. Island Willie hung out with DiNatale for a reason. Guys talked and bragged, and others could put two and two together. I assumed the thief had talked or bragged to somebody who passed the info along to DiNatale. Of course, DiNatale wouldn't answer our question about how he got the lab book.

I had a client to think about. "Should we call the professor—"

"And tell her we got the lab book? Hell, no. Not until we know more. Person X could be the professor."

"Damn, I didn't think of that."

"We got the hottest commodity Thornton Racetrack has ever seen, and we better not lose it. Keep it under your shirt or in your pants. Don't let that black beauty of a book out of your hands. Got it?"

"Got it."

"It's our bargaining chip. We just need to figure out how to use it and what it says." Uncle Mike puffed on his cigar. "By the way, you know any Ukrainian biochemists?"

41

AFTER THE TRACK, UNCLE MIKE AND I DROVE TO the neighborhood on the near west side situated along a filthy stream that served as a sewer for several manufacturing plants. We drove up to a house with flaking paint and screens hanging off the windowsills.

A late-model Lincoln Continental was parked at the curb. We saw Lou in the passenger seat. We parked and walked up. As Lou exited the vehicle, the entire vehicle, and chassis bounced as if exhaling a sigh of relief.

The driver, a nervous, small man, raced ahead of us to the house with his gun drawn.

A woman in a ratty bathrobe with a cigarette dangling from her lips opened the door and waved. "C'mon in, everybody, let's get the party started."

Lou ducked down when he entered the house and seemed to take up half the living room. We followed Lou and the driver through the tiny room and down the hall.

The woman lectured us from behind. "No reason for guns. If you want to beat on him again, go ahead. He's in the bedroom. Just try not to raise a ruckus. I don't need to hear from the neighbors again. I got enough problems."

Inside the bedroom, Lou pointed toward the bed. "This here is Otis Horan."

A man was sitting upright on the bed with a cast running up his right arm to his shoulder and chest. His right arm extended straight out from his shoulder, his forearm bent upward at a ninety-degree angle at the elbow, his hand reaching toward the ceiling. The result was an appendage frozen in a permanent gesture of "Hi". He also sported a heavy neck brace and a bandage over his left eye, covering part of a bushy eyebrow. Everything in his expression was the opposite of "Hi." He wiggled the fingers on his right hand, perhaps to keep the blood flowing.

Uncle Mike walked up. "Well, Mr. Horan, we finally meet."

The man sneered back. "Call me Otis."

The driver put his gun away and told Lou he'd wait outside in the car. Lou nodded.

Otis Horan had been in and out of prison several times for a string of burglaries.

"Okay, Otis. This is Eddie, and my name is Mike. We're here to learn about the lab book."

"I gave it to them," Otis growled.

"We know. Now we want to hear your story."

"What's there to tell?"

"A lot. You recognize Eddie?"

Otis smiled. "Yeah. Thanks for the envelope. All I want is the name of the guy who ratted on me to—"

Lou stepped over and grabbed three or four wiggling fingers of Otis's right hand and gave it a quick twist.

Otis screeched as if his chicken wing might be plucked from its socket.

"Okay, okay," Otis said, breathing hard.

Lou stepped away.

"Let's make this quick," Uncle Mike said. "We don't have all night to watch you writhing in pain."

"I do." I couldn't help myself. Otis had given me orders the night of the drop, and it didn't sit well.

"Alright," Uncle Mike said, "tell us how you stole the lab book."

"Fuck me. My lady friend—"

A voice came from the kitchen. "If you kept your dick in your pants—"

"What was her name?" Uncle Mike asked.

"I don't mind telling you. She left town. Took the seventy-five hundred and ran. Fucking bitch. I'll catch up with her."

"You won't catch up with anyone for a while. What's her name?"

"Laverne Baker. She worked as a janitor and had a friend who worked at the lab."

"You got a cell phone number and last known address for Laverne?"

"Yeah. It won't do no good, though. She flew the coop. Now that I think about it, the bitch probably wasn't using her real name." He had his phone on his lap and showed us her contact info. I jotted it down.

"What about her friend in the lab?"

"I don't know her name. The friend wasn't a part of it."

"You got a photo of Laverne?"

"Yeah," Otis snickered. "A couple of good ones." He held out the cell with his left hand.

Uncle Mike took a look. "You got any of Laverne with her clothes on?"

The voice from the kitchen echoed through the tissue-thin walls. "Slime bucket."

"Hell, no."

"Let's start from the beginning. Go through the theft step by step."

"I ain't admitting nothing."

Lou took a step toward the bed.

Otis talked fast. "I just want this all off the record, okay? Shit, take it easy. I'm in real pain."

Lou took a step back and settled into a chair that squeaked under his weight.

"Go ahead," Uncle Mike said.

"Laverne was the one. Her friend told her how the lab owner, a professor—a hot-looking foreign babe—always had this lab book with her. When she checked reports and found something funny, she made a note in her lab book. People took notice." He laughed. "I guess they told each other, 'Don't fuck up or your name will end up in the professor's lab book.' They were scared of this woman." Otis snickered again.

"After you stole it, you decided to sell it back?"

"Yeah. What else am I going to do with the damn thing? I thought we'd make a quick score. Laverne and I could take a trip."

"Rotten piece of shit," the woman in the kitchen screamed.

"Fuck off," Otis squealed back. "We started getting nervous when people started asking us about it. I guess maybe I talked about it to a few people. I think I know who ratted me out. He'll get his—"

"What people started asking?"

"Some bookies I know. They never gave me the time of day before, and now they're buying me drinks. Offered to buy me dinner. Then I wised up. These guys wouldn't be as nice to me as Lou here."

Lou nodded and examined the fingernail of his right index finger.

"How did you and Laverne plan to steal the lab book?"

"Like I said, it was all Laverne's idea. Laverne went in to meet her friend for drinks after work, and I followed her into the labs."

The kitchen voice yelled, "Get him out of my house when you're done. Throw his ass in the gutter."

I wanted to oblige the poor woman, but we didn't have time to clean up the neighborhood.

"What about the lab's security guards?" Uncle Mike asked.

"Yeah. Laverne said they wcrc changing shifts or something. I did the lock on the office door. Laverne had given me this lab coat."

"You picked the lock on the professor's office door?"

"Yeah. It was almost too easy. It was at night. I ran out. I should've kept things simple. But I wanted a big payday. Like I said, people began talking."

"You weren't going to agree to the twelve thousand five hundred final payment?"

"No way. I began to think I could get fifty thousand if I held out. But I guess Laverne got nervous. Bitch grabbed the money and blew town. She didn't have my experience in these things—"

"You said it was too easy?"

Otis nodded. "The night we were there. No guards. I walk in and walk out. The lab book was right on the desk. I locked the door on my way out, like I always do. It was all real clean."

42

THE PROFESSOR HAD TOLD US THAT HER DESK drawer had been jimmied open. She even showed us the markings.

The professor said she always locked the lab book in the drawer.

We went over things again with Otis. Uncle Mike pulled all his old tricks. After asking a series of easy questions, including a few about how Otis must've taught Laverne the finer points of extortion that Otis appreciated, Uncle Mike asked, "So when you broke into the professor's desk…"

Otis said, "The lab book was on the desk. No need to hunt around. Laverne told me what the lab book looked like."

Uncle Mike tried several more tricks to see if Otis would contradict himself, but he didn't waver. It wasn't as if he'd face any additional charge for breaking into a desk, since he'd already broken into the office.

On our drive back to O'Connell's, Uncle Mike wasn't happy.

"The one thing we get out of Otis is that the professor lied to us about the lab book being in the desk drawer. I expected Otis to lie—not our client."

We'd come to respect the professor. She seemed to be the white knight in all this, working to find new ways to analyze blood samples from racehorses and giving a talk to Vandy's Late Money Boys. Why would she lie about something so simple? Perhaps she'd even gone to the added trouble of gouging those amateur marks around the lock of the desk drawer.

"We can't ask her about it," I said. "We'd have to tell her about the thief and what he said. Then we'd have to admit that we have the lab book."

"Yeah. We need to forget about Otis. The guy is a thief and probably lied to us. I've seen it before—the perp says that the victim made everything too easy as if the victim is responsible. We used to get it all the time with stolen cars. 'They left the keys in the car.' Like the car thief had no choice but to steal it."

It seemed that whenever we were able to shed some light on the investigation, all we got was another question.

—

That night at O'Connell's, I made time to thoroughly review Irv's docs. One of Orman's owners, Old Prairie Stables LLC, was owned by D. Kovalenko. The "D" was the first initial of the professor's middle name. I wondered how much work it took to find the owner's name. There were a number of limited liability corporations, like Diamond V, where Irv's team couldn't find an owner's name, despite their extensive efforts.

Old Prairie Stables was the owner of ClassicMasterD, the horse that had finished second and made me a star.

According to Irv's docs, the professor did in fact come from "real" money. The accountants had determined she had holdings of close to five hundred million. That didn't include other funds and assets squirreled away in other corporations or trusts.

Uncle Mike was seated at the bar watching a college football game. I asked him to join me in the office and then I showed him Irv's information on Old Prairie Stables.

"Good work, Eddie. There are clues hidden in these races after all—nice. What does it mean?"

"Good question. My first thought was, why does somebody with real money like the professor own a string of claimers at Thornton with a low percentage trainer like Orman? Her lab does blood tests—isn't that a conflict?"

"A big one. If anyone bothered to dig around in Thornton's dirty laundry."

"Here's another question," I said. "If ClassicMasterD had enough potential for me to pick the horse, why didn't Sal and Vandy claim the horse? Sal and Vandy made it their duty to poach Orman's live horses at the claim box. Was it because Jessie gave them additional insight on each Orman horse?"

Uncle Mike scratched the few hairs sprouting around his ears. "Jessie had been murdered, so Sal and Vandy didn't have her input on ClassicMasterD."

"Yes, at the time I was doing Vandy's test, but ClassicMasterD had run in prior claiming races. I looked up each of the horses owned by Old Prairie Stables based on the info Orman gave us. Old Prairie owns about ten or fifteen horses, all trained by Orman. The majority of these horses are claimers, but none have been claimed by Sal and Vandy. In fact, Old Prairie horses seem to be untouchable."

"What do you mean?"

"None of the Old Prairie horses have been claimed by any barn at Thornton Racetrack."

"They know the owner of Old Prairie is the professor, and they know she has the power?"

I nodded. "No wonder the professor's lab book is such a hot item. The trainers recognize the power she has over them."

"What does it mean?" Uncle Mike asked. "Does it mean our

professor is dirty? If somebody claims her horse, their lab tests could be in jeopardy."

"She's using a shell company for a reason. Tonight, I'll dig into her lab book and see what else I can find."

"Good luck. If you have any chemistry questions, remember, I need my beauty sleep."

43

UNCLE MIKE COULDN'T GET OUT TO THE TRACK every day when the horses were running. We had O'Connell's Tavern to run and tried to budget our time the best we could, but since I had the advisor deal with Vandy, I was the one who had to attend the races.

It meant I had to handicap last night, and I wasn't able to spend as much time on the professor's lab book as I had hoped. I would be able to spend more time on it tomorrow since it was a non-racing day.

Today, I was at the track alone. Vandy didn't have a horse running, but he was around. In the third race, I had a good-looking filly making the drop from Maiden Special Weight down to Maiden Claiming named Lady Margie, trained by one of Thornton's up-and-coming trainers.

Lady Margie had thirteen starts and had been dropped to the claiming level six starts ago and just missed. In her next four starts, at the Maiden Special Weight level, she showed speed, but faded in the stretch. Each of these four starts had been run at different racetracks in the Midwest and included a couple of uninspiring tryouts on the turf.

Her last two starts had both been at Thornton Racetrack, giving Lady Margie a chance to finally get fully acquainted with the track surface.

There were a couple of other horses making the same drop in class from Maiden Special Weights to Maiden Claiming, considered the biggest class drop in horse racing. These other horses would take a lot of the action, allowing Lady Margie, who was zero for thirteen and beginning to look like a career maiden, to get decent odds.

In the first race, I'd picked a six to one shot that led all the way and then got nipped at the wire by a twelve to one shot. I'd made the right pick. It was just one of those things. I'd made a substantial bet with Vandy on my Island Willie account.

Vandy didn't seem upset; in fact, he'd even given me a pat on the back. It seemed out of character for him. He always wanted more and hated to lose.

When your frontrunning horse gets nipped at the wire, as my horse did in the first race, and then you have another one with a similar running style—Lady Margie—you're not exactly anxious to relive the experience.

I could simply bet Lady Margie at the Thornton windows and not bet that much. I always reserved my Island Willie account for joint bets made with Vandy in order to keep tabs on our fifty-fifty split.

I decided to talk with Vandy about Lady Margie.

Vandy studied the horse closely in the program and then asked, "What do you think? Are you hot or lukewarm?"

I liked the fact that he relied on my opinion more and more. "I have to tell you, the way our horse lost in the first race has me wondering if the track is a little heavy." Sometimes the track retained added moisture, causing horses on the front end to tire.

"But I also think Lady Margie will be alone out front."

"Let's do it. We'll only go three hundred to win. It's still early."

I agreed. Horseplayers had a thing about a winning day. It had to do with momentum and psychology. If you put together enough winning days over the course of a meeting, you felt like you were getting ahead.

The more I thought about Vandy's reaction to our loss in the first race, the more I wondered if he'd bet the exacta on those two horses. I never felt as if I was getting the full story from him.

I made the bet on Lady Margie. The horse wired the field and graduated at five to one odds. Vandy was happy but pissed that he'd reduced the bet from our usual five hundred to three hundred dollars.

After receiving congratulations from Vandy, I bought a burger at the grill and was slathering it up with ketchup and mustard and onions and anything else I could find to kill the burned-grease taste when I spotted them. It was a group of more than ten guys, each one maintaining an equal distance from the man in the center, who strode tall and straight for being five-foot-five inches tall, his eyes straight ahead. It was The Hippo. They were headed up to the second floor of the clubhouse and the private suites.

I resisted the urge to follow the gang. Oddly enough, DiNatale's boys and Island Willie were absent today. That was probably a good thing.

I called my uncle.

"Hold on, let me get into the office," he said.

I waited, biting off a chunk of burger-grease and condiments between a bun.

He got back on the cell. "Okay, The Hippo is there?"

"Maybe The Hippo is making a power play." This was the first time I'd seen him at the track during the races. He'd promised a showdown with DiNatale.

"It's possible. Why don't you go up there in five minutes—or, better yet—go up there just before the next race. That way, if they ask you why you're up there, you can tell them you wanted to have a better view of the race. Find out what they're up to."

It was a good excuse. "Sure. Want me to talk with them?"

"No, stay as far back as you can."

None of the corporate owners we'd given Irv to research showed The Hippo as an owner. Like DiNatale, he'd probably used a straw man to avoid having his name show up on any LLC.

I walked up the stairs and read the racing program at the same time. A horse from Diamond V Stables, DiNatale's company, had scratched from the upcoming race.

As I reached the top of the stairs, I got a call from Vandy.

"Eddie, I need to get something down on the number six horse in the next race," he said.

I looked at the six in the program. "Dreaming Moon? That horse hasn't won in two years."

"Just do it."

There wasn't much time before the race, but I told him I would.

I almost didn't notice the man standing close by. He was one of The Hippo's guys, standing sentry duty near the walkway from the stairs into the clubhouse.

"Hey, you. What did you say about Dreaming Moon?" the man asked.

"Nothing. Just getting a bet down." The horse was at thirty to one and seemed to me like a waste of money. I went online through my phone—which was a pain since I usually used the laptop—but I managed to remember the passwords and my code and got the bet down on my Island Willie account just before the start.

The man watched me close. "You bet on the six horse?"

I didn't want to admit to making a bet on a horse I considered a sucker bet. "I just came up to watch the race."

"This is a private affair."

"Fine. I'll go back down."

"Wait a minute. You bet Dreaming Moon, right?"

What was the big deal? The horse hadn't run better than last place in his last four races. It was owned and trained by Orman. "I was considering it, but the horse looks like shit," I lied.

"I think you better talk to the boss," he said.

I didn't have much choice but to go with him. I couldn't start a fight. Even if I got away, I couldn't exactly get lost in the crowd downstairs.

They made me wait until after the race. Of course, Dreaming Moon, a white horse, ran like he was on jet skis and won by a city block, paying sixty-four dollars and change to win.

They explained my mortal sins to The Hippo. How I had talked about the horse with someone and then seemed to place a wager on my phone.

The Hippo studied me. "I know you. You were with that island fuck the other day." Through gritted teeth, he said, "What the fuck? You talked about Dreaming Moon?" He looked around at his men. "Did somebody here say something? Who was it, kid?"

"Nobody here said anything, sir." I thought the added "sir" might help my cause.

"No? Did you have a dream about Dreaming Moon? Is that what you're telling me?

"I didn't play him."

"Show me. Get your phone out and show me your app. You better not be fucking with me."

I pulled out the WagerEasy app on my cell. I didn't dare show him my Island Willie account, where Vandy and I had just won a bundle.

"No bet at all on the race? What're you doing up here?"

"I just wanted to watch the race." The guys were laughing at me now. I felt like a complete idiot—I was supposed to go upstairs and see what I could find out and stay back, not become the center of attention.

"Why don't we toss him off the balcony outside? See if he bounces?" One of his bloodthirsty men said. This got a lot of laughs. They were having fun at my expense. It was only about a sixty-foot drop. I knew I couldn't fight the entire crowd, although I'd take a few of them with me if they actually tried it.

"Who were you talking to?" The Hippo asked.

"My uncle," I lied.

"His uncle?" Someone called out. "He needs a ride home." Everybody laughed again. They were a jolly crowd after celebrating the victory of Dreaming Moon.

"You're the guy who roughed up Hugo. I learned some things. What's your name again?" The Hippo asked.

"Eddie O'Connell."

"O'Connell?" The Hippo thought for a few seconds and then snapped his fingers. "That's right. He's Mike O'Connell's nephew. Burrascano told me something. Damn, I can't remember what it was."

Somebody said, "Mike O'Connell? Shit, boss. He used to be a homicide detective."

"I guess he didn't inherit his uncle's smarts, huh?" The Hippo said to more laughter. "All right, we had our fun. In honor of Mike O'Connell and due to our big win out here today, I'm going to let you go." He stood and pointed at me. "Next time— there better not be a next time. I don't want to see your face hanging around me again, understand?"

"Yes, sir," I said, and walked away.

"You lucked out, kid." My original escort told me as he led me to the stairs.

I had almost asked The Hippo a question. I wanted to ask him if he was at the workouts the other morning to see a particular horse. Dreaming Moon had worked out that morning.

—

Later that day, I heard that a man had been killed in the construction area beneath the old grandstands. He'd been knifed in the throat, the same way Donnie Egan's throat had been slashed in the parking lot of Old Shagbark Country Club. Today's victim was a man named Gerald Wilcox, visiting from New York.

The breaking news photo of Mr. Wilcox seemed familiar. Then I remembered, and Uncle Mike agreed. He was that fast talker at Vandy's reception, the one we overheard talking with his buddy.

At first, I thought it must've been The Hippo and his boys, and I felt like the luckiest person on earth and the smartest for being respectful and then leaving when I did. Then I thought of Island Willie. He said there would be consequences if you didn't play fair. The fast talker mentioned Island Willie and the manipulation of the exacta pools. Plus, the man had been killed at the same place—the construction area—where we had our little talk with Island Willie.

Island Willie had talked about killing pigs with a knife. The more I thought about it, the more these murders seemed like something Island Willie might do. Lou would be perfect for the part of the Hawaiian pig-hunting dog.

I hadn't seen the gambling guru around that day. Had he patched things up with The Hippo? I could only speculate; I had no hard facts. If The Hippo and Island Willie did meet, maybe it meant Island Willie and DiNatale were no longer getting along.

44

THE NEXT MORNING, I MET WITH UNCLE MIKE IN his office. I'd spent the previous night working on the professor's lab book. We'd also arranged for a party later that afternoon at O'Connell's Tavern to celebrate two things—the birthday of Isabel's daughter and Sal being released on bond.

St. Clair's law office suggested that Sal do something with his family—something low-key that would divert his attention from the murder case. We were told to talk about mundane topics that Sal enjoyed, like sports or travel, anything that didn't touch on the subject of horse racing or his murder case.

Then Pam Ferguson called us. "I understand you're having a family party. Remember—stay away from the murder case. We don't want you to discuss our investigation with Sal, and we don't want Sal discussing his defense with you. A fact that might seem irrelevant to you or to Sal could be something useful to the defense. And don't get him worked up. Cases can be lost if the defendant has a few drinks and gets a loose mouth. Anyone can take a video at any moment, and a social media post could infect the jury pool."

Uncle Mike hung up the cell. "Well, Eddie, do you think we got the message? Will St. Clair call us next?"

"We should be able to remain calm and boring."

"Before we take a snooze, let's talk about the lab book. Were you able to decipher anything?"

I always liked Uncle Mike's ability to shake things off and move on to the next topic as if his brain operated on an automatic Rolodex. He wasn't going to dwell on The Hippo's bet on the long shot or yesterday's murder of the New Yorker. He wanted us to stay focused.

"I have to tell you it has been frustrating." I placed the lab book on the desk along with my notes. "It's like finding ancient scrolls, except the writing is in Ukrainian. Look at this—look at these drawings." I opened the book and turned it around to show Uncle Mike. I flipped to the pages I'd bookmarked.

"What the hell? Are those cobras?"

"Some of them."

In black ink, the professor had drawn intricate drawings of snakes. The drawings were the size of a postage stamp; others took up almost half a page. Several showed a cobra coiled in profile, its head raised high, or leaning to one side as if swaying to the mysterious tune of a snake charmer. Other pictures showed a closeup of the snake's head about to strike, its mouth open, exposing long, sharp fangs.

"It's creepy, isn't it?" I'd been mesmerized by the drawings, hunting through the entire lab book, more than a couple hundred pages, to find them and study them.

"What do you mean 'some'?"

"They aren't all cobras. Many are from Australia."

"She's got artistic talent."

"You should see the poison frogs." I showed him a couple of those pages. The little critters were covered in what looked like war paint—striking colors and designs that told predators to steer clear.

"She colored these frogs with magic markers?"

"The pictures of snakes, frogs, scorpions, and spiders appear each time her lab does yet another trial experiment. The professor is clearly pissed off, and the pictures seem to drive her."

"What is all this?"

I didn't want to get Uncle Mike bogged down in too much detail. He already thought I was nuts for playing the horses, and what I was about to say wouldn't help. "Snake venom or other venom, diluted somewhat, will help mask pain and provide a sense of euphoria. It's perfect for juicing a horse on race day, and it's almost impossible to detect because it doesn't last long in the system."

"You're kidding me."

"No, I'm not. Trainers have been suspended when regulators found vials of venom in the tack room. But that's only because a disgruntled employee ratted on their boss."

Uncle Mike cradled his head in both hands. "C'mon. They squeeze these frogs?"

"They synthesize the active ingredients in the venom these days. They don't have to go out and capture frogs anymore."

"That's a relief. At least the frogs are getting a pass."

"The minute a regulator's lab identifies the synthesized stuff and can test for it, the black market tweaks the molecule, and they're back in business."

"This is a nightmare. How long has this been going on?"

"The drug culture in racing has been going on since they started horse racing in the 1800s. It's called greed."

Uncle Mike's shoulders slumped. "I must be getting too old. I can't take it. Tell me the professor's lab book has an answer."

"I can't tell for certain. From the dates I found, there are references to races. They're from different tracks over the past year. I looked up the results of those races, and usually a long shot was involved. Their trainer was having 'a very good day.' She must've received blood samples from somebody on site. Not exactly approved procedure—the professor had gone rogue." I rifled through the pages. "Here, look at this."

Uncle Mike leaned over and studied the page. "Now, we're getting somewhere."

The page was crammed with the usual scientific measurements and chemical symbols, similar to the other densely packed pages, but this page ended in a Ukrainian word that was underlined three or four times, followed by several exclamation points. The word "YCNIX" was highlighted with bold lettering that took up a quarter of a page, encircled by drawings of snakes slithering away off the page.

"I looked up the word. It's Ukrainian for *success.*"

Uncle Mike stared at me. "This book is so hot it's burning a hole in my desk. Don't let it out of your sight."

45

WE HAD DECORATED THE PARTY ROOM FOR Juanita's birthday. The check-cashing store next door to O'Connell's had closed after a twenty-year run. The owner had spent more time in our bar complaining about new regulations than he had trying to drum up business. His loss had been our gain. We'd worried about taking on more monthly rent, but the space turned out to be a big hit with our customers. Weekend reservations had to be made at least a month in advance, and for Christmas, even longer than that.

The balloons and party hats always helped. Everyone at today's party made a good show of it. We congratulated Juanita, the birthday girl, and sang a rousing rendition of Happy Birthday. It was a good crowd—Nicole, Sal, and Isabel, as well as Aunt Maureen and some of our retired regulars like Mrs. Reilly and Marge, who had made the chocolate cake from scratch.

Sal sang louder than any one of us. It was hard not to stare at him and try to analyze him. How was he holding up? Was his smile real, or was he thinking about what he'd lost and left behind and the big hill he still had left to climb to keep his freedom? I thought of my role in helping him to scale that mountain and couldn't help but feel self-doubt creeping up on me. Were we doing everything we could do for Sal?

Marge and Clara Reilly worked as a team to dish out the ice cream and cake.

"This is too much," Isabel said. "Pizza and cake. Juanita, we are very lucky. Say thank you."

"Thank you," Juanita said, trying to stand and then kneeling on a chair. "Chocolate is my favorite."

"What did you wish for?" Aunt Maureen asked.

"It's a secret."

"That's right. Don't tell anyone or it won't come true," my aunt said.

"I can tell you, can't I?" Juanita asked, her eyes wide.

My aunt smiled and leaned in close to the little girl. "Yes, your secret is safe with me. Birthday parties are special, so it's okay.

She whispered in my aunt's ear.

Clara Reilly brought the ice cream over to me. She and my aunt looked so alike they could have been twins. "Say when," she said, dropping a big scoop of ice cream on my cake.

"When."

Clara leaned over and whispered in my ear. "I hope you get the bastards."

I looked up in shock. Her face was set in stone, and she dropped another large scoop onto my plate as if to cement the point home.

"You'll be the first to know," I said.

"Good."

Nicole, seated beside me, squeezed my leg. She must've overheard Clara.

We celebrated Juanita's birthday and kept up the laughter and good times, while beneath the table this hideous monster lurked.

"Juanita, don't let your ice cream melt," Isabel said.

Juanita took a spoonful. "We're going to live in a big house, isn't that right, *mami?*"

"Don't talk with your mouth full," Isabel said.

Juanita opened her mouth to show everyone the cake and ice cream train wreck.

Nicole laughed. "We need to think about birthday presents."

"For me?" she giggled.

"Yes, for you."

Nicole had told me that Jessie would've wanted this party.

That's when Marini walked in and waved to me. He went up to Marge and Clara. "Just a small piece."

"Who invited you?" Marge asked and then laughed to herself.

"We always have a party crasher when we have parties here," Aunt Maureen said. "It makes things fun."

"And I'll go to the same school all the time," Juanita said.

"Say hello to Mr. Marini, Juanita."

"Hello, Mister Martian," she said. We couldn't help but laugh.

"Happy Birthday, Juanita," Marini called out.

I'd asked Marini to meet me at the party and suggested we go into the bar to talk.

He looked at me expectantly, as if I might have something good to say about that dreary manuscript of his. I dreaded talking to him because I hadn't finished his manuscript, and I wondered if I'd ever be able to plow my way through it.

We stood off to the side in the bar. "What did you think?" he asked.

"Sorry, I haven't gotten through—"

"What? Then why did you—"

"Did you hear about Donnie Egen?" I asked him.

Marini nodded. "Yes."

"This guy is Wynton, isn't he?"

Marini's mouth dropped open, and then he stared at the floor. "How did you know?"

"It's pretty obvious, isn't it?" Both Marini's fictional Wynton and Egan had a son who was a star quarterback making millions. Both were big-time sports bettors. Egan had been at Vandy's Late Money Boys reception—sports betting was the next step on their agenda.

"I'm sick over it. I met Donnie years ago when I first started out in the sports department. He was betting, and we'd meet for beers at the usual sportswriter joint downtown. Donnie would pump me and others for scuttlebutt—you know, info on injuries or gossip about the players. A guy caught up in a fight with the wife might have a shitty game on Sunday—that sort of thing."

"Right. What about lately?" Marini had a way of veering off track. Uncle Mike and I needed to find out more about the slasher murders of Egan and Wilcox. We didn't think they were related to Jessie's murder, since Jessie had been shot, and to our knowledge, didn't gamble, but we needed to cover the bases.

"I still see him at the old watering hole. He's a character. He was losing his ass for a while. But then, thanks to his son and other players he'd gotten to know on the team, he started winning big on college. He'd found a new bookie offshore."

"Do you know why he was at Old Shagbark Country Club?"

"Yeah. He said this guy Wilcox invited him. Something about a group of really high rollers. He was psyched. It meant he'd hit the big time."

"You know, Wilcox was murdered in the same way at the track yesterday." Both had their throats slashed. It was what Island Willie had talked about—the way those pigs were hunted in Hawaii. Wilcox had been involved in manipulating the exacta pools and then betting offshore.

"I heard." Marini scratched his beard. "I'd told Egan I wanted 'in.' I wanted to go along on his college action. I had him scheduled for a podcast."

"You should count yourself lucky."

"I should get a beer."

46

A FEW DAYS LATER, UNCLE MIKE AND I WENT TO Elena's to meet with Ronnie Orman. Orman had been ducking us for the last week or two since Sal's arrest. Yesterday, Orman called us back. We'd suggested that we should meet in Orman's office—he'd moved into Sal's old office. Orman told us he'd rather meet at Elena's.

We showed up at the backstretch cafe, and this time around it was Orman who was late. He did call to apologize and told us he was on his way over.

When Orman entered Elena's, it seemed everyone in the place called out to him. "Hey, Ronnie or Mr. Ronnie" or "Good morning, Mr. Orman," depending on the person's status level on the backstretch. Orman called back to them, went over and shook hands, exchanging a few words, while making his way slowly to our table.

This was an entirely new man. Today's version was brimming with confidence. Orman had graduated.

Maybe the folks on the backstretch had always thought of him as Sal's assistant, a young man trying to make it, but always walking in the shadow of his mentor. Now Orman ruled. Sal was gone, and Orman had his horses and his owners. He knew Sal's tricks of the trade and could ply those well-guarded secrets to his advantage. He'd become the trainer everyone wanted to work for.

There was no need to talk about taking the horses to Turfway or the Fairgrounds for the winter. Sal wouldn't have time to keep his hand-in by training horses in the judge-friendly state of Louisiana. His bond required that he stay home, and he'd be busy attending court hearings in preparation for his upcoming trial.

We exchanged greetings, and Orman sat down in our booth. "Eddie, you've been doing an excellent job for Vandy. If you want to know the truth, keeping Vandy happy was one of my biggest worries. If Vandy's not happy, I'm in big trouble."

We talked about a couple of recent claims that Vandy had made with my input. We also talked about their recent workouts and where he'd place them in upcoming races. He ordered coffee and a sweet roll.

"You guys need to order the sweet rolls," he said.

"I've had them. They're great," Uncle Mike said.

"Mike, I appreciate your research," Orman said. "At first, I was somewhat skeptical, but you've got a knack for this work. I understand you hear from Isabel about certain horses on a regular basis?"

Uncle Mike was a natural. He'd taken up with other backstretch workers, in addition to Isabel, and supplied information on the progress of other horses. I'd begun to see the morning workouts in a whole new light.

"Isabel is still my main point of contact. I pass the info on workouts along to the expert here," Uncle Mike said.

"Isabel learned from the best," Orman said, a pained expression coming over him. "May Jessie rest in peace. Isabel is the best hire I've made in a long time. Thanks for recommending her,

Eddie."

"I'm glad you offered her a job," I said.

Orman leaned over the table, lowering his voice. "When I took over for Sal, I wasn't sure if I could handle it. I was between a rock and a hard place. Who do I hire from Sal's old team and how would my people adjust? It's easy to ruffle feathers when you hire new people, and then overall morale suffers. I didn't know if Sal's old owners would stick with me or move on, especially a guy like Vandy."

"But you got to know Vandy when you worked for Sal, right?" I asked.

"Yeah, but we weren't close. I was just another worker to him. Invisible. All of a sudden, I have his horses. I had to impress him and maintain the first-class service he'd grown accustomed to with Sal. Yet, I didn't want to over-extend myself either. Taking on Sal's horses came with the feed bills, vet bills—extra everything. Emergencies happen. Owners don't always pay on time. I didn't exactly have a rainy-day fund."

"You've had a good record with Sal's horses." It had only been a couple of weeks since Sal turned over his horses and, although Orman's win percentage wasn't up to Sal's leading trainer stats, he was close.

"I don't have to worry about Sal and Vandy claiming my horses anymore. I've been able to be more creative," he said. "I've been putting in long hours, but it's been worth it."

"You dropped a horse in class the other day—Veronica's Mission." It was a horse owned by Old Prairie, the professor's stable. The horse had gone off at even money and won easily. No one had claimed the horse. We wanted to see how Orman would respond and if he'd tell us more about his relationship with the professor. Unlike every other trainer on the grounds, Orman didn't have to worry about incurring her wrath with those rumored groundbreaking blood tests.

"It's all in the timing," Orman said, anxious to talk. "When you're doing well, people get suspicious. Why is he dropping Veronica's

Mission so drastically? They assume that I don't need a winner to help pay the bills because we're doing so well. Instead, they think I'm dumping the horse and that Veronica's Mission must have a serious problem. I could see why they might think that, since the horse did have some issues a few months ago, and that's why we gave her some time off. I thought her works showed she was ready, and the betting public agreed, but no one took a chance on the claim."

I liked Orman's explanation. It made sense, but he neglected to mention the professor's clout or how every trainer was running scared. Orman had the perfect cover story. As the professor's trainer, I thought he might cook up a cover story for his client, and he had.

"What about the thirty to one shot last week—Dreaming Moon?" I asked.

Orman sipped from his coffee. "Remember how you told me I needed to disguise the form of my horses? It looks like I'm doing a pretty good job of that, doesn't it?"

"You own and train Dreaming Moon. Vandy said you gave him a tip on it." It was a lie, but that's what investigators do. A smart trainer might decide to tell his top owner a few things now and then to keep them happy.

Orman shrugged and took a bite of his sweet roll. "I didn't, but I probably should have. The horse surprised me. I think the favorites got caught up in traffic trouble."

It wasn't what I saw in the race, but I let it go. Instead, I said, "The Hippo said he was grateful."

"You know him?" Orman began coughing.

"Yeah, he was out here. We talked."

"What's your connection to The Hippo?" Uncle Mike asked.

Orman sipped from his water. It gave him time to think. "I'm in trouble. The police are back. Two guys got their throats cut. A guy named Egan, and another guy named Wilcox. They're both gamblers. Why talk to me?"

"Detective Saboski?" Uncle Mike asked.

"Yeah. The detective questioned me about Jessie. It was when I was working for Sal. I had a thing for Jessie. I was stupid. Nothing happened, but Sal found out about it. It was the reason we parted ways."

Uncle Mike leaned forward. "Saboski is asking you about this now?"

"Sal's attorney is scraping up reasonable doubt garbage. The cop questioned me about that, and of course he wants to know about these other murders. Somebody told them The Hippo was around my barn."

"The day Dreaming Moon ran?" I asked.

"Each day blurs into the next. I'd have to check my records."

I knew what Uncle Mike was thinking. Sometimes suspects give you information to conceal their own guilt. Plus, Orman must know that Uncle Mike and Saboski had a connection.

"You ever talk to The Hippo?" I asked.

"No, no way. I stay away from those guys." Orman looked around the restaurant as if there were spies everywhere. He leaned in closer, his voice low. "I'm seeing Isabel. The cops got me under surveillance."

I studied him. "When did you start dating—"

"Recently. I always lived and breathed the horses. She and Juanita are special. Now this."

"I'm sure it's all innocent," Uncle Mike said.

My uncle, the veteran interrogator, cozied up to Orman, a "person of interest," with all the cunning of one of those snakes in the lab book. I was impressed.

"The cops don't see it that way. What do you think? Do I need a lawyer? They say I'll need to testify."

"Lots of witnesses testify. They don't each get lawyers or need to," Uncle Mike explained. "Where were you when Jessie was killed?"

Orman's eyes grew wide. "That's what the detective wanted to know. Oh, God. I don't have a witness. I was taking a nap. Shit, I was up before dawn. What do they expect?"

47

THE NEXT DAY, WE STOOD OUTSIDE THE TRACK beneath an overhang with Island Willie. Rain came down in intermittent sheets, and during each brief lull, the races were run. The track had turned from sloppy to a quagmire.

Island Willie, dressed in his winter clothes, consisting of the wool Chicago Bears stocking cap and down jacket, swayed back and forth on his bad feet. He held a black umbrella with one broken spoke over his head to ward off the windswept mist intruding upon our bit of shelter.

"Damnit, what am I doing out here today?" Island Willie said. "I can't tell you how many Advils I got in me. Fuck."

"You wanted to meet out here," Uncle Mike said. "Why can't we meet inside where we met before—in that construction? I didn't see any crews at work."

"Yes, at least it would be dry. However, I'm afraid the police have taken over that space, and you know my superstitions when it comes to the authorities."

"I like watching the ponies splash around in the mud," I said.

Uncle Mike puffed on his stogie. "The police have taken it over because a man was murdered."

"Unfortunate. That's right. I read something about it. A messy affair," Island Willie said.

"His name was Wilcox," I said. "Another man named Donnie Egan was killed the same way at Old Shagbark Country Club. I heard that he was working with some of his son's fraternity members, winning on Same Game Parlays." It was something I'd read in Marini's manuscript.

Island Willie's head turned slowly in my direction. He studied me and then said, "You don't say. I don't recall that in the media. I'm partial to in-game parlays myself."

I bet he was. It was the sucker bet extraordinaire in the NFL.

"Hey, Willie," Uncle Mike said. "You got a ticket you can show us *before* the next race? I'd like to get a bet down on the horse."

I recalled how Island Willie had shown us his winning ticket *after* the race. It still stuck in Uncle Mike's craw. I was surprised Uncle Mike didn't ask more questions about the murders of Egan and Wilcox, then I remembered what he'd said before— you can talk to Island Willie all day—he'll talk, but you won't learn a thing.

"Sorry, guys. From what I've seen of Eddie's wagers, he doesn't need any help." He started coughing and then took a swig from his water bottle.

"I hope my cigar—"

"No, no problem," Island Willie said. "The smell of a cheap cigar and manure were meant for each other. Eddie, when we last talked, I talked about 'notice.' Although I appreciate the chance to chat, I'm afraid that's the reason for this meeting."

I wasn't happy to hear about "notice." What did I do?

"It was a race last week, I'm afraid," Island Willie continued. "It seems there are questions about the race. A high volume of wagers were made on a horse by the name of Dreaming Moon—"

"I made the usual wager."

"I know, I know. You only won sixteen grand. No big deal, but it's similar to other wagers made by other accounts—they've all been flagged."

How much did The Hippo bet on that horse? The way his little entourage was celebrating, they must've bet a bundle. They hadn't bet at the Thornton mutual windows, because the odds remained near thirty to one the entire time.

"I'm sorry, Eddie, Mike," he said, wincing and standing on one leg while twisting his bad foot. "Your account has been frozen."

"What?" How could I explain this to Vandy? "What questions about the race? I haven't heard about anything."

Island Willie cleared his throat. "The track might not investigate, but we do."

The wind kicked up, and a heavy mist joined our party.

I couldn't believe this. "What kind of bullshit—"

"This is outrageous," Uncle Mike said.

"Read your paperwork, Mike," Island Willie said.

I could see my role as Vandy's gambling advisor coming to a screeching halt. "I'll withdraw the amount in my account minus the sixteen grand—"

"Sorry, Eddie," Island Willie said. "When these things come up, the entire balance is frozen. I told you—play fair or there will be consequences."

"There's more than twenty-five grand in my account, not counting the money I won yesterday," I said.

"It's out of my hands," he said.

"That's a cop-out," I said. "You run the place."

"Where's that paperwork?" Uncle Mike hunted through the pockets of his coat.

Island Willie's busted umbrella flapped in the wind. "I'd like to help you both. I've explained my fondness for Mike and my appreciation of what he did for me, and Eddie, your wagers show real talent."

"Did you freeze The Hippo's account as well?" I asked.

Island Willie scowled. "I never divulge information on another customer."

Uncle Mike stood with his hands on his hips, the cigar planted firmly in gritted teeth. He'd given up the search for the paperwork. "What? What the hell do you want, Willie?"

"Find me the lab book. Then we'll talk."

48

ISLAND WILLIE TOTTERED OFF, ONE DELICATE, pain-filled step at a time. Lou held the door open for him as the island maharaja, probably wearing every stitch of clothes in his wardrobe, stumbled inside.

"What the hell are we going to do now?" I asked.

"Let's go over there," Uncle Mike said, pointing to a place another twenty yards away toward the old grandstands. "I worry about why Island Willie chose this particular spot. I guess I'm paranoid."

We walked under the overhang in the opposite direction from the finish line.

"This is good," Uncle Mike said. "We can't give Island Willie the lab book, that's for sure. No telling what he'd find in that damn Pandora's box. We might end up with a dozen murders on our hands."

The lab book detailed which trainers had juiced their horses, and on which races, and if these trainers had kept the track odds high by betting with someone in the black market like Island Willie, then Island Willie and others like him, might take revenge. It made me wish we could get the entire lab book translated, but that would take the professor or a team of Ukrainian chemists.

"You think that the murders of Egan and Wilcox were Island Willie's work?" I asked.

"Could be. I told you, murder follows Island Willie around. You heard what he said about the consequences. Egan got inside information according to Marini and his manuscript, and we overheard that Wilcox manipulated exacta pools."

"DiNatale is providing protection for Island Willie. Why didn't he give Island Willie the lab book?" I asked.

Uncle Mike puffed on the cigar. "Good question. I'd ask DiNatale if I thought I could ever get a straight answer out of the guy."

A tractor towed the starting gate to the sixteenth pole for the start of the next splash-filled scramble around the track.

"Island Willie said that 'accounts were flagged.' Do you think he'd freeze The Hippo's account?"

"Island Willie didn't like that question, did he?" Uncle Mike said. "Maybe DiNatale and Island Willie are working together to make a statement. DiNatale says the track is his place of business. Maybe The Hippo is infringing on his territory."

"All I need is for The Hippo to blame me for the freeze."

"You think that could happen?"

"Yeah. The Hippo was ready to kick my ass just for saying the name of the horse prior to the race. If he finds out I lied to him, and that I did bet the horse, and that I'd bet with Island Willie, he'd work me over just on general principles." It wasn't The Hippo I was worried about; it was the ten men who followed him around. Even I couldn't fight ten guys.

"The Hippo blamed Island Willie for killing Egan. What do you make of that?"

"Egan hadn't paid his debt to The Hippo's bookies.

According to Marini, Egan won a lot on his offshore account. He could've used that money to pay the debt, but like any degenerate, they wait until it's absolutely necessary before they tap the bankroll."

"Island Willie says you have to play fair," Uncle Mike said.

"Vandy was the one who gave me the bet on Dreaming Moon. He wanted me to place it with Island Willie."

"Right. Maybe Vandy is using you. Vandy could've been the one with his throat slashed. Or maybe Vandy's account with Island Willie was frozen previously, so he signed you up."

"Remember, I signed up with Vandy for the investigation. I'm not Vandy's chump."

"Okay. Still, you're the bad guy in the eyes of Island Willie and maybe The Hippo. Although I assume your Island Willie account wouldn't be frozen if it wasn't for this lab book."

"What about Orman? He might have an account with Island Willie as well."

Uncle Mike flicked ash onto the cement. "Orman said he was surprised at how well Dreaming Moon ran. What bullshit. I'm not believing much of what he says."

"Orman told us now that Vandy and Sal aren't claiming his horses, he can be creative. A vial of venom sure helps creativity."

Uncle Mike pulled down his hat and pulled at the collar of his coat. "We don't know if Orman juices his horses, do we? The lab book didn't list his horses or Sal's. Of course, the lab book doesn't have any races after Jessie's murder. But Orman evaded our questions about Dreaming Moon and The Hippo."

"Orman is feeling the heat from Saboski. Thank you, attorney St. Clair."

"It could be that Orman has borrowed money from the wrong people," Uncle Mike said.

"Like The Hippo?"

"It's time to deal," Uncle Mike said. "If we don't move first, The Hippo will."

A horse stopped and took a dump near us. The horse seemed to be making a statement with nature's call. I was tempted to bet on him.

Uncle Mike laughed. "I guess that horse is ready to run. Orman has stepped into a pile of horseshit. Let me ask you this. Is Orman the luckiest S.O.B. ever?"

"He has everything Sal had, and he has Isabel, too."

Uncle Mike stomped his feet. "I'm getting cold, but I want to stay outside to watch this race."

49

WE MET WITH VANDY IN A VACANT CORNER OF THE clubhouse, far from those who might recognize the track's claiming wizard, and far away from those who might just happen to eavesdrop on our conversation in hopes of obtaining a tiny tidbit of information about today's card.

Uncle Mike and I sat down. Vandy dropped his carryall bag on the table and sat.

He reached out his hands, palms up. "Okay, this must be bad to haul my ass all the way over here. What's up?"

"Our account with Island Willie," I began. "The bet on Dreaming Moon was flagged. I guess others bet on that thirty to one shot."

"What do you mean, *flagged?*" Vandy stared first at me and then at Uncle Mike.

We went over it in detail—that there were questions raised about the race. Island Willie had told us that a number of accounts had been flagged and that an "investigation" was commenced by him and his partners.

"What kind of bullshit is this? I haven't heard about anything. The track paid out the money to the bettors. The purse has been divvied up. There isn't any *investigation.*"

"That's what I told him," I said.

"Let's withdraw our other funds and get the hell out—"

"That was my reaction—but our entire account has been frozen."

"Why? What does the amount won on Dreaming Moon have to do with the monies we've already won?"

"I have no idea. Maybe Island Willie has done it to apply pressure?" I explained about consequences and the piece of paper.

Vandy pointed a finger first at me and then at Uncle Mike. "I thought you and your uncle were in tight with this guy. You were all joking and laughing, remember? That's what I was led to believe. If there were problems or conditions, why wasn't I told? I have alternatives."

Vandy was boiling over.

I explained again about the fact that the horse sat cold as ice on the tote and then won by a city block. Vandy said nothing in response. He simply shrugged. Those facts made the entire race appear questionable to me, but I didn't say that. Nor did I say that after the race, I'd enjoyed the smug feeling of being "in" on a fix—a wonderful feeling for a change.

"I thought we had momentum, Eddie. I thought we could work together, trust each other. Now you serve up this plate of bullshit?"

Vandy was the coach, and I was the scrub who just came off the bench for his big chance and then missed two last-minute free throws that would've tied and won the game.

"What I'd like to know," Uncle Mike said, "is who owns these other accounts that have also been flagged?"

"Yeah," Vandy nodded, his lips pursed. "What happened, Eddie? You make the bet over a loudspeaker?"

"Look," I said, "all I did was place the bet. It was your bet, not mine. I didn't give you any gambling advice on Dreaming Moon." I should've told him about The Hippo and how the mobster and his boys were all over the horse. Maybe Vandy would like to confront The Hippo about it.

"Did Orman give you the horse?" Uncle Mike asked.

Vandy shrugged. "I don't know. I've been out here a long time. I got my sources."

I pointed my own finger back at Vandy. "That won't get us anywhere. I didn't make the bet over a loudspeaker, either. You think I'm nuts? The guy who gave you the horse—that's the one who has a big mouth, not me."

"If it was Orman, you should think about leaving him. He's in with a bad crowd," Uncle Mike said.

Vandy didn't like Uncle Mike's comment. If it wasn't Orman, who was it?

"From day one," Vandy hissed, "I've made things crystal clear— I expect results. If I can't get results, I go elsewhere. I don't know what your history is with this Island Willie, but I'm not coming out on the short end of this. It's your account, and you owe me."

I was getting pissed. This was too much. "You asked *me* to set up the account. You said you ran 'hot'. It was a fifty-fifty split. We were 'in' this together."

"You were my guy at Thornton. I gave you a chance. I put my money and reputation on the line. I gave you the opportunity. I gave Nicole the chance to get in on the ground floor of the next big thing in sports betting. You want to throw all that away? Then pay me my share."

"Talk to your source," I said.

Vandy got up. "By the way, I'm shipping Winning Spirit to a little track in western Canada. There's a stake race that's perfect for him." He slung his bag over his shoulder and walked off.

It was a rotten thing to say, even in the heat of anger. Racehorses were sent to Canada for slaughter.

50

THAT EVENING, I WAS BACK WALKING THE STREETS of Sal's neighborhood. I had checked off most of the houses on Sal's cul-de-sac. This effort had taken several tries in an attempt to catch people at home. Tonight, I'd once again try the street behind Sal's house.

According to Uncle Mike, a good investigator had to "go through the motions" even when the work seemed hopeless. The idea of "going through the motions" didn't exactly put me in a good mood. My mood was already dark over the Island Willie freeze on my account, and Vandy's reaction. All my handicapping and winning picks had been flushed down the drain in one fiery argument. My chance to "peer" inside Vandy's claiming operation and his connection to the Late Money Boys had gone up in smoke with it.

I refused to pay Vandy his half out of my own pocket. That was out of the question. I didn't have twenty grand sitting in my personal account to pamper Vandy. Maybe Island Willie's investigation would go nowhere, and he'd release my account. Why not wait a few days?

Vandy had seemed desperate. His demand that I pay him was ridiculous. The one-time wizard of the claiming game was facing extinction thanks to the Late Money Boys, and now he couldn't even get his hands on his winnings. I'd check Irv's docs again on his financial situation.

I trudged along and rang doorbells like a salesman trying to sign up customers. What was sold door-to-door these days? Vacuum cleaner salesmen and Fuller Brush Men were extinct. I lived in an apartment, and no one ever made a cold-call.

Even at this prime-time dinner hour, many houses sat dark and empty. Were they out to eat? I'd driven by before, and no one ever seemed to be at home. Was it twilight soccer practice?

Maybe nobody answered their doors because they were busy working remotely in their home offices, tucked away in the basement or a back room. I didn't want to ring more than twice because then they'd get angry. I couldn't ring just once because then they'd think it was an Amazon delivery.

No one knew Sal in the neighborhood, and Sal didn't know anyone. According to my talks with those I did happen to catch, the street was filled with people who waved at each other but never talked. I promised myself that when Nicole and I bought a house, we'd get to know our neighbors. I'd give them a free drink ticket to O'Connell's, if that's what it took.

What difference would it make if I did find somebody who knew about a break-in at Sal's house? It wouldn't be enough—it wouldn't be evidence that Sal's gun was stolen. But it would be something. It would confirm a portion of Sal's story about the gun.

I told myself for the hundredth time how much I loved a wild-goose chase. It was a detective's job, and this was a part of the job—the part that really sucked.

The large home at the end of the street behind Sal's house

was dark, but I went up to the front door and rang the doorbell anyway. I rang a second time and was about to leave, but heard a dog bark inside. Then I thought I heard footsteps.

I forced a smile in greeting as the outside light came on and the door opened. The man held back a large black dog baring its teeth, barking wildly and attacking the storm door as if I was a mortal enemy.

"Get down, get down," the man pleaded, tugging at the dog's collar. "Down, Jaime. Down."

I thought about getting a head start on Jaime.

He started to inch the storm door open while shoving poor Jaime to the side with his legs. Jaime dove beneath and got his snout through the crack in the door in a desperate effort to get free and rip out my liver.

I stayed calm. "I just have a couple of questions." I held up a notebook.

The man held the dog's collar and pulled with all his might. "No surveys." His face was turning red. He wore a torn shirt and ripped jeans.

I talked fast and loud. "It's not a survey. It's about a break-in."

"A what? A break-in? Get down, Jaime." He managed to push past Jaime and get outside. Jaime jumped at the storm door again and again, barking and slobbering. "I'm sorry about that."

The smell of beer and marijuana hit me. "No problem," I lied.

"A break-in? In this neighborhood?"

I filled him in on what had happened more than a month ago. Sal's backyard abutted a small part of his backyard, and we spent some time trying to nail down exactly which house was Sal's.

"We could walk back there, but it's full of dog shit," he said. "Nobody's home right now and Jaime—"

"I understand." I wanted to suggest a straight-jacket or a

muzzle for Jaime, but then again, I was the intruder and Jaime was just doing his job. "My client is a well-known horse trainer."

"You don't say? He's a neighbor?"

"Yeah." I was amazed that people could live among strangers.

"Cool. The wife and I have been talking about giving our girls riding lessons."

I told him that Sal wasn't that type of trainer and what he did.

"He trains racehorses? You mean like the Kentucky Derby?"

"Yeah."

"Damn. And they do that around here?"

"Yes, at Thornton Racetrack."

"Where?"

I gave him the general location of the track, and he was astounded that horse racing was going on in the city. Since he was a younger man and his house was one of the biggest in the neighborhood, I asked what he did for a living.

He shrugged, and a sick smile of embarrassment flickered. "Sure, why not? It is a nice house, isn't it? Usually, I don't like to talk about what I do, but since I don't know you, I'll tell you. I'm the Mr. Mom in the family. My wife has a really good job downtown in the tech industry. Big bucks. As long as I pick up the kids on time, get to the grocery store and walk Jaime twice a day, I'm good." He giggled.

At least one of us was high. "Did you see anything weird in the backyard? During the break-in, they got into a tool shed. Made a mess of things."

His face scrunched up in thought. "No, no strange tools, or anything."

Jaime continued to rattle the storm door, and I thought now might be a good time to leave.

"Wait, wait a minute," he said. "One of my girls did find something. I got two—one is in the fifth grade and one is in middle school. They love horses. They draw pictures of them all the time—it's a girl thing, you know. Wait here for one minute. Let me get it."

He squeezed his way back inside, and Jaime did a number on his pants leg. After the man pulled free, they both ran up the stairs. I reached over to make certain the storm door was shut tight.

After a few minutes, he came back down with something in his hand. Jaime jumped at the object as if it might be food or part of a game. The man held it higher, which only made Jaime jump higher and claw at his chest.

Once again, the man wrestled with his best friend to get outside. He handed it to me.

It was a trophy, more than a foot tall. There was a statue of a horse on top. The plaque on the base of the trophy had Sal's name and the name of the horse. The person who'd ransacked Sal's house must've found it in the tool shed and thrown it over the back fence.

This was exactly what I needed. "Do you know when your girls found this?"

"Are you kidding? The day they got it, the 'Gold Pony' went viral on TikTok. Will it help?"

"Perfect." I told him about the court proceeding and that he might need to testify.

"Cool. The wife thinks all I do is sit around here all day and get high."

51

WHEN I GOT HOME THAT NIGHT, I COULDN'T WAIT to tell Nicole. Finally, we had something to celebrate—some small glimmer of hope. We had Trophy Man.

Nicole clapped her hands when I told her the story. She gave me a big kiss.

"Thank God," she said. "I've had this constant throbbing in the back of my head. It's like half the lights are out around me. I think the darkness lifted a little just now. How did you find Dad's trophy?"

I explained how I went door to door behind Sal's house. I gave Jaime, the dog, a starring role—if it wasn't for his barking, I might've walked away and his owner would've taken another toke.

"Does Dad know?"

I shook my head. "No. I talked to Pam at St. Clair's office. She said that I had to leave it to them to tell Sal. They didn't want it to sound too good. It will depend on the judge. Excluding the gun from evidence is the key to the case, I guess. Pam downplayed the trophy, but I could tell she was excited and nothing gets Pam excited."

"You deserve a lot," she whispered, kissing me again in a way that I hadn't experienced for some time. "First, I need a glass of wine. You want one?"

"Sure. Uncle Mike was lukewarm about the trophy. He thinks the judge will let the jury sort it all out." Her father's murder charges hung over us like a dark shroud. She needed a break, but I didn't want to give her false hope.

She closed her eyes tight as if she needed a moment to make sense of it all. "Uncle Mike can be so serious." She took a deep breath. "I used to think Dad's suspension was awful. If that's all I had to worry about, life would be good." She raised her glass. "Here's to Trophy Man."

We toasted, and she sipped from her wine glass. "I haven't thought about it for a while, but I like to think about it—those days long ago—before I left for Vegas. I had my own place then, and I was working for Dad. I'd go over to Dad's house for dinner, and Jessie would make one of her special dinners."

She'd mentioned the wonderful meals Jessie would make, with Tres Leches Cake for dessert. "Ronnie used to be there, right?"

"Yes. Sometimes Vandy would come over. When we had something to celebrate." She leaned back against the counter. "When we got a new horse in the barn, we'd treat him or her like royalty. We'd coddle the horse, let our saddle horses or our dogs or goats into its stall to get acquainted. We talked to them. We did everything but make love to this poor claimer who'd gone from track to track, running races as if they were on a treadmill. We'd give the horse time off. Allow the horse a chance to play before we got back to business."

"And when the horse won, you'd celebrate?" She'd told me this story many times, and she knew how much I enjoyed it.

She'd told me the names of the dogs and the barn's goat. These stories told me how hard it must've been for her to leave everything behind to chase her poker dreams in Vegas.

She nodded. "I suppose all good things have to come to an end."

We stepped over to the couch with our glasses and sat down.

"Orman told us he had a thing for Jessie."

Nicole laughed. "Yes, Jessie said it was nothing, but Dad made a big deal out of it. Jessie was flattered, actually. That's why Ronnie left. Why did that come up?"

"He's being questioned by the homicide detective—Augie Saboski. St. Clair and Ferguson are using it to show reasonable doubt. They might call Orman as a witness."

"Good. I don't know what it will prove, though. That happened a number of years ago."

"Orman also said he started dating Isabel."

Nicole threw her head back and laughed. "What? Are you kidding me? Good for them."

"Did Isabel mention it at the party?"

"No. I can't blame her. Any mention of Ronnie would go against St. Clair's rules. Remember? No talking about the track or the murder case or anything else that would stir up Dad."

"That's right."

"You know, I was thinking—the funny thing about Dad's gun turning up? You know about his brother committing suicide—our family's secret? Dad would never tell anyone this, but Jessie used to hide his gun."

That might explain the house being ransacked. If someone knew about the gun and wanted to find it to frame Sal, they would've had to search the house for it.

So much depended on the judge. If the judge didn't exclude the gun, Sal might have to take a plea deal.

She set down her glass and pulled at my shirt collar. I leaned down and kissed her.

We parted, and she looked up at me. "Tell me that you and Uncle Mike are going to solve this thing." Tears welled up in her eyes. Her mini-high was over.

She couldn't bring herself to say the word "murder."

"Yes, we will."

Our investigation had gained leverage, and we intended to use it. Uncle Mike had called DiNatale to set up a meeting.

52

WE DROVE UP TO AN AUTO BODY SHOP RECENTLY christened Diamond V Auto Parts, located a mile or two from Midway Airport. Cars were lined up four-deep around the establishment and down the block. An older woman in a house dress stood outside and waved to us when we pulled in and showed us where to park. We slipped into a spot between a dented minivan and a sports car with a missing fender.

She walked over to us, a cigarette in hand. "What do you want?"

"We're here for a meeting," Uncle Mike said.

She gave each of us a closer look. "Wait here."

She strode back to the building, took a final drag on the cigarette, placed it in a receptacle beside the door, and then walked inside. The joint was jumping, as they say. Cars moving in and out of the garage, a radio blaring tunes and the smell of fresh paint in the air.

"I'm beginning to think these Diamond V companies might

be real," Uncle Mike said.

"Maybe he's consolidating Burrascano's holdings," I said.

The woman waved to us from the side door. We walked up. She led us past the main office and down a short hall with several small offices.

DiNatale sat in a swivel chair in a mini-office wedged between two other offices. He was on his cell, nodding and saying, "Right, right." After we stepped inside, the woman closed the door behind us. DiNatale held up one finger to signal he needed a moment.

After fifteen agreeable seconds, he yelled into the cell, "Do what I tell you, damnit."

He ended the call and stood up to greet us. "What is it? You find Jessie's killer?"

"We've got some questions." Uncle Mike said. "There's a lot of people around."

The mobster nodded. "The shop makes money—that's all I care about."

Uncle Mike said. "Okay to talk?"

We took a seat on the chairs that fronted the desk.

"Guaranteed, no bugs." DiNatale stood and made his way to the front of the desk. In the small space, his cologne overwhelmed the toxic smell of paint and exhaust fumes. "Look. I got problems. The Hippo is pissed his cash has been frozen. I pledged to protect Willie, and now the big mouth wants me to turn him over."

Uncle Mike said, "What can we do about it?"

"I got a loose agreement with The Hippo, but it could fall apart any moment." He hesitated. He gritted his teeth and seemed to fight back a wave of anger. "I promised Burrascano. I'm talking about peace. You got to watch yourselves."

"You're afraid The Hippo—"

"He wants the book because Willie wants the book."

Uncle Mike held up one hand. "Stop. What if it's not just

about The Hippo's frozen account? What if The Hippo wants the book for another reason?"

"Like what?" The mobster folded his arms across his chest.

"What if The Hippo wants to "work" with those guys who juice their horses?"

DiNatale thought for a second and then began to move around and shuffle his feet in that familiar dance. "Yeah. He strong arms the trainers who juice. And he bets the horse."

"You were going to take an active role in the track—for Jessie," I said.

"I don't know how Burrascano fucking did it," DiNatale said, seething. "Keeping these fuckers in line."

In a calm voice, Uncle Mike said, "They don't listen."

DiNatale pointed a finger at Uncle Mike. "Right. They think everything's up for grabs. If it was up to me, The Hippo would take a header into the grease pit. Island Willie would swim back to the islands, and I could get back to business. But that's not Burrascano's way."

Uncle Mike leaned forward. "You said you weren't bound by Burrascano's commitments…"

DiNatale nodded. "That's right—yeah."

"We were at the workouts the other morning a couple of weeks ago. We were with Island Willie. The Hippo came out and threatened us. I'm sure your guys told you about it," I said.

DiNatale's face reddened. What could Lou or his men say— that they let The Hippo spout threats, and they did nothing? They never knew what DiNatale might do when he got pissed. Sometimes, the messenger gets killed in their line of work.

Uncle Mike used his best cop voice. "The Hippo said to tell you there'd be a showdown."

"Fucking cocksucker," DiNatale muttered.

"He was at the track with his men when Dreaming Moon won at thirty to one," I said. "They took seats on the second floor."

"The son of a bitch."

"Eddie was lucky to get out of there," Uncle Mike said.

"Your horse scratched out of the race won by Dreaming Moon," I said. "What did they tell you? Did they tell you Dreaming Moon was a winner?"

"The fucker." DiNatale pounded a fist into the palm of his hand.

"We hear The Hippo sells fentanyl on the backstretch," Uncle Mike added.

"Damnit. I did hear about that." DiNatale twisted around and pulled out his cell. I worried he might call his men to make things "right" with The Hippo this very instant.

"Take it easy, Vic," I said, holding up one hand again.

"Who is it?" DiNatale demanded. "You know who killed Jessie?"

"Hold it, hold it," Uncle Mike said.

"What?"

"Listen."

53

WE ARRANGED TO MEET DETECTIVE SABOSKI AT Elena's.

Saboski took a seat across from us. "Okay. You guys probably know where I'm coming from."

"No, we don't," I said.

"I've got another murder in the grandstands. This guy wanders past warning signs of ongoing construction and danger. He goes up the stairs, past a chain draped over the entrance, into the grandstands where the floor is ripped up, the TVs are hanging by a thread from the ceiling, wires hanging down, and no place to bet—and he gets stabbed repeatedly in the neck and bleeds all over."

"Funny how that happens," I said. Maybe Saboski was making a case for contributory negligence by Wilcox. "What about the similar murder at the Old Shagbark Country Club?"

"We're waiting on forensics, but it looks like the same killer."

"Talk to us about that other case," Uncle Mike suggested.

"The one with the trainer and the assistant trainer. Unlike the other two murders, this one involved a shooting. You remember the one that happened on the backstretch."

"Cut it out, Mike. You know what that trophy means."

My uncle wasn't smiling, but I knew he was enjoying the hell out of this moment, and I took a backseat. Trophy Man strikes again. Thanks, Jaime.

"I can't think of what it might mean. Can you, Eddie?" Uncle Mike said.

"Nope," I said.

"I guess the Backstretch Murder isn't a simple matter after all?" Uncle Mike asked.

Saboski shifted in his seat. "Cut it out. I got my tail chewed."

"You did?" Uncle Mike asked. "Tell me about that. I thought our captain was such an understanding person." Uncle Mike tilted his head to one side quizzically.

"You suck, Mike. You too, Eddie." Saboski took a deep breath. "I realize those sweet little neighbor girls didn't jump the privacy fence and break into Sal's tool shed and then decide to take one of the trophies from the box. I also realize the manure pile I'm stuck in. There's a record of the trophy on TikTok from the date of discovery and every day thereafter like it was breaking news."

Uncle Mike nodded slowly. "And what would that trophy mean—in a certain place where somebody wears a robe?"

Saboski cleared his throat. "It means one of two things. It means that the gun should be excluded because the defendant—Mr. Nicoletti—was telling the truth about a break-in and his house being ransacked."

It would leave the DA with a whimsical case of circumstantial horse shit.

Uncle Mike nodded along. "Or..."

"Or, it means that the officer in charge was doing a sloppy job."

St. Clair would have a field day on cross-examination of the lead detective—one August Saboski.

Uncle Mike shook his head and made a clicking sound with his tongue. "I guess one of us here needs to make amends. Isn't that right, Eddie?"

"I wouldn't know. I've been busy with that bowling team."

"C'mon, guys, give me a break," Saboski said.

Uncle Mike shook his head. "Okay. Ready to work together, Augie?"

54

THE NEXT RACING DAY AT THORNTON, ORMAN HAD a couple of horses on the card that would be prohibitive favorites.

We showed up at the track for the first one of these races. DiNatale, who had his men on site to watch over Island Willie, would report a sighting of The Hippo to us.

The first Orman horse, owned by Vandy, finished second, resulting in a juicy exacta when a long shot won. I'd seen that scenario before, but I wasn't out here to bet the races. I was out here to set up a meeting.

The other Orman horse running that day was owned by Diamond V Stables. The horse won easily with a driving finish. I headed down near the finish line and hung out along a walkway, where the trainer would need to pass by. Track security usually prohibited non-track personnel or non-owners from using this walkway, but we had clout, thanks to Arlene.

After Orman stood beside the horse and got his picture

taken with his groom, Alejandro, and his assistant, Isabel, Orman walked back down the walkway. I met him inside.

"Another winner," I said. "I wanted to congratulate you."

"Eddie? You aren't supposed to be here." He studied me and saw I wasn't really in a congratulatory mood. "Did you have a bet on the winner?"

"No, I'm here to deal," I said.

"I have nothing to say to you." Orman walked on.

Isabel overheard. "I'm sorry, Eddie. He's not in a good mood today."

I said, "Isabel, can you pass along a message to Ronnie? I've got a certain lab book, and I'm willing to pass it along to him in exchange for information."

She nodded.

I didn't want to leave anything to chance. "Tell him we'll be able to do the exchange tonight at ten o'clock. I'll be alone on the second floor of the clubhouse in Suite 3A, overlooking the finish line."

"You have a lab book, and the exchange will be tonight," she repeated. "Suite 3A. I'll tell him."

"Thanks," I said. "Tell him to come alone."

"I'm sorry for Ronnie's behavior. I don't understand," she said.

55

AT TEN O'CLOCK, I WAITED IN SUITE 3A ON THE second floor of Thornton Racetrack with the professor's lab book. It was one of a number of premium suites. The expansive room outside held rows of tables and chairs for fine dining. A bar on either end of the room kept race day crowds supplied. Betting windows were located on the far side of the room, opposite the glass. Glass doors provided access to several rows of box seats outside that angled downward toward the track, ensuring diners inside would have an unencumbered view of the races.

I was a sitting duck. The door was ajar. Through the window behind me, the track below was dark.

Quick, short steps approached. There was a knock on the door.

"Come in."

The door opened wide. It was Isabel.

Seated at a round table, I asked, "Where's Ronnie?"

"Hi, Eddie. Ronnie sent me. He said to apologize. He didn't have time. Since I'm now Ronnie's assistant, he sent me."

"Congratulations. Have a seat."

"I don't have much time." She sat with her large gray vinyl bag on her lap. She focused on the black leather-bound book on the table. "Is that the lab book?"

"Yes. I don't have to tell you what's in it, do I?"

She shook her head. "Everyone knows."

"I always thought there was something funny about the gun. You know—the one used to murder Jessie?"

She kept her eyes on me and nodded. Her hands held her bag below the table.

"It didn't show up until Orman had Sal's horses."

Isabel shrugged. "The Lopez boy —"

"He's just a kid. I asked myself—could a boy that young hold on to a gun, a murder weapon, that long? It was what—more than a couple of weeks?"

She looked away. "I don't know."

"You had the gun. Hugo was stalking you. You used it to kill Hugo." Quintella had said Hugo was "gone."

"What? Are you kidding?"

"You came to America to escape the cartel, but there was no escape." The cartel would take Hugo's body and wouldn't call the police. They stopped selling meth as punishment and to pressure their backstretch customers for answers. They would demand to know who shot Hugo.

Hugo was dead, and it wasn't due to my right hand. It wasn't The Hippo either. So who was it?

"You must've lived in fear. You needed protection." The Hippo jumped into the void left by the cartel to sell fentanyl.

Her face was constricted with emotion. She whispered, "Just give me the lab book."

"I wanted Ronnie to answer questions. Did you know The Hippo showed up the morning you were working Dreaming Moon? That wasn't very smart timing."

"Why torture me like this?"

"You couldn't be a source for Island Willie because you were working with The Hippo."

She looked out the window into the dark.

"What did you use to juice Dreaming Moon? The Hippo won a lot that day."

She stared at the lab book.

"We have the blood sample. The professor will be able to tell us. The police are searching your room right now."

Now I had her full attention. Her hands moved under the table.

"What kind of venom was it?" She could walk across the hall to plant the gun on the Lopez boy. She could give Sal's horse the meth that resulted in the suspension. Jessie would be caught off guard.

She pulled out a gun. Her lips tight. "Cobra venom."

I held up my hands. I didn't want to be her next victim. "Give yourself up. Do it for Juanita."

Her voice rose in volume. "Is it a sin to want a better life for your child? Yes, I did it. Any mother would. What choice did I have?"

I knew a lot about a mother's love, but I had to imagine it. I pushed the lab book toward her.

She held the gun. Her hand wasn't shaking. "Give me your phone and your gun."

I slid both across the table and then kept my hands up. I must be crazy.

"Now you have nothing. Don't follow me if you want to live. My friends are outside."

"The Hippo?"

She slipped the lab book into her bag and held the gun on me as she backed up toward the door.

Uncle Mike was in Suite 5B, listening in and recording the conversation. Saboski was on the conference call.

"I'm coming out," Isabel called out. She slipped through the door.

The second floor erupted in gunfire.

56

"WE'RE OVER HERE," SOMEONE YELLED. IT sounded like The Hippo; a voice near the windows.

I crawled toward the door. I closed it gently, but left it slightly ajar. Then I reached up and switched off the light. Isabel had brought her insurance policy, and I'd brought mine.

"Give up," DiNatale roared back from the other side of the room.

The voices of the two mobsters were lost in the gunfire. They were past the talking stage. Despite Burrascano's careful planning, a succession battle would be fought, and it'd play out right here.

I hugged the floor and peeked through the crack in the doorway. The lights were off. Flashes of gunfire lit up both sides of the room. As my eyes adjusted, I could see tables tipped on their side to provide cover, shadows racing like human rats. A chandelier burst into a thousand bits.

Isabel was a few yards away, lying face down. She'd strutted into a crossfire. Blood had started to pool around her.

My suite remained on their radar. Shots nipped at the door jamb outside. My heart raced. I'd expected a war of words, not guns. I expected The Hippo to give up Isabel. That DiNatale would take over.

"We got the old man," someone yelled from The Hippo's side of the room.

Uncle Mike—I had to reach him. Both sides loved their guns, and this was their chance to prove it. The Hippo wanted what DiNatale had. DiNatale wanted to cement his rightful place in Burrascano's shoes. Peace wasn't even a concept.

I needed to get to Isabel. She was still breathing. I could drag her back into the room. Get my gun—plan my next move. *Damnit, think.*

The Hippo's men wanted the lab book. One of them might rush me. I opened the door inches at a time.

Like a spider, I crawled out of my fortress. *Stay down.* Wood splintered around me. Bursts of gunfire filled my ears. I reached across the floor and grabbed hold of Isabel's ankle.

A man screamed. People were getting killed.

I tugged the dead weight. Adrenaline spiked. The body slid across the tiles. I yanked the body back into my lair.

She moaned. I got her into the room as a flurry of shots raked the door and hallway.

"We got the old man," The Hippo called again. He was on the side of the room that led to the box seats. Outside, you could jump sixty feet and break a leg; otherwise, you were trapped. The Hippo's plan didn't include logistics. The Hippo took Uncle Mike as a hostage to ensure a safe exit.

DiNatale had the advantage and wasn't in the mood to bargain. His answer was more gunfire. He'd brought plenty of men.

Isabel pulled at my shirt. "Eddie," she gasped. "Pray for me." Her voice caught. There was a gurgling sound.

I turned her over. There was so much blood. I tore at her shirt. A gaping wound in her gut spouted blood. I pulled off my own shirt, balled it up and used it as a compress. It was soaked in no time. Her breathing stopped.

"Isabel?" I pounded her chest. Tried mouth to mouth. *Damnit.*

She died on the floor. I found my gun, my phone, and the lab book in her bag. My cell was no longer on conference. I emptied the bag of all her stuff, put the lab book back inside. I had to get to Uncle Mike.

Shirtless, the bag's straps around my neck, I swung the bag onto my back and then crawled through the door and along the bloody floor on my stomach.

No chance to pray. Time to join the party.

I headed past the other suites, in the direction of The Hippo. The gun battle had shifted, focused on other areas of the open floor. The Hippo's men had been able to make progress on the far side of the room. There was another stairway there if they could get to it.

DiNatale's men had taken up strategic positions around the bars and near the exits. Our side had the element of surprise. I didn't know if we were winning or favored—the tote board wasn't working.

The suite where Uncle Mike had holed up was empty. Paper was strewn about, and his cell phone was cast aside. Did Saboski know Uncle Mike had been taken? I heard sirens outside.

I slid down toward the first set of glass doors. Thank God The Hippo's men were pointed in the other direction.

Outside in the box seats, I could get a view of things. Where were they holding Uncle Mike?

The gunfire inside was muted by the glass—a clear, hard plastic of some kind. So far, despite the cracks and potmarks, it had held up against the barrage.

I crawled along the aisle between the boxes and popped my

head up to see between the seats. I had to peer around the numerous spider cracks. Unlike the secretive, chemical warfare of the track, this war was hell to behold. No soundtrack other than men shooting. Some were holed up behind tables. If I could free Uncle Mike, I'd be in a position at the back of the room to outflank The Hippo's men. *Dream on.*

The sirens came closer. The police would need to proceed with caution, or some of them would end up like Isabel.

At the end of the first row of box seats, I saw Uncle Mike. He was behind a table, bound and gagged. Two men were with him. Another set of glass doors at the end of the aisle would get me within ten yards of them. I couldn't shoot both of them at once, but every second counted.

I slithered to the glass doors. The second I went inside, they'd turn in my direction. I waited. One of the men was shooting and said something to the other. He scurried away to another set of tables. Here was my chance.

Bent down low, I pushed through the glass doors into the shooting gallery. I fired just as the man holding Uncle Mike twisted around. It was The Hippo.

I hit him in the shoulder. His gun clattered to the floor.

I was on my knees, both elbows on the floor. In my right hand, my gun was pointed at him.

He looked down at his gun a few feet away.

"Go ahead," I said.

57

WE WERE ON TIME FOR OUR SCHEDULED MEETING at the professor's office. We planned to return the lab book to her, but we wanted answers.

The meeting started off with each of us apologizing to the other. We apologized for the length of time it had taken us to obtain the lab book, and the professor apologized for not getting us more information about the IT folks she'd feuded with over the faulty university network security.

"How did you do it?" she asked. "No additional ransom payment?"

"When the thief failed to call us to set up the second and final payment, we used our other contacts in the industry," Uncle Mike said.

"I hope you didn't place yourselves in jeopardy," she said.

"No, our contacts had obtained the lab book and then gave us the name of the thief," Uncle Mike said.

"It was strange," I said. "At first, we were contacted by a

woman and then, at the time of the drop and the down payment, we were contacted by a man."

The professor hesitated. Maybe she didn't appreciate my tone. "Did you meet them both?"

"No, only the male thief—a small-time crook," I said.

"What's his name?" she asked.

"Names aren't important. He said his accomplice, a woman named Laverne Baker, worked for you?" I was playing bad cop. Uncle Mike had established more of a rapport with the professor, so the dirty work would be left to me.

The professor shrugged. "No one with that name comes to mind. We do employ many lab workers who clean up or do other minor work. I could check our records."

"The thief told us he picked the lock to your office late at night during a shift change."

She shook her head. "During a shift change? I'll look into that."

"He also said that your lab book was sitting on the desk. He said the theft was clean and easy."

"What? I told you I keep my lab book in the drawer." She pulled her sweater tight around her shoulders. "I don't understand. There were marks on the drawer before. It is an antique. Maybe I just forgot. I wasn't thinking."

"Another thing," I continued, "many people at the track had heard about the lab book."

Her lips grew tight. "You can't trust thieves. They probably wanted to see what they could get on the open market."

"You never told us you owned a string of horses at Thornton." I enjoyed playing the bad cop.

"What?"

"Does the name Old Prairie Stables ring any bells?"

She looked at Uncle Mike and then back at me. "How did you find out? I do have an interest. You two are well-informed, aren't you?"

"You own claimers?"

She nodded slowly. "Yes. Also, two-year-olds and allowance horses—"

"No one would claim your horses—"

"The claiming game is a tough game." She bit her bottom lip. "Ronnie Orman handled those horses. You should talk with him."

"No one claimed your horses because you let it be known you ran a major lab."

"That sounds strangely unethical even for the track," she said in an attempt at humor.

Uncle Mike's stone-cop face didn't find it funny. "A little larceny seems to be written in the track's bylaws."

"I'm guilty as charged, Mike." She flipped pages of her lab book. "I am so relieved. If the illegal bookies obtained the lab book, they might do something…"

"Against those who doped their horses and then placed bets with them?"

She nodded. "I want to catch the bad actors all at once. As you can see, I can now test successfully for some of these designer drugs they use. It's the key to cleaning up the track."

"That is just what the sport needs. One more question. Did you know Jessie?" I asked.

She fished around in a drawer and pulled out a package of cigarettes.

Uncle Mike edged forward in his chair. "C'mon, Yana, you can tell us. As you know, the murderer has been caught. Tell us."

The professor stared up at the ceiling and tapped her fingertips on the desk. "Yes, you do deserve an explanation. You might not like it."

"Try us."

She took a deep breath. "The reason my horses weren't claimed by Vandy, unlike other horses trained by Orman, was simple—Jessie and I were close friends. We talked often. When I learned she was murdered, I was heartbroken."

"Why didn't you tell us?"

"Jessie swore me to secrecy. She had to deal with Vandy, an important owner of Sal's barn. She wanted to clean up the track as much as I did."

"Did Jessie get you those blood samples?" I'd traced the tracks where the races took place. They matched Sal's seasonal moves.

The professor nodded. "She risked a lot to get those samples for me. My testing of those samples—ones taken from horses she suspected of doping—made all the difference. I'd get into a lot of trouble for doing these tests. They weren't submitted to my lab through approved channels."

She was nervous. I thought of those school regulations and the need for any lab to be squeaky clean and tightly secured, what with the controversy over the enforcement of the new federal horse racing laws. She had risked her career and possibly her own safety.

She took a deep breath; tears welled up in her eyes. "I worried that I was the one who was responsible for Jessie's death. That someone caught her taking one of those unauthorized blood samples."

"That wasn't the reason behind Jessie's murder. You don't have to worry about that," I said.

"Yes, I read about it. You both deserve so much. At one point, I went over the edge. I talked about my new blood tests at the Alumni Elite meeting. I let those CAW people know it was out there and held secrets—that the tests were in the beta stage and results had been obtained."

"That won't help you catch all the bad actors at once," I said.

She ran her fingers through her hair, pulling on a stray lock. "I know. I lost control. The procedures for getting new tests approved takes time. I wanted to scare the living daylights out of them. Even those who got caught and ran to other states—

they'd fear discovery by the black market. If someone like Island Willie got such a lab book or was able to test—"

"Now who is well-informed?" I was shocked she knew of Island Willie. "Island Willie has run back to the islands," Uncle Mike said. "He got what he wanted. His presence scared the hell out of those who don't play fair."

I thought about the murders of Egan and Wilcox. Uncle Mike and I chalked those up to Island Willie, but we had no way to prove it.

She pulled out a cigarette and placed it in the holder. "I'm afraid I'll have to go outside to smoke this. But first, let me show you something."

She opened a cupboard behind her desk. It held a steel safe, one of the best on the market.

58

I STOOD OUTSIDE THE COURTROOM IN THE Leighton Criminal Courts building with Nicole, Sal, and Uncle Mike.

"Eddie," Uncle Mike called out, "why are you pacing? Why don't you sit down?"

They were seated on the bench outside the courtroom, but I couldn't take it. Five minutes on that bench and all the memories would come flooding back. I'd had my own run-in with the criminal courts years ago on a trumped-up charge of aggravated battery. I'd gotten lucky. I'd gotten off with a last-minute plea deal.

I knew what was going on in the minds of the zombie people streaming past me down this hallway. One moment of desperation, one moment of anger, or poor judgment, could change the course of your life. I'd been lucky.

St. Clair and Ferguson walked up, the attorney holding onto her assistant's right arm. A paralegal I recognized from their law office pulled a heavy suitcase packed with files and laptops.

There was a group hug that was difficult to describe. Joy was written on each face along with sadness over the events.

Ferguson watched St. Clair's every move to be sure she didn't stumble, then reached up and placed a hand on my shoulder and squeezed. "Isn't it strange when justice happens?"

Saboski had gotten a search warrant and searched Isabel's dorm room. He'd been on the conference call before The Hippo grabbed Uncle Mike. The police found the hypodermic needles and a bottle of a strange substance. We lived in a world where fentanyl could be cooked up in a kitchen in Mexico by first year chemistry students. Chasing new drugs was like playing whack-a-mole. I hoped the professor's new test would change all that.

If Isabel had been smart, she would've disposed of the stuff and she wouldn't have met me to get the lab book. But she was under The Hippo's thumb. He wanted more juiced horses like Dreaming Moon. If she didn't cooperate, he'd tell the cartel she'd murdered Hugo.

Saboski received the credit. In the papers, there was a mention of newly discovered evidence; otherwise, Uncle Mike and I remained mostly anonymous.

What DiNatale and The Hippo worked out was something we'd never know. When I captured The Hippo, the gun battle ended.

St. Clair barked, "Sal, don't look so nervous. Today is a done deal."

Her announcement seemed to break our solemn mood. She even hugged me. "Eddie, you guys are still my A-Team."

Bro hugs followed with Uncle Mike and Sal. Sal had tears in his eyes and told me, "I can't believe it. My nightmare is over." Sal would get his horses back.

I'd called Vandy to tell him my account with Island Willie was no longer frozen. Vandy wanted to work together again. Fine, as long as Winning Spirit went to aftercare.

Uncle Mike shook his head at me. "You and your gambling, Eddie."

Nicole and I hugged tight for a long time.

She whispered, "You think my football picks are magic—how did you pull this off?"

I shrugged. St. Clair and Ferguson had begun to go inside the courtroom with Sal.

"You're sure you want to stay outside?" Nicole asked.

"Courtrooms and me don't get along. I'll wait right here."

"Okay. Love you," she said. "You're sure you're okay with everything?"

"Yes, I'm okay with it. Love you, too." We were planning to sign the papers today for a rental house.

"It's not a big house, but I think Juanita will love it," she said. "And it's so close to the school."

We were going to do whatever we could to help Juanita. Arlene had provided legal services for the migrants with children in the dorms. In her Last Will, Isabel had appointed Jessie as custodian for Juanita, and named Nicole as the alternate custodian. We hadn't obtained court approval yet, but we hoped things would work out.

It's what Jessie would've wanted.

ACKNOWLEDGMENTS

I really appreciate the support I've received from so many. I'd like to thank my critique partners who see the pages before the second or third draft. These brave readers include the Tuesday Night Mystery Critique Group and my Thursday Night Critique Group. Special thanks to my beta readers: Scott Brendel and Sue Thomas. Many thanks to my mentors in the publishing world: Karla Jay, Wendy Barnhart and Barbara Nickless. I would also like to thank my fellow writers at Rocky Mountain Fiction Writers, Rocky Mountain Mystery Writers of America and Bouchercon for the meetings and conferences they've presented over the years that have provided me with insights into the craft of writing.

To my fellow handicappers, best of luck. Stay in control and seek help, if needed.

To my editors, developmental editor Steve Parolini and copy editor Susan Brooks, thank you. To my design team, book cover by David Ter-Avanesyan and Interior by Susan Brooks. For the audiobook version of the book, Susan Brooks and my narrator Josh Innerst. Thanks for your hard work.

Lastly, to my family. My wife, Kathi, and sons, Greg and Mark.

You make it all worthwhile.

ABOUT THE AUTHOR

Tom Farrell has worked as a golf course starter, a chemist and clerked at City Hall in Chicago, while attending law school and the local horse tracks. He is the author of The Wager Series, including the award-winning *Wager Tough* (Book One), *WagerEasy* and *Wager Smart*. He was voted the 2024 Writer of the Year by Rocky Mountain Fiction Writers. The series offers an insider's view of gambling on sports, horse racing, and poker, with a nod to the small-time player and the need for caution.

www.tomfarrellbooks.com